FROM THE BORDELLOS TO THE GALLOWS . . .

Wild, beautiful, wayward and daring, Polly Smith is the talk of London town.

She is also a common thief.

Born of royal blood but raised by a charitable villager, Polly doesn't question her lot in life—until she is cast out on the streets, forced to fend for herself.

From the cobbled squares of London to the stone cells of Newgate Prison, this eighteenth-century beauty soon learns the ways of the world as she encounters a parade of colorful characters. Some try to help her; many try to use her. Only one man wants to believe in her innocence in this scandalous world. Scorning the hot stares of noblemen and ignoring the cold looks from their wives, Polly discovers scoundrels and connivers lurking around every corner.

Her enemies long to see her dancing in the wind, hanging in the clutch of the gallows. And men have been hanged for smaller crimes than hers.

She has to escape the law. She has to escape her own innocence. For in Polly's world there's a thin line between virtue and vice.

DANCING ON THE WIND

Sarah Chester

Tudor Publishing Company
New York and Los Angeles

Tudor Publishing Company

ISBN: 0-944276-22-9

Printed in the United States of America

First Tudor printing—October, 1988

CHAPTER ONE

THE AUTUMN LEAVES WHIRLED DOWN FROM THE trees in cascades of red and gold. Mossy, rounded gravestones leaned at crazy angles on the smooth-cropped turf of the churchyard like old drunken men hunched against the buffets of the wind. Far above in the steeple tolled the great bell, at times the sound bellowing down into the ears of the mourners, at others sent high in the gale to clamor over the dying countryside. Then with a final noisy peal the bell fell silent, and the funeral service for Meg Jones, wise woman of the village of Upper Batchett, began.

The mourners from the village had come to pay their last respects. They huddled on one side of the grave, leaving a lone figure with bent head isolated on the other. Polly Jones, who until Meg's death had believed herself to be the old woman's niece, brushed a tear away from one brown cheek and glared angrily at the group on the other side of the grave. It was only on Meg's death they had told her she was a foundling and no relative of the old woman. They had always disapproved of Polly. She was too wild, far too beautiful, too wayward, and too amused and contemptuous of narrow village ways and spiteful village gossip.

But fear of old Meg's charms and spells had kept their dislike well hidden. Now, with Meg gone, not one cared what happened to the girl.

Polly shuddered as the earth fell on the coffin. She had never felt so frightened or alone. Why would no one listen to her? Why would no one explain why Meg had had two cruel bruises on her neck the day she died? Why had old Meg looked up at her with dying eyes and whispered, "My lady, I am sorry"?

My lady. Polly had thought long and hard about that. Meg had gone to Meresly Manor on the day of her death to see Lady Lydia, wife of the earl of Meresly. The news that the earl had returned to Meresly, which he had not visited in years, had thrown Meg into a fever of excitement. Polly had assumed Meg meant to find employment for her at the manor. But Meg had returned dying, and Meg had said, "My lady," and Meg had two wicked bruises on her old neck.

The sound of a procession of carriages making its way along the road outside the churchyard broke into Polly's thoughts. "That'll be them from Meresly Manor going back to London," said one. Polly whirled about and ran to the churchyard wall and climbed up on it, oblivious of the cries of outrage from the villagers.

Lady Lydia sat up straight as her carriage came to a halt. "What's to do?" she cried.

"A funeral," said her husband laconically. He put his head out of the window and shouted up to his coachman, "Who is dead? Anyone I should know about?"

The carriage dipped and swayed as the coachman climbed down from the box. After a few moments, his round red face appeared at the carriage window on the earl's side. "Some old woman of the village," said the coachman. "A Mrs. Jones."

Bertram Pargeter, Lady Lydia's but recently dismissed lover, riding on her side of the carriage, noticed the sudden flush of relief on Lady Lydia's face, saw the way her eyes began to sparkle, saw the fear of the last few days begin to leave her face. A quick movement to his left distracted him. He looked sideways. On a level with his face was a gypsy-looking girl, climbing up onto the churchyard wall. Her mass of chestnut hair was wild and tangled and her large violet eyes fringed with heavy lashes looked out of a nut-brown face. Something made him remove his hat and give her a slight bow. Her workworn hands clutched the stones at the top of the wall tightly and she looked down and past him to where Lady Lydia sat in the carriage. Lady Lydia glanced up and saw the girl. She quickly raised her fan to shield her face and said something. The carriage moved on. Bertram touched his horse's flanks with his red-heeled boots and cantered along beside it again. After they had gone a little way away, he slowed his mount and twisted in the saddle and looked back. The girl was still there, a solitary figure, her cloak whipping about her on the rising wind. He turned back and looked again into the carriage.

Lady Lydia was sitting very still. Her long jewelled fingers clasped and unclasped the sticks of her fan. Fear was back in her face.

Bertram, all his senses sharpened by jealousy and hurt, turned over that strange little scene in his mind. He scented a mystery, and that mystery might give him the means to torture his cruel mistress as much as she had tortured him.

After the funeral, Polly returned sadly to the little cottage in which she had passed sixteen years of her life with old Meg Jones. There were no funeral baked meats, no sympathizers. Without looking at her, the villagers had filed out of the churchyard and had gone their separate ways.

The cottage had very little left in it, Polly having sold the furniture and pots and pans to pay for Meg's funeral. She had just slung the one remaining pot over the fire to make some fennel tea and was easing her feet out of her shoes—she had been wearing shoes for almost the first time in her life, knowing it would be regarded as disrespectful had she turned up at the graveside in bare feet—when there came a great pounding at the door.

Sure that it must be some villager calling to give comfort—for people could not really be so unfeeling—Polly went to answer it. Two small squat men stood on the doorstep. She recognized the squire's bailiffs and her face hardened.

"You've got a week to get out," said one, picking his teeth with a straw. "Tenancy o' this cottage belonged o' Meg for life, and seeing as you is no kin to her . . ."

Polly slammed the door in their faces. "We'll be back in a week," she heard them call. "You've only got a week."

Tears, thought Polly, could wait. She must plan what to do. She must find work. Why had Meg never sent her out to work in the fields like the other village girls? That was what had caused the village people to dislike her; she had been allowed to run wild and do as she pleased. Why had poor Meg paid for her education at the parish school? Of what good was book-learning to the penniless? Polly remembered one of the servants from Meresly Manor when the earl was in residence bragging in the village that London servants could live like kings.

"So London it is," said Polly aloud. And with that decision, a little of the pain eased at her heart. London was surely a glittering city full of palaces and gardens where people ate off gold plate all day long. London would mean escape from the sneers and stares of the villagers. "Foundling," their eyes accused. "Foundling and bastard, most like."

The pot began to boil. She put some dried fennel leaves in a cup and scooped boiling water on top of them with a ladle. She put her bare feet on the hearth and sipped her tea.

No, thought Polly, I cannot leave for London without going up to Meresly Manor. Something happened to Meg that day. Mayhap there is something there to give me a clue.

The blind eyes and curved smiles of the marble statues which lined the drive to Meresly Manor looked down on the figure of Polly Jones an hour later as she hurried toward the great house, her skirts flying about her in the chill wind.

In answer to her knock, a caretaker, a gruff London servant, told her curtly he had never heard of Meg Jones and slammed the door in her face.

Polly stood huddled against the wall of the manor, Meg's old shawl wrapped tightly about her shoulders. She turned at last and walked off down the drive. But once out on the road, she made her way along the wall of the estate and climbed back into the grounds at a point where she could not be seen from the house.

By slow and circumspect degrees she crept toward the manor. She made her way round the back and crouched below a terrace until the dark autumn evening set in.

Shivering, she waited and waited. Then she cautiously crept up to the French windows and tried the handle. To her relief, the windows were not locked, the caretaker being lazy and secure in the knowledge that none of the locals would risk a hanging by breaking in. Polly felt all fear of discovery leave her.

She cocked her head and listened. The murmur of voices came faintly from somewhere downstairs. Polly felt at her waist for the dark lantern she had tied there. She fumbled with her tinder box, wincing as each noise of the striking flint sounded unnaturally loud in the silence of the drawing room in which she found herself.

At last, a faint light shone on her surroundings.

But she realized she did not know what she was looking for. The clue to what had happened to Meg surely lay in London, in the earl's town house among his family and staff of servants, not here. She had overheard someone in the village saying that the earl was not expected to return to Meresly Manor, and although he had a great mansion and estates in Norfolk as well, Lady Lydia would not live there either, but preferred to spend the year round in Town.

Polly raised the lantern high. A portrait caught her eye, a long portrait which dominated the room. She gave a superstitious shiver, thinking for a moment she was seeing herself, then looked down at her shabby clothes to reassure herself that the silken-clad creature in the picture was another being entirely. She looked closer. Violet eyes like her own, looking out of a face like her own, stared haughtily down at her. But the lady in the picture had black hair, and her gown was panniered and elaborate, her skin white, and her hands with their long tapering fingers delicate and blue-veined. It was a portrait of Lady Lydia, the lady in the carriage which had passed the churchyard, the lady who had covered her face with her fan.

Feeling uneasy, Polly turned her back on the picture and once more looked about the room. Her eyes fell on the soft gleam of gold on a small table. She picked up the gold object and looked at it. It was a snuffbox. She hesitated, holding it in her hand.

Some fear of God had come to her with Meg's death. Then it struck Polly that surely there was no God, or certainly not any God of love as preached from the pulpit. There were so many precious trifles just lying around while such as she faced starvation. What was so very wrong in taking what would mean so much to her and so little to the earl of Meresly?

She slipped the snuffbox into a capacious pocket, more like a deep pouch, in her petticoat which had recently served to hold a rabbit she had poached from the squire's estate. The weight of the gold snuffbox in her pocket gave her a warm feeling, as if the glow from the polished gold had managed magically to spread its radiance through her whole body.

Her sharp eyes spied a pretty china shepherdess and then a pair of silver candlesticks.

"Enough!" she told herself after she had stowed them away. She made silently for the window.

But just as she was about to blow out her lantern, it occurred to her that selling shabby household goods, pots and pans and Meg's old clothes, in Hackminster, the nearest market town, was one thing; turning up dressed as she was to sell precious objects was another.

She would need suitable clothes.

Then she froze.

A man's voice called, "Jist making sure them doors is locked," and she heard the faint voice of a woman answering. The caretaker and his wife.

Polly blew out her lantern and crouched behind a chair. For the first time it struck her that being found with the stolen objects would send her to the nearest gibbet. She gently drew out everything and placed it under a chair. She waited while she heard the care-taker rattling about, checking the locks and bars. Surely he would come in to lock the drawing-room windows.

But after a short while, she heard him clattering down the stairs to the servants' quarters.

Polly waited for an hour after that.

Then she lit the lantern again, went quietly out of the drawing room and began to ascend the shallow oaken stairs to the bedrooms above.

The old stairs creaked and she had to wait and wait, heart pounding, to make sure the caretaker did not come running.

She wandered about the great bedrooms, looking in wardrobes and closets. There were a few beautiful gowns left by Lady Lydia, but after longingly finger-ing the material, Polly decided she would attract too much attention with such fine clothes. No one with-out a carriage and a train of servants wore such clothes. She climbed on up until she reached the attics—and luck was with her. In a large wardrobe on the very top landing were a few maids' caps and gowns and one warm black wool dress. Polly took the dress and a cap and apron. Bolder now, she searched the servants' rooms until she found a thick cloak. It was a man's cloak, but it would serve well. The sight of these servants' clothes gave Polly cour-age. London servants must be very well treated to be able to leave any clothes behind in a place to which they might never return.

She tied up the bundle of clothes with string and inched her way back down the stairs, the sound of her own heartbeats so loud that she feared the drumming might wake the caretaker.

She nearly stumbled and fell when she reached the drawing room, so great was her haste to escape, but she did not forget to pick up the snuffbox, candlesticks and china figure from under the chair. Then she blew out her lantern and fastened it back at her waist.

Once out in the cold night glittering with frost, Polly forced herself to go slowly, making her way out of the grounds by the way she had come in.

The wind had died. Everything was frosty, sparkling and glinting in the moonlight like marquesite.

The heavy weight of stolen goods bumped against her thigh. Polly felt a tremendous sense of exhilaration which grew and grew as she walked rapidly down the road toward home—that home so soon to be taken from her.

She leaned over the bridge which spanned the River Mere and looked at the rushing water. "I shall beat them all, Aunt Meg," she whispered. "You'll see. I'll get to London and find out who marked you. Who was it? Lady Lydia? Did you think I was her when you was dying and you called me my lady? Or was it one of them grand London servants?"

An owl hooted from the trees, sending a shiver of sound over the whitening landscape.

Polly heaved the bundle of clothes up onto her shoulder and strode out down the road. She began to whistle a jaunty, military air. For she felt as brave and elated as a soldier who had just fought his first battle.

*   *   *

Two of society's "pretty fellows" met at White's Club in St. James's Street, London—that haunt of High Tories, adventurers and hangers-on—to turn their weak brains to a problem.

The Honorable Jonathan Barks was the owner of the problem. His friend, Mr. Percy Caldicott, was the gentleman who was to solve that problem.

Both were still exhausted after the brain-straining of the previous day. It had been spent in playing that intellectual game of Inventing the Lie. One started at a coffee house over at, say, the Temple, where one delivered oneself of the lie—in this case that the French had secretly taken over Dover—and then followed the lie as it spread from coffee house to coffee house and club to club. They had followed it all over London and watched with glee as it grew in magnitude, only to find to their chagrin that their beautiful lie had been exploded by evening by none other than the marquess of Canonby, who had damned it as rubbish. And what the great marquess damned as rubbish was promptly accepted by the rest of the *beau monde* as being just that.

"Pity about Canonby," drawled Mr. Barks. "Curst spoiler of sport."

"What's yar problem," yawned Mr. Caldicott, revealing a large mouthful of shattered teeth like the shelled ramparts of a besieged town.

"Him."

"Who?"

"Canonby."

"Oh. Want to get revenge of the fellow for shooting down our lie?"

"Strap me vitals! No! Want his favor."

"At court?"

"Yas."

Mr. Caldicott nodded wisely. He had often heard the moans of Mrs. Barks that she had not yet been presented in the royal drawing room. Everyone knew the marquess of Canonby had great influence.

"Wife complaining again?" he asked. He gave a spasmodic jerk of his head, took the implement euphemistically called a back scratcher out of his pocket, and applied it vigorously to his high-ladder toupee. A small gray louse rattled onto the table between them. Mr. Caldicott caught the insect between finger and thumb, popped it in his silver lice box, and snapped shut the lid with the satisfaction of a deer stalker bringing home a stag.

"Never stops complaining," said Mr. Barks gloomily. "That's why I keep her in the country. But she writes to say she's coming to Town next month and if she ain't presented at court, she'll move her mother and herself up to Town permanently."

"Gad's 'oonds!"

"I found out that Canonby will be thirty-one at the end of the month, so I thought if I could hit on a present for him that would really please him, then I could ask him for a favor."

"True. Vary true."

"Well, think of something."

Both men furrowed their brows in thought, making little cracks appear in the white enamel on their faces. Had they been washed and scrubbed, both men would have appeared different, Mr. Barks being fair and Mr. Caldicott swarthy. But blanc, rouge, wigs and powder, tight-lacing, high heels and the same affectations made them appear peculiarly alike.

"He's got everything," said Mr. Caldicott slowly. "We must hit on something rare, something that's hard to come by in this day and age."

"What about a virgin?" tittered Mr. Barks.

Mr. Caldicott looked at his friend in awe.

"Strap me. Blessed if you ain't got it and with no help from me."

"Got what?"

"The present. Get him a virgin. Not one of those pretend-virgins, not one of those whores, not a child neither, but a real slap-bang untouched fresh-as-day virgin."

"Where in God's creation do you find one of those?"

"Mother Blanchard."

"Ah. But she'll charge high, that abbess will. Very high."

"Let me put it this way." Mr. Caldicott leaned forward and rapped his friend on his embroidered knee with the ivory sticks of his fan. "It's either a high price for a virgin, or it's the wife and mother-in-law in Town—for life."

"You have convinced me. We had best go and see the abbess now."

Outside the club, the gentlemen climbed into two sedan chairs, Mr. Caldicott with his tall wig poking up through the trap at the top. The Irish chairmen

with their exquisite burdens hurtled along the pave-
ments in the direction of Covent Garden at a great
rate, shouting, "Make way! Make way!"

That famous "abbess," Mrs. Blanchard, listened
carefully to the gentlemen's request. She looked more
like a country housekeeper than the owner and man-
ager of one of London's most notorious brothels. She
had a round apple-cheeked face and blue twinkling
eyes, and wore a sober gown of lilac silk with a
decorous cap of white linen.

"I want beauty as well as virginity, mother," said
Mr. Barks after he had agreed to her staggering
price. "And no money until I have inspected the
goods!"

"Of course not, my dear gentlemen," cooed Mrs.
Blanchard. "I shall go on the hunt this very day."

Polly Jones decided that her days of crime were
over. As she sat on the London-bound wagon beside
the waggoner, Mr. Silas Brewer, she thought with
some wonder of how dangerously easy it all had
been. She could not depend on such luck again.
Now, she had enough money. She would never steal
again. The day after the robbery, she had walked
halfway to Hackminster before hiding behind a hedge
and putting on her maid's disguise and wrapping
herself in the stolen cloak. Her hair was scraped up on
her head in a demure knot under the white cap. She
buried her old clothes in the field.

Then into Hackminster, seeking a jeweller in the
back streets rather than one where there might be too
many curious people about. With maidenly lowered

eyes, she produced candlesticks, snuffbox and figurine, saying meekly that her mistress, who wished to
remain anonymous, was in sore need of money. Na-
tive cunning made Polly refuse the first two offers as
being too low and she settled for the third.

In case their loss had already been reported, she
decided it would be risky to find a place on the stage
coach, although she could easily have afforded it.
She had walked several miles along the London road
before she had hailed the wagon she was travelling in
now and persuaded the genial Silas to take her up.

By the time the wagon lumbered over the cobbles
of the City of London, Polly had heard most of
Silas's life story and the two had become fast friends—
although Silas, a wizened little man who had talked
for hours about his home in Shoreditch and his wife
and three daughters, did not realize he had learned
very little about his pretty companion.

"Can ye write?" he asked, as Polly swung down
from the wagon, carrying a basket with her money
and a few belongings.

"Yes," said Polly.

"See here. I've got this scrap of paper." He held
out a grimy piece. "Write down me name and address, and if you're ever in need o' a friend, come to
me."

Polly wrote down his name and address and thrust
the paper in her bosom.

"I'm going to find work as a servant, Mr. Brewer,"
she said proudly. "I'll come and call on you and
Mrs. Brewer, for you've been ever so kind to me.
But I won't need help. I can take care of meself."

She gave him a cheeky grin and a wave of the hand, and the restless, shifting London crowd swallowed her up.

But when Polly had gone a little way, she stopped and looked about her in bewilderment. She was sure this was not the *real* London. That other London of parks and palaces must lie elsewhere. Where should she start looking for work?

Fog was coming down, blurring the streets. The roar of the great carriages and brewers' sleds rumbling over the cobbles was deafening. "Make way!" yelled a gouty-legged chairman, forcing her to dart off to one side. "Make room there!" screamed another fellow, driving a wheelbarrow full of nuts straight at her legs. Shouting voices in the streets assaulted her ears with a cacophony of sound. *Have you brass pot, iron kettle, skillet or frying pan to mend? Two a groat and four for sixpence, mackerel! Stand up there, you blind dog. Will you have the cart squeeze your guts out? Buy my flounders. Turn out there, you country putt. Kitchen stuff, ha' you maids.* And above all the shouts, the terrifying blasts of a trumpet, the trumpet player carrying a placard advertising the rare sight of a calf with six legs.

Polly found herself near a church. She retreated up the steps to the shelter of the porch and looked out over the bustle of the City of London. The streets presented a picture of luxury and dirt, color and grime, rags and riches. The brilliant clothes of men and women of the upper class, the colored and gilded coaches, the liveries of the footmen and of the Negro pages, the gaudy signs which hung above every house and shop—these wonders were offset by the thick mud of the streets, the overflowing filth of the kennel, the sore faces of the beggars, the reeling drunkards, and the draggle-tailed hawkers and ballad singers.

But there was an excited, restless, strung-up excitement in the air which seemed to emanate from the very stones. Polly, defeated and dazed, nonetheless loved it all.

"Excuse me, my dear," said a motherly voice at Polly's ear.

Polly started and turned round.

A plump, pleasant woman stood there, smiling at her.

"You look lost," she said. "May I be of some assistance?"

"Oh, yes," said Polly gratefully. "I want employment as a servant and I don't know where to start."

The woman smiled again. "Just up from the country, are you?"

"Yes, ma'am."

"Well, now, we are both lucky. I am housekeeper to a certain noble lord and am looking for a bright and willing girl. There's a comfortable tavern near here. Why don't we go along together and find out if we shall suit each other?"

Dazed with her good fortune and reassured by the woman's motherly appearance, Polly agreed.

Soon she was drinking her first glass of gin and confiding in this comfortable woman who was so attentive and easy to talk to.

"It seems to me," said the woman, "that you are just what I am looking for. What is your name?"

"Jones, ma'am. Polly Jones. My real name is Mary, of course, and I am nicknamed Polly."

The woman patted her hand, her little blue eyes twinkling in her round apple-cheeked face.

"And my name is Blanchard. Mrs. Martha Blanchard of Covent Garden. Now, we'll just have another gin and we'll be on our way . . ."

CHAPTER TWO

THE FACT THAT THIS HOUSEKEEPER HAD A CARriage to take her home did not surprise Polly in the slightest. She assumed grand servants such as housekeepers must be on an almost equal footing with their masters.

Mrs. Blanchard had fallen silent. Polly gazed eagerly out of the carriage, always looking for the palaces and gardens of her dreams. But the fog was closing down as the carriage made its way under the ghastly severed heads of executed criminals stuck up on the gate at Temple Bar. Then, before they swung off the Strand to enter the crowded lanes of Covent Garden, Polly had one little glimpse of heaven.

A lady was alighting from a carriage, holding out her hand to take the helping hand of a young gentleman. The carriage lamps were lit and so the little tableau was surrounded with a soft circle of gold light. The young gallant was wearing a flowered waistcoat, tight to the figure, under a white satin coat. He had lace ruffles at his wrist and a foam of lace at his neck. He carried a gold-laced three-cornered hat. His sword had a gold hilt sparkling with jewels, and a sword sash of white silk embroidered with gold lay across his chest. He had silk stockings and gold-buckled shoes. His young clean-shaven face smiled out from below the shadow of an exquisitely curled and powdered Ramillies wig. But it was his lady who held Polly's fascinated gaze.

Her gown had a flowered silk body and cream-colored skirts trimmed with lace. She had light blue shoulder knots, an amber necklace, brown Swedish gloves, and a silver bracelet. Her flowered silk belt of green, gray and yellow was tied to one side in a large bow. Her white powdered hair was covered with a large straw hat decorated with large green and yellow flowers. The carriage jolted on and the scene was lost to view. But it was a picture out of a fairy tale and Polly no longer saw the filth and grime or flinched at the noise and roar of the streets.

"Here we are, dear," she realized Mrs. Blanchard was saying. Polly stepped down and Mrs. Blanchard followed. The house was tall and narrow with over-hanging gables. Mrs. Blanchard produced a large key from her pocket and opened the door, then ushered Polly inside.

The hall was in darkness. There was a scraping of flint and then an oil lamp blossomed into life. Picking it up, Mrs. Blanchard pushed open a door that led off the hall. "Come into my little parlor," she said over her shoulder to Polly.

Polly walked in and looked about her in amazement. Surely a housekeeper could not possibly be allowed such a principal room on the ground floor. Mrs. Blanchard was lighting branches of candles. Long, heavy brocade curtains were hung at the windows. The room boasted three red silk sofas and even had a thick carpet on the floor.

Then Polly's heart began to race. Her country upbringing had given her an almost animal sense of danger. She felt it in the closed and scented air of the room.

"I do mind, Mrs. Blanchard," said Polly carefully, "that I left some of my traps over in the City. I'll just be off to fetch them."

Mrs. Blanchard smiled and pulled hard on a bell rope. "As you will," she said, "but first, let us take a dish of tea."

"No, I thank you, ma'am," said Polly firmly. She walked to the door, which opened before she reached it. Her way was blocked by two men in footmen's livery. One was very tall and thin, and where his left eye should have been was a mess of criss-crossed scars. The other was small and broad with broken teeth, a blue chin and a low forehead.

"Come back and sit down, Polly," said Mrs. Blanchard.

"No," said Polly. "I . . ."

She broke off as she saw the smaller of the two men was holding a pistol, and that pistol was pointed straight at her.

She backed away, collided with a sofa and sat down abruptly. "She looks galleyed," grinned the man with the pistol. "Introduce us, mother."

"Certainly, my dears. This is Polly Jones. Polly, the smaller gentleman is Barney and the tall one with the beautiful eyes is Jake."

"You don't want me as a servant," said Polly, fighting for calm. "Am I to be raped?"

This caused much hilarity. "No, no, my chuck," said Mrs. Blanchard, wiping her streaming eyes. "I promised you you would go into a nobleman's service and so you shall, if you're a good girl. Take off your cap." Barney raised the pistol menacingly. Polly slowly took off her cap.

"Unpin your hair."

Polly drew out the wood pin from the knot at the top of her head. Her heavy chestnut tresses cascaded about her shoulders.

"Better and better," murmured Mrs. Blanchard. "Now take off your cloak."

"Aren't we at least going to play cards?" asked Polly sarcastically. She had heard gossip from the village boys that in London some of the grand folk would play cards, the loser each time having to take off a piece of clothing.

"A wit, i' faith," said Mrs. Blanchard in a hard voice. "Do as you're told, girl."

Polly took off her cloak. Over her black gown she was wearing the leather tight-laced bodice of the country girl.

"I think she could do with a dish of tea, mother,"

said the man called Jake, drooping his one good eye
in a wink.

"You are become soft-hearted, Jake," grumbled
Mother Blanchard. Her two henchmen sat down on
one of the sofas facing Polly while Mrs. Blanchard
got out the teapot, took out cannisters and pot, and
then put a small silver kettle to boil on a spirit stove.

Polly's mind raced. She must be calm. She must
wait and watch for a means of escape. At last, Mrs.
Blanchard handed her a cup of tea. Polly drank it,
grateful for the taste of the refreshing, scalding liquid.

"You must tell me why you have brought me
here," she said loudly.

Neither of the three said anything. They watched,
and waited. Polly saw Barney lower the pistol. She
stood up to make a dash for the door but her head
whirled, the ground rushed up to meet her, and she
plunged down into a great black pit of nothingness.

Mrs. Blanchard stooped over her. "Off with you,"
she said to Barney and Jake. "I want to examine the
goods in peace and quiet."

Polly Jones came slowly awake. She felt sick and
groggy. At first she did not know where she was
and wondered why her surroundings were so unfamiliar. Then it all came rushing back—London, Mrs.
Blanchard, Barney and Jake, and the tea!

She sat up and groaned and clutched her stomach,
feeling dizzy. After a while, the sickness passed. She
found she was in a narrow bed and that she was
naked. A blush of shame crept over her from the
soles of her feet to the top of her head. She pulled a

blanket about her and climbed out of bed and looked about. The small grimy window was barred. The door was locked. Apart from the bed and one chair, and one chamberpot under the bed, there was not another piece of furniture.

Gone were her money and her belongings.

From downstairs came noise and music. Polly threw back her head and screamed "Help!" at the top of her voice. No one came running. No voice answered.

She sat down on the edge of the bed, feeling tears prick at the back of her eyes. "No, Polly Jones," she said aloud. "Now is not yet the time for weeping."

There came the scrape of a key in the lock. Polly scrambled under the bedcovers and pulled them up to her chin.

Jake came in with a pile of clothing over one arm and a tray of food. "Eat this," he said curtly, putting the tray on the floor. "There's wine and it ain't drugged. I'll be back for you in fifteen minutes. Be ready."

"What for?" demanded Polly.

"For yer eddication."

"Education? What in?"

"Geography," said Jake, and fell about laughing at his own wit.

Then he went out and shut the door behind him and locked it.

Polly got out of bed and examined the clothes. There was a sack gown made of tabinet with box pleats forming the straight back, a muslin shift and a lawn petticoat with huge bell ruffles at the end of its three-quarter-length sleeves. Polly put on the clothes, pulling the ruffles of her petticoat out of the sleeves of her gown. The gown was cut very low, exposing the top halves of Polly's round firm breasts. In the summer at Upper Batchett, she had worn only her leather bodice and petticoat and had exposed just as much skin. But Mrs. Blanchard was the serpent who had entered Polly's garden of innocence, and for the first time she felt immodest. She bent down and, lifting up her skirt, tore a long strip of lawn from her petticoat and tucked it into the top of her gown to form a kerchief. She looked at the food and wine, wondering whether it had been drugged. But she was ravenously hungry and knew she must keep up her strength for whatever lay ahead. There was a large piece of cold meat pie, a heel of bread, and a jug of wine. Polly demolished the lot. She sat nervously on the bed, waiting anxiously to see whether she would become dizzy again, but time passed and she began to feel remarkably well.

There was a fumbling and scraping at the lock, the door swung open, and both Barney and Jake stood there. "Come along o' us," said Barney, brandishing his pistol.

Polly walked before them, her head held high. Somehow she would escape this terrible place, out into that magic world peopled by wonderful creatures such as the couple she had seen in the Strand.

They urged her in front of them down a narrow staircase and into a room on the first floor. It was small and dark and lit only by one candle. Mrs. Blanchard sat on a stool next to a curtain which covered one wall.

"Now, my dear," she said on seeing Polly, "you are to be trained to please a fine gentleman and you must learn our arts."

"What did you do to me when I was drugged?" asked Polly harshly.

"Nothing," said Mrs. Blanchard calmly. "I had to make sure you were a virgin, and you are, still. That is your worth. Come here, girl, and kneel on the floor by me."

"Virgins ought to 'ave virginal minds," said Barney suddenly from behind Polly. "Don't see no reason for this."

"Stow your whids," grated Mrs. Blanchard, her voice coarse and sharp. "Keep her covered. Polly, kneel by me or you get your brains blown out."

With a defiant shrug, Polly did as she was bid.

Mrs. Blanchard drew aside the curtain over the wall, revealing a small peephole. "Put your eye to that, Polly girl, and keep it there."

Kneeling, Polly put her eye to the hole. She found herself looking directly into another room, at a sofa on which a man was lying while a female, naked to the waist, lay across him. He was drinking from a bottle of wine, occasionally setting it on the floor to fondle the girl's breasts. The girl was about Polly's age, and her eyes had a dead-fish look about them. Then the man stood up and said something and the girl got up as well. She hitched up her skirts and then lay down inelegantly on the sofa, one thin stick-like leg over the back. The man fumbled in his breeches and then mounted her.

Polly watched them indifferently. Had she been a

town girl, the scene might have horrified and disgusted her. But she had seen animals mating too many times to find anything unusual and interesting about the spectacle before her. She had stumbled over too many coupling bodies on the hayfields to be alarmed. And yet a part of her mind, as innocent and untouched as only a virgin's can be, wondered what all this had to do with love and honor. Her knees hurt from kneeling on the floor. She wanted peace and quiet to think. Obviously these people would expect some sort of reaction. So Polly cried out, "I cannot bear it!" and pretended to fall over in a faint.

"Oh, the pore thing!" she heard Jake exclaim.

"Don't seem right," grumbled Barney.

"Figs. What has come over you gallows-birds," snarled Mother Blanchard. "You've been with me only two days and already you are turning soft. Do you know how much I'm going to get for handing this lovely into the marquess of Canonby's bedchamber? A fortune!"

Polly lay very still. So she was to be sold. She thought hard. If she could not escape from this brothel—for she knew beyond all doubt where she was—then all she had to do was bide her time until she was delivered to this marquess. Neither Barney nor Jake nor Mother Blanchard would be expected to follow her into the nobleman's bedchamber. There would be only Polly, and one aristocrat who would not expect any resistance.

Jake spoke from somewhere behind her. "This marquess wants a bit o' novelty, mother. Stands to reason he wants a proper virgin, not one versed in the tricks o' the whoring lay.''

'' 'S right,'' drawled Barney.

"But if she knows how to please him," said Mrs. Blanchard, "she may be in the way of putting some more money our way. If she don't know how to please him, he may be shot of her quick."

"Naw," said Jake. "Them lords can get all the whoring they want. Like to do the eddicating themselves, if you ask me."

"When did you turn philosopher," grumbled Mrs. Blanchard. "Oh, very well. Lock her up in her room. My buyers are coming soon to see her. Her skin's still tanned. I could cover her up with blanc, but she'd look better natural. Throw a jug of water over her.''

Polly quickly pretended to recover consciousness.

Barney escorted her up the stairs to her room. "A poor life for a man," said Polly, confronting him, her hands on her hips.

"If you'd faced transportation as I 'ave, you'd not sneer," said Barney grimly. "The law don't bother Ma Blanchard and so they don't bother me."

"What was you arrested for?" asked Polly.

"Thieving wipes."

"Stealing handkerchiefs. Pooh!" said Polly airily. "I did better'n that."

"Go on, a child like yourself!"

'' 'S true. I took two silver candlesticks, a china piece and a gold snuffbox and sold 'em, 'cept your mistress took the money away with my basket.''

"You kin hang for that."

"Why wasn't *you* hanged?"

"Ma Blanchard was looking for workers so she hired witnesses outside the court to say I hadn't done it. Did the same for Jake. Jake and me's bin together since we was in the orphanage. So we come to work for her just this week. Don't you go thieving, Poll, 'cause that road leads to Tyburn.''

"You mean I ought to lead a clean and decent life by becoming some nobleman's whore?"

Barney shifted his squat bulk uneasily. "Ain't too bad," he said. "You gets food and pretty clothes. Save all them baubles he gives you, if you like, and then me and Jake'll take them to a fence for you."

"A what?"

"A chap that buys stolen goods."

"Fiddle-de-dee. I'll sell 'em to a regular jeweller like I did the last."

"Yes, but what if his nibs ups and says you stole them? And what was you about to pop stuff at a proper jeweller for? When it's found missing, they'll ask the jewellers and they'll give a description o' you."

"Barney!" Mrs. Blanchard called from downstairs.

Barney darted from the room, locking the door behind him.

In the long and weary days of her imprisonment that followed, Polly tried to engage Barney and Jake in conversation but they answered her curtly and refused to stay longer than necessary.

Christmas came and went, the event marked for Polly by a small sprig of holly placed on a slice of plum pudding. She looked sharply at Barney, know-

ing that Mrs. Blanchard would hardly have added
this frivolous touch, but he only looked away and
said gruffly, "Won't be long now, Poll."

The reason for the long delay was that the marquess of Canonby had decided to go out of Town and
celebrate his birthday in the country. But he was to
hold a party at the end of January, and Mr. Caldicott
and Mr. Barks planned to present Polly to him then.

At the turn of the year, Polly was at last brought
downstairs. Mr. Barks and Mr. Caldicott were going
to call to inspect her. Her now-white skin was bathed
in lemon juice to make sure it stayed that way. Her
long tresses were twisted up in hot clay rollers. Then
a little hairdresser who appeared terrified of Mrs.
Blanchard unwound the rollers and proceeded to back-
comb Polly's hair up over a black silk cushion. When
it had reached the desired height, it was dusted with a
cloud of white scented powder. Then she was strapped
into long stiff stays which pushed up her breasts.
Over a blue quilted petticoat went a white satin stomacher laced from side to side with blue cord. The
exquisitely frilled three-quarter-length sleeves of the
petticoat were drawn through the sleeves of a gown
of blue lutestring, looped up at the hem with garlands
of silk daisies to show the petticoat. Blue shoulder
knots ornamented the sleeves at the top and three
strands of pearls were tied around her neck with a
white satin ribbon. Small posies of daisies were placed
in her hair just above her ears. She wore fine white
silk stockings and black pointed shoes with high red
heels. One of the prostitutes who was acting as lady's
maid for Polly's embellishment muttered jealously in

her ear, "Enjoy it while you may. You'll soon be one of us," and Polly looked at the girl's young-old face and wasted figure and shuddered.

At last she was seated on one of the red silk sofas in the "boudoir," and Mr. Barks and Mr. Caldicott were ushered in.

Mr. Caldicott drew in his breath in a little hiss and Mr. Barks stood and goggled. Polly's violet eyes looked enormous in her white face. There was a small black patch at the corner of her mouth but her face was free from paint. Another black patch ornamented the swell of her left breast, revealed by the low-cut gown.

She looked disdainfully at the two men. "This is a lady," said Mr. Caldicott sharply. "You'll run us into trouble, mother."

"She's nothing but a country girl," said Mrs. Blanchard with a shrug. "I saw her arrive in a wagon and followed her. Fine clothes make her. She's only got to open her mouth and you'll know she's not a lady."

"Odd's fish," said Mr. Barks in awe. "My good wife will be presented this year without a doubt. What loveliness!"

"When are you taking her?" snapped Mrs. Blanchard. "She's been here for ages, eating her stupid head off."

"Two days' time," said Mr. Caldicott. He slapped his knee. "We'll put her in a box like a regular present."

"Fool," said Mrs. Blanchard. "The girl would suffocate 'fore she got there."

But Polly's beauty had urged Mr. Caldicott's imagination to great heights. "We'll put her in a cage,
like they do with the wild beasts at the fair. A gilt
cage on wheels. And we'll drape it with a satin cloth.
'Your present, my lord,' you'll say, Barks. You
whip back the cloth. His eyes will be dazzled. You
will have his favor for life!'."

Mrs. Blanchard looked amused. Barney and Jake
looked stunned. To Polly, it was all some horrible
dream. And yet that dream still held one little glim-
mer of hope. She would be outside soon, and perhaps
outside there was hope of escape. These monsters
were used to keeping girls prisoner. But an aristocrat
would not be so vigilant. Perhaps if she behaved very
badly, he would throw her out into the street and then
she could find her way to Shoreditch and to Silas.

The audience was over. Polly was taken back to
her "cell" by Barney and Jake. They gazed at her
with something approaching reverence. "Blessed if
you ain't the prettiest thing I ever did see, Poll," said
Barney.

"Please do one thing for me," pleaded Polly. "I
don't want my money back. Find where Ma Blanchard's
got my basket and see if you can find a scrap o'
paper she took off my body with a Shoreditch address on it."

"Bit dangerous," said Barney uneasily. "Fact is,
Polly, me and Jake ain't suited for this here lay. Ma
Blanchard's beginning to say we're soft about you
and is threatening to have us whipped."

"Oh, just look for that scrap o' paper," pleaded
Polly.

The two men shifted restlessly. "Don't seem much," said Jake. "We'll look, but don't you go trying to run away, for we'll have to shoot you or Ma Blanchard would shoot us herself. While we're away, you've got to get out of those fine clothes but leave your hair as it is. Ma ain't going to pay for another head. And if you tear it out, she'll whip you."

"No, she won't," said Polly cynically. "She wants the goods to stay unmarked."

Jake grinned. "You're learning fast, Poll. But think on't. Better a bit o' discomfort than having it all done over again and Ma screeching and hollering."

"Anything," said Polly wearily. "Just find me that paper."

When her two jailors had left, she carefully slipped off the new clothes, laid them on the bed, and put on the sack dress.

After an hour, the door opened and Barney and Jake came in. Ever vigilant, Barney kept her covered with the pistol while Jake picked up the clothes. Then Barney threw a grimy scrap of paper on the floor. "Think that's it," he said gruffly.

Polly scooped it up and put it in her bosom. With a bit of luck, she might be in Shoreditch in two days' time.

Even Mrs. Blanchard was impressed with the arrangements for Polly's departure. She was placed in a gilt cage like a circus cage, and seated on a gilt chair. The cage was then draped with white satin. The combined forces of Mr. Caldicott's servants and Mr. Barks's servants were there to escort it with flaming torches through the streets of London. Barney and Jake leaned out of an upper window of the brothel and watched and watched until the cage and its entourage had turned a corner of the street and disappeared from view.

Jake struggled to express unfamiliar feelings. At last he wiped his nose on his sleeve and said, "Don't life seem a bit cold and dirty wiffout her?"

"You're soft," sneered Barney, but he bit his thumb furiously and then spat with accuracy on the head of a passing beadle to relieve his feelings.

CHAPTER THREE

THE NOISE AND CLAMOR OF THE LONDON STREETS rose once more about Polly Jones as her cage was wheeled westwards. At one point she thought freedom might be at hand, for she heard some hoarse masculine voices yell, "Hey, what ha' ye? A wild beast? Let us see!" Then there were the sounds of blows and curses as her entourage fought off what sounded like a great many attackers. Her cage tilted dangerously and she clutched at the bars for support. But soon the noise of fighting died away and once more she felt herself being trundled onwards.

What would Aunt Meg think? wondered Polly. For all her white witchcraft, Meg had been a religious woman and attended church every Sunday, making the rebellious Polly go with her. But Polly had paid scant attention to the service, flashing her eyes at the village boys instead. She had just begun to enjoy the power of her beauty when Meg had died. But her beauty had turned out to be a disaster. Polly tried to pray but found she could not. God had let Meg die. God had sent the squire's bailiffs to turn her out. If she prayed, then God might know where she was and send down some more divine punishment. Polly turned her thoughts to Silas Brewer. There were kind people in the world, decent people who led blameless lives. Somehow she would get to Shoreditch, and once there, she would find respectable employment. Then she could find out where Lady Lydia and the earl of Meresly lived and see if she could think up a way to get close to them, to question them about Meg's death.

The streets were quieter now. Suddenly, the cage jerked to a halt and she felt it being lifted up off the wheels. "Steady now," she heard Mr. Barks cry. "Don't want to damage it."

It, thought Polly miserably. I have no soul, no rights; I am become an "it."

Then she felt warm scented air about her and the clamor of mincing, affected voices, male and female.

"What on earth is that idiot Barks up to?" said Lady Lydia Meresly.

"He has brought a caged present for Canonby," said Bertram Pargeter. "He doubts, no doubt, to gain influence at court."

"Tiresome man. Come and play me at vingt-et-un, Bertram."

"Lady of my heart, I would rather play once more in your bedchamber."

"You are bold and coarse. I have warned you before that our liaison is at an end."

"Why?" pleaded Bertram. "There was much between us."

"All history," laughed Lady Lydia. "Come, Bertram, you grow tedious."

Bertram flushed to the roots of his powdered hair. He wanted to strike her, to kiss her, to fall to his knees and beg her to smile on him once more. He had high hopes of that little scene in Upper Batchett and had returned there to ferret out scandal. But all he heard was a tale of some old witch who died after leading a blameless life. The girl in the churchyard had been some foundling bastard, so coarse in spirit she would rather gawp at the great folk than mourn her protectress. No one could remember having seen Lady Lydia in Upper Batchett before that last visit for years and years, and she had never had anything to do with any of the local people.

The marquess of Canonby's mansion in St. James's Square was a blaze of lights. He was rich and gave elaborate parties with three card rooms, a saloon for dancing and an excellent supper. But his affairs were always correct and formal. His guests covertly watched his immobile face as he surveyed the satin-shrouded cage and wondered whether Barks and Caldicott had run mad. The elegant marquess would hardly relish the present of a wild beast.

"My lord," said Mr. Barks, sweating with excitement. "I have a present for you."

And what do I do with this animal? wondered the marquess crossly. Send it to the menagerie at the Tower, I suppose.

But aloud, he said politely, "You do us great honor, Mr. Barks. May we expect the unveiling?"

"Certainly, my lord," gasped Mr. Barks. "Stand back, ladies and gentlemen."

The cage was placed in the center of the saloon. Couples, anxious to resume dancing, stood about, half curious, half irritated.

Inside the cage, Polly tensed.

The satin cover was twitched aside. Polly Jones looked out at the beau monde, and the beau monde stared back.

"I do not know this lady," said the marquess harshly.

"But you will, my lord," crowed Mr. Barks. "She is yours. A virgin!"

So this was the marquess of Canonby. Polly surveyed him calmly, trying to assess how easy he would be to outwit. He was tall and very handsome. Under his powdered wig, his face was lightly tanned. His eyes were green, flecked with gold and heavy-lidded. He had a high proud nose and a firm, uncompromising mouth. He was dressed in a blue silk coat embroidered with gold. His shoulders were unfashionably broad and square for this age when men considered sloping shoulders a sign of genteel birth. His legs encased in blue silk breeches and white-clocked stockings were well shaped and muscular. A foam of white Mechlin lace was at his throat and fine Mechlin lace fell at his wrists under the wide embroidered cuffs of his coat. His long white silk waistcoat was elaborately embroidered with crimson and gold flowers and fastened with a long row of gold buttons. Diamonds blazed in his cravat and on his fingers, on the jewelled hilt of his dress sword and on the gold buckles of his shoes.

The marquess looked curiously at Polly, at the alabaster skin, the pink virginal mouth and the strong swell of two excellent breasts. His one thought was that this virgin must have cost Barks a fortune.

Then he realized the caged girl was staring beyond him. He swung about.

Lady Lydia Meresly stood there, her hand to her brow. As he watched, she clutched at Bertram Pargeter's sleeve and said faintly, "Get my husband. Get Meresly. Take me home."

Bertram caught her about the waist, his eyes darting first to her white face and then to Polly's. Lady Lydia's hair was powdered, as was Polly's. The resemblance between them was marked. And then Bertram realized he had seen Polly's violet eyes before. He was sure this was the girl from the churchyard. His grasp on Lady Lydia tightened with excitement and she moaned faintly.

"Do as the lady says," snapped the marquess. "Ah, Meresly. Your wife feels faint and would go home."

The earl of Meresly, a tall handsome ruin of a man, came quickly forward. He thrust Bertram rudely away and picked up his wife in his arms.

The marquess turned his attention back to Polly. He signalled to two footmen. "Take her to my bedchamber," he said, "and lock her in. I'll deal with her later."

Mr. Barks winked and nudged Mr. Caldicott gleefully. Both men unlocked Polly's cage and stood back. "Thank you, Barks," said the marquess in chilly accents. "Most original. Now, if we can but remove that cage, the dancing may commence."

Polly sat in a chair by the fire in the marquess of Canonby's bedchamber and looked about her with wide eyes. The room had been decorated in the latest Chinese fashion. It was dominated by a great black and gold lacquered bed with a pagoda-like canopy. The flock wallpaper depicted little Chinese figures crossing and recrossing bridges. The furniture was upholstered in yellow silk. Polly, feeling bolder, stood up to explore. On the mantel were a couple of beautiful gold and enamel snuffboxes. On a table by the bed was a shoe horn of ivory with a silver handle. On a chest of drawers stood a jewel box, the lid up and the contents blazing in the candlelight.

Polly's magpie senses quickened. All about her lay the means to freedom and independence. Only a few of these trinkets would set her up for life. The marquess had so much, he would not miss a few pieces. Fear left her. She remembered all the elation she had felt when she had stolen from Meresly Manor. Her gown boasted slits at either side which led down to pockets in the petticoat. Moving quickly, she slipped into her pockets one of the snuffboxes, the shoe horn, one ruby ring, a small bird made of jade with emerald eyes, and a silver patchbox.

She heard someone at the door and quickly resumed her seat, a guilty flash staining her cheeks. A footman came in carrying a tray. Polly looked hopefully past him but there was another footman in the doorway, standing guard. The footman placed the tray, which held a selection of cakes and a small decanter of wine, beside Polly and turned to leave the room. "Feeding the prisoner, are we?" jeered Polly,

but the shutting and relocking of the door was the
only reply.

Polly eyed the wine doubtfully. What if it were
drugged? She decided to take a little sip and wait for
results. The wine was sweet and heady. She took
another sip and another. There was no reaction other
than a pleasant warm glow spreading through her
stomach. The cakes were delicious. Polly finished
them all down to the last crumb. The chair in which
she was seated was comfortable and the fire was
warm. The noise and music of the party filtered only
faintly up to her.

She tried in vain to keep her eyes open, but after a
few minutes, she was sound asleep.

The marquess of Canonby entered the room half an
hour later and stood looking down at her. Her long
black lashes were fanned out over her cheeks. She
slept as quietly and innocently as a young child.

He hated to disturb her sleep, but he wanted rid
of her. Barks had made him feel like some sort of
slave trafficker. It was fashionable, for example, to
have black servants, but he swore he would take to
employing them only when they were as free as
Englishmen, and there were a growing number in
society who held the same opinion. The very idea of
this girl having been bought for his pleasure sickened
him, although surely she could not be as innocent as
she looked.

He shook her gently by the shoulder. "Wake!" he
commanded. Polly's eyes flew open. What a strange
color they were, he mused. Violet. Like Lady Lydia's. Some malicious guests had been quick to point

out the resemblance between the girl in the cage and
the earl of Meresly's wife, but the marquess and
most of the others put this down to spite. Lady Lydia
had few friends and so she was often the victim of
malicious comment. And it was not unusual for ladies to faint in an age when fashion demanded tighter
and tighter lacing and smaller and smaller waists.

Polly sat up, looking at him warily.

He pulled up a chair and sat next to her. "Where
do you come from, child?" he asked.

His voice was deep and well modulated. His eyes
were hooded and remote.

"I come from the country," said Polly. "I was
took by a Mrs. Blanchard when I arrived and she
tricked me by saying she could find me work in a
nobleman's household. She runs a brothel in Covent
Garden."

"I know," said the marquess curtly.

"I suppose you do," said Polly with such contempt in her voice that he added, "I am not, however, one of Mother Blanchard's customers. Go on."

"Well, I was kept prisoner for ever so long," said
Polly, stifling a cavernous yawn. The marquess found
himself disappointed at the rough country accents of
her voice. Provided she never opened her mouth, she
could pass for a lady anywhere. "Then," Polly went
on, "I was tricked out in this finery and put in a
cage and brung here. I knew I was to be a present
for you." She studied his brooding expression.
"Look, my lord," said Polly urgently, "you don't
need me. There's plenty o' women would bed with
a lord."

"Thank you. I am glad to know my title makes me irresistible."

"Oh, it's not just that, my lord," said Polly.

"Were you thinking of my devastatingly handsome looks?" he asked sarcastically.

"No," said Polly candidly. "I was thinking about all your money."

"Did Mother Blanchard not think it necessary to instruct you in the arts of pleasing men? You are blunt to the point of rudeness."

"Well, she tried," said Polly, beginning to feel comfortable. She kicked off her shoes and luxuriously wriggled her toes. "There was a peephole in this room and she made me look through it. There was a man and a woman fiddling about." Polly's brow wrinkled. "Ever so sad, it was."

"I meant, pleasing in manners. But I am beginning to believe you *are* a virgin. Why was it sad?"

"I don't know, somehow. See, this wagonner took me up on the London road and he talked about his wife and children in such a way—loving, like. I know in here," said Polly, pointing to the region of her heart, "that's how it should be."

"You seem remarkably unafraid of me. Why?"

"Life has begun to seem . . . dangerous. I've learned to live a little bit at a time. Here I am, warm and rested, in a pretty room with pretty things." She cast a covetous eye around the remaining objets d'art and wondered whether she should have taken more. He followed her glance and his eyes sharpened a little before returning to her face.

"Why did you leave the country?"

"My aunt died and the squire's men came to turn me out of the cottage."

"But as your late aunt's niece you have a right to the tenancy!"

"Maybe," said Polly with a toss of her head. She had no intention of letting this grand lord know she was a foundling. "I heard how London servants were well clothed and fed so I decided to travel to Town."

"And what did you do before the death of this aunt? How were you employed?"

"I didn't do nothing," said Polly. "My aunt wouldn't let me. She sent me to the village school. But the day she died, she went to Meresly Manor and I thought she had changed her mind at last and meant to find me work."

"Your aunt obviously had enough for both of you. What did she do?"

"She was the wise woman of the village. She told fortunes, and made potions. People come . . . came . . . from far and wide to see her."

Polly thought of Meg, patient wise old Meg, and unshed tears brightened her eyes.

"Enough." He stood up. "I have no need of you. You may go."

Polly stood up as well and looked at him in a dazed way. "You don't want me?"

"Not in the slightest."

Polly felt an irrational stab of pique. Her experiences at the brothel had strengthened rather than shaken her knowledge that she was beautiful. Despite herself, she threw him a coquettish look and sank into a deep curtsy.

A slight look of distaste crossed his eyes. Polly slipped on her shoes and minced to the door on her high heels.

"A moment," said the marquess. "You may leave behind the belongings you have thieved from me."

Polly's face flamed. "How dare you call me a thief," she raged. "I am as innocent as the day. I am . . ."

"I am giving you just one more chance to hand over my bits and pieces, you little magpie."

Polly gave him a haughty stare. "Fiddle, my lord, I cannot hand over what I have not got."

He crossed the room quickly to stand in front of her. She threw up her hands to protect her face, thinking he meant to slap her. But he bent down, picked her up by the ankles as she screamed and screamed and shook her hard, dangling her upside down. Unmoved by her screams or by the delectable view of a shapely pair of legs in white silk stocking and scarlet garters or by the sight of a well-rounded bare white bottom, the marquess watched as snuffboxes and all rattled out over the floor. Then he dumped her unceremoniously on the floor.

Polly scrambled to her feet and pulled down her skirts. "You are no gentleman," she said. "Your servants drugged that wine and slipped those things in my pocket."

"Not only a thief but a liar who would try to ruin the reputation of my servants! Get out. Get out before I throw you out!"

With her head held high, Polly stalked from the room. She minced along the passage and then took off her shoes and began to run. She ran silently down the great staircase to the hall. In a saloon upstairs, the lords and ladies were performing charades and the servants had been encouraged to swell the audience. No one noticed her going. She saw an anteroom door standing open containing hats, cloaks and shawls. Quickly she slipped inside and rummaged through the pockets until she found a guinea piece. Then she selected the best of the cloaks and swung it about her shoulders. Gently she opened the street door and crept outside. Two chairmen had just deposited their burden outside a neighboring house and were making their way off.

"Chair!" called Polly. "Chair!"

The Irish chairmen gasped at the idea of carrying anyone as far as Shoreditch until Polly produced the guinea and held it up. They hurriedly agreed. Polly wearily climbed inside and was borne off through the nighttime streets.

"Well, my lord," leered Mr. Barks when the marquess rejoined his guests. "How did you enjoy your present?"

Much as he disliked the whole idea of the gift, the marquess felt it would be churlish to say so. Besides, Mr. Barks had obviously spent a great deal of money.

"I did not have an opportunity," he said. "Your present ran away."

Mr. Barks staggered and put out his hand to support himself. "Ran away?" he echoed faintly.

"Yes, my friend."

Despite his distress, Mr. Barks was emboldened

by that "my friend." "Tol rol," he said airily. "We shall find her for you. Did I tell you my good wife is coming to Town and is desirous of an entrée to the royal drawing room? I know you have great influence at court and so . . ."

"I have no influence," said the marquess icily. He turned on his heel and walked away.

Polly sat in Silas Brewer's little kitchen with her bare feet among the ashes and smiled sleepily about her. She felt warm and safe. Mrs. Betty Brewer stared open-mouthed at Polly's gorgeous robe and fashionably powdered hair.

Opposite Polly sat Silas Brewer, worry creasing his brow.

Polly yawned. "All I need is a good night's sleep," she said.

Silas shifted uncomfortably. "Well, it's a bit difficult, Polly," he said. "I hate to worry you after all the fritful adventures you has had. But that there—" He jerked his head toward a curtained recess. "Is where *we* sleep, that's me and missus and childer. Ain't no room for no one else, nor would it be fitting like. Now, I did hear of a merchant, a Mr. Gander, over in Cheapside what is looking for likely girls as servants. Get what rest you can, and I'll take you there tomorrow."

Polly went very still. She wanted to burst into tears, to cry out that she was safe at last, that she did not want to go back out into the wicked world so soon. She looked about her. This little kitchen must be all the room that Silas had. It was neat and shining, a small oasis of warmth and decency in a wicked city. Polly closed her eyes, and images of Mrs. Blanchard, Mr. Barks, Mr. Caldicott, Jake and Barney danced in front of her eyes. I must not whine or complain, she told herself severely. I must not be a burden to Silas.

"I'll need to have clothes fitting for a servant," said Polly aloud. "See here, we can sell these I'm wearing. You can keep what money is left after I buy what's necessary."

"I can get a lot of money for those," said Silas. "But we'll keep the change by for you. That cloak will fetch a bit. A good thing that brothel keeper was so generous."

Polly flushed slightly and looked away. Something told her that if she confessed to stealing the cloak, then Silas would take it back. Silas was poor, but he must go to bed each night with a free conscience. In that moment, Polly resolved to get that job with the merchant and work hard and diligently and earn every penny.

When Polly finally fell asleep in a chair in front of the fire, and the Brewers nestled together in their communal bed, the clocks were striking midnight. In Boston, in America, a gentleman was just finishing his supper and deciding to look through the post which he had neglected to open that morning.

Mr. John Carpenter, former curate of the parish of Upper Batchett, now the Reverend John Carpenter of St. Charles in Boston, had admired and respected old Meg Jones. When he had left for America, he had told her to write to him from time to time to let him know the progress of her odd little foundling, Polly. He had left when Polly had been a chubby toddler of three years. As time passed, he had almost forgotten about Meg.

Now, as he stared down at her letter, memories came rushing back, memories of Meg brewing up her aromatic herbal potions in a black iron pot over the fire in her cottage, Meg who looked like a witch and had the heart of a saint.

He read her letter carefully, and then read it again in growing amazement. "Dear Mr. Carpenter," it began in thin spidery writing, "I fear I am Not Long for This World, having Frequent Palpitations of the Heart of which I have said Nothing to Polly. She is the Legitimate Daughter of the Earl and Countess of Meresly, and her real name is Lady Mary Palfrey, Palfrey being the Family Name of the Mereslys. It came about that Lady Lydia Meresly was with child and her husband was at the Wars. He had his mind set on a Son, and my lady was affeart that should she give Birth to a Daughter, then he would have the marriage Annulled. She membered me for she came here when she was but a little girl with a Party of Fine Folk to have her Fortune told. She told no one but me she was Quick with Child, and went into Hiding in Meresly Manor. No servants had she, only old Meg to attend her. It was a girl, Polly, and she made me swear an oath to drown it and Paid me Well. I knew if I refused, then she would Kill the baby herself. So I kept Polly and I brought her up. I thought she would grow up to be a natural Aristocrat but I have let her run Wild and she has coarse ways and coarse speech. I learn that Lady Lydia is coming back to the manor and I am going to Plead with her, for I have Learned she gave her lord two daughters, twins, and he did nothing Bad and is said to Dote on them. Why should they have the jewels and dresses and my poor Polly none of what is rightfully hers? You said one day you would Come Back on a visit. Please find my Polly and see Right is Done by her. Do not Write to Lady Lydia for she may yet Do Harm to the Girl, for perhaps her lord will not believe her and Think that Polly is a bastard Lady Lydia is trying to Conceal. I have learned My Lady has been in the way of taking Lovers from time to time, for my lord has become a wrecked man, no longer Powerful and Strong, and lets her do Much as she Pleases.

"Say a prayer for My Soul. I meant well. Yr. Humble and Obedient Servant, Meg Jones."

Mr. Carpenter carefully slipped the letter into his pocket. No one must see it. By coincidence, he had already made plans to return to England in two years' time. Meg had waited this long. She could wait a little longer for his help—if, of course, the old lady were still alive.

CHAPTER FOUR

THE EARL OF MERESLY HAD SUFFERED FROM AN apoplexy from which he had recovered. But it had left him slow and vague, roused only occasionally to shrewdness and awareness of matters about him. It was during one of those bouts of normality when he had ordered his wife to dismiss her lover, Bertram Pargeter—although the earl believed the young man to have been a fashionable lover; that is, in name only.

The morning after the marquess of Canonby's party, the earl remembered the appearance of the prostitute in the cage, for anything coming out of Mother Blanchard's stable must be a whore. And yet the girl had reminded him vividly of how Lydia had looked when they were first married. Possibly there was some family connection. One of Lydia's brothers' bastards, no doubt. His own features were stamped

on various children around his estates in Norfolk, but
at least none of them had surfaced in London to
plague him.

He sipped his chocolate and flipped through the
morning's letters. One from his caretaker at Meresly
caused him to start up against the pillow and let out
an exclamation of rage. He had recently written to
the caretaker, Harry Sellen, to warn him to expect
the arrival of an architect. His recent visit had roused
in the earl an affection for Meresly Manor and he
planned to make additions and restorations. Deciphering
with difficulty the ungrammatical scrawl, the earl
was able to make out nonetheless that Sellen had
taken inventory of the furniture and belongings at
Meresly Manor prior to the architect's visit. Missing
were a pair of silver candlesticks, a china figurine,
and a gold snuffbox. The earl rang the bell beside his
bed and ordered his secretary to attend him immediately. When his secretary, an intense young man
called Paul Jenner, arrived, he showed him the letter
and commanded Mr. Jenner to travel to Upper Batchett
immediately and take matters up with the parish constable. The earl had enough remnants of shrewdness
left to know that his caretaker would not risk a
comfortable post by stealing, and the fact that one of
the peasantry must have had the gall to risk a hanging
was almost beyond bearing. If the parish constable
could provide no clues, then the Bow Street Horse
Patrol must be brought in.

Mr. Barks at that same moment was gloomily
trying to remove last night's fur coat from his tongue

with a tongue scraper. Mr. Caldicott, who was seated at the end of his friend's bed, turned slightly green at the spectacle presented by Mr. Barks and quickly averted his eyes.

"That Blanchard woman ain't getting the rest of her money," growled Mr. Barks, throwing the tongue scraper at his soft-footed valet, who fielded it expertly.

"You mean you didn't pay her?"

"I paid her some, but I said she would get the rest the day after the goods was delivered. Had to make sure the goods arrived in one piece. And they did! I mean, she did, that whore Polly Jones. No wonder Canonby was so sour. 'Have no influence at court.' Ya! 'Course he has, and 'course he'd have used it like a shot if that strumpet had not up and run off. There's gratitude for you! Didn't she have the best gown, the best tete? Pah! Pooh!"

"Well, it's no use pahing and poohing," said Mr. Caldicott, stretching out one silk-stockinged leg to admire the height of the red heels on his shoes. "How do we go about getting her back?"

"Getting her back?"

"Yes, my dear parrot. You are not going to let some jade from the hedgerows outwit you?"

"Friend of my bosom, we can hardly run to the law and say we want our strumpet back!"

"No, but we have help at hand. Think what a rage Ma Blanchard will be in. No Polly Jones, no money. Rouse yourself and we will go and see her and make sure she sets her henchman on the trail."

Mrs. Blanchard was not cursed with much sensitivity, but she had enough of it to have been touched

on the raw by Polly. Polly's open disgust and contempt, not to mention the way she appeared to have
gained the admiration and affection of Jake and Barney, had annoyed Mrs. Blanchard intensely. Her prostitutes and staff went in fear of her; her customers
treated her with all the respect due to a brothel keeper
who supplied high-quality goods. She was not used
to being treated with contempt.

She had stayed up late the night before, following
Polly's adventures in her mind, seeing her deflow-
ered, crushed and weeping.

When she heard that Polly had run off, her rage
and venom knew no bounds. She forced herself to
reassure Mr. Barks and Mr. Caldicott that, yes, she
would get Polly back.

"And then we'll sell her ourselves, mother," said
Mr. Caldicott, "and when we sell her, then you'll
get your money."

Five minutes after they had left, Jake and Barney
suffered the lash of their mistress's tongue. They
were ordered to search the town in every pawn and
second-hand clothes shop for that gown, for Polly
surely would have sold it to give her enough money
to survive.

Later that day, the cause of all this concern stood
before Mrs. Gander, the merchant's wife, head meekly
bowed.

Polly was dressed in a demure chintz gown under a
black-laced bodice. Her luxuriant tresses were hidden
under a mob cap. She felt tired after a night's fitful

sleep in the chair in front of the fire and a hectic
morning selling and buying.

Mr. Gander had made his money by importing
silks, jade, and ivory from the East. The latest demand for chinoiserie had made him a fortune. Like
quite a lot of men with a capacity for making money,
he lacked brains in every other direction. But his life
was trade and he was content with that. Not so Mrs.
Gander. Risen from humble beginnings, she craved
the status of a great lady, and unfortunately aped the
current fashion in the West End of dressing like a
miss in her teens. Her gown of apple-blossom satin
was cut very low, exposing a bosom the color and
texture of stretched leather. She had great masses of
iron-gray hair, powdered lavender. She had a moustache which she assiduously bleached, convinced that
the resultant orange color would not show, and covered her face with a thick layer of white enamel
through which the orange moustache nonetheless
showed like a wintry dawn. She had servants enough
but was convinced that the road to gentility lay in
having too many.

"Your references, girl," she demanded. Polly produced a paper and handed it over. She had bought
one sheet of paper and had lied to Silas that she
meant to write home, not having told Silas anything
about her background, only her adventures since she
had come to London. She had forged a reference
from a Mrs. Rendell of Hackminster, saying that one
Polly Jones had been an excellent chambermaid, clever,
willing and honest. Mrs. Gander had no reason to be
suspicious of the reference. Girls of Polly's status

were usually as illiterate as Mrs. Gander was herself. She could not read a word Polly had written, but made a great show of pretending to do so.

After humming and hawing, Mrs. Gander said, "I have room for a girl in the kitchen. Our French chef is extremely exacting and you must not upset him. My housekeeper will show you your quarters. Where is your baggage?"

"It will be sent on, mem," said Polly, dropping a curtsy and lowering her eyes. She had only taken enough for the clothes she stood up in and for that one sheet of paper. The rest she had given to Silas.

While they both waited for the arrival of the house-keeper, Polly glanced about her. The drawing room in which she found herself was on the first floor and the steady roar from the traffic came up from Cheapside below. Although she had only a muddled recollection of the marquess's town house, she did remember the impression she had had of light and color, comfort and beauty. Here all was overfurnished, dark and cold. A small fire of sea coal struggled ineffectually with the icy air of the room. A black marble clock in the shape of a temple rapped out the seconds and minutes. The floor was sanded and uncarpeted. Outside, a great wind appeared to rise out of nowhere and howled down Cheapside, sending miniature whirlwinds of debris up into the air. Polly looked out of the new sashed windows—the mullioned ones had been removed the year before—at the bits of straw and paper dancing in the high wind and felt a longing to be just as free and mindless.

The door opened and a woman who looked just

like Mrs. Gander, except that she was dressed in black bombazine and had bunches of keys dangling from her waist, came in.

"This is Polly Jones, Mrs. Fritt. Show her where she sleeps and then take her to the kitchens, where she will start work immediately as a maid."

Polly looked at Mrs. Fritt and felt laughter beginning to well up inside her. The country people said frit when they meant fright, and the housekeeper seemed to have an appropriate name. Polly's large eyes glistened with tears as she tried to stifle her laughter.

"Don't snivel, girl," snapped Mrs. Fritt. "Come with me."

Polly curtsied to Mrs. Gander and followed the housekeeper from the room. She was led upstairs, higher and higher, until at last the housekeeper pushed open an attic door. "That's yours, over in the corner," she said. The room was small and very dark. Polly could dimly make out a pallet of straw in the corner indicated. So much for the grand life of London servants, she thought dismally.

"Now, come down to the kitchens, girl," said Mrs. Fritt.

"My name is Polly," said Polly sharply.

The housekeeper stared at her for a long time until Polly's eyes dropped. "You will be called what we think you ought to be called. Follow me."

Polly's new master—the chef, Monsieur Petit, called by one and all Monsoor Petty—was a tall, thin, neurotic man in a long apron and skull cap. He was, in fact, not French at all, and had been christened

Josiah Biggs. But the Ganders had advertised for a French chef and so French he decided to be. The strain of keeping up a fake foreign accent combined with his frequent resorts to the gin bottle kept him in a constant state of suppressed rage. He would have been a good plain English cook, but he knew the French were famous for sauces and so he served everything in a sauce, including the roast beef.

From the start, he seemed determined to take all his frustrations out on Polly. He ordered her hither and thither, shouting out orders and then counter-manding them. Every sauce he made was liberally laced with spirits, and Polly reflected that she had never known before that it was possible to get drunk on a dish of roast beef. Her lot was only just better than that of the scullery maid and knife boy. A birch rod stood by the huge open kitchen fire and evidently Monsoor Petty delighted in using it, as Polly found out when he gave the poor little knife boy a lashing.

When Polly at last had a quiet moment as she stirred pudding mix in a basin, she thought about the marquess of Canonby. She thought about all the delicious trifles she could have stolen. But Silas and his family had touched a chord of decency in Polly's soul. For their sake, she would work honestly and well.

A housemaid appeared at her elbow. "Your basket's arrived, Polly," she said. "You kin take it upstairs when you go."

Basket? What basket? Polly wondered.

But she was not to be allowed a rest from her duties until nine in the evening. Wearily, she climbed up the stairs. There were three other girls in the attic room: a fat, beefy housemaid called Betty; a thin, acid-tongued parlor maid called Mary; and another kitchen maid, little more than a child, called Joan.

"Can't we light a candle?" pleaded Polly, feeling her way in the dark.

"We got a rushlight," said Mary, striking a tinder. "But it's got to be put out in ten minutes' time. Mistress often comes looking."

By the feeble light of the rushlight in its pierced cannister Polly was able to make out a wicker basket on her "bed." She opened it up. There was a little pile of clean linen, and a small worn copy of the Bible. On a torn scrap of paper was written, "Bless You, Silas Brewer."

Polly felt the tears hurt her throat. Silas could read but he could not write. He must have gone to the trouble to pay someone to write that little message. No time for crying, she told herself. She carefully removed her clothes and lay down in her shift under the thin blanket, clasping her hands behind her head.

She wrinkled her nose. Her sense of smell had not yet been dulled by the city. The room reeked of unwashed bodies. She herself had been bathed before being sent to the marquess of Canonby. In the country, she had simply stripped off and scrubbed herself under the pump whenever she felt like it. Meg had said that frequent washing was a protection against disease and lice. When would she ever have an opportunity to wash again?

The world is full of people leading lives like this,

thought Polly. They do not cheat or steal or lie. If they can bear it, then I must.

But Polly was quickly to learn another kind of stealing.

She stole time. She flattered Monsoor Petty so much that he ceased to berate her, saved her the best of the food and left her some time to think and dream. She stole another personality, pretending she was someone quite different, someone sunny and happy and cheerful. She started to sing at her work when the housekeeper was not around. Monsoor Petty began to join in, forgetting to maintain his French accent and roaring out the words in pure Anglo-Saxon. Soon she found that pretending to be happy was a good road to being really happy.

Winter began to lose its grip and a pale sunlight flooded the cobbles of Cheapside, turning them gold. The first really warm day, she waited until the house was asleep and went out to the pump in the yard at the back and scrubbed herself and washed her hair.

Then the parlormaid left. She did not give notice, simply disappeared. And Polly Jones was elevated to the position of parlormaid.

Monsoor Petty was devastated. He was falling madly in love with Polly, and used the close confines of the kitchen quarters as an excuse to lean against her at every opportunity or brush his arm against her generous bosom when handing her bowls of batter to stir.

Mrs. Gander felt at first she had made a mistake. Her women friends were quick to point out to her the beauty of her parlormaid and say it was dangerous to have such a jewel serving her husband. But Mr.

Gander was tickled at the attention and admiration
Polly received from his business friends, and commanded she be dressed in prettier and prettier gowns.

Polly longed for her kitchen job back, away from
the hot stares of Mr. Gander's friends and the cold
looks of dislike from his wife and her companions.

The earl of Meresly quickly forgot about the theft
from Meresly Manor, but his assiduous secretary did
not. Finding the parish constable too slow and sleepy,
Mr. Jenner returned a second time to Upper Batchett
with Mr. Tarry of the Bow Street Horse Patrol.
Assuring the secretary that matters could now be left
in his hands, Mr. Tarry set to work. Unlike his
colleagues, who were near-criminals themselves and
made most of their arrests through intimate knowledge of the underworld, Mr. Tarry used his intelli-
gence. He was a fat, lazy-looking man with a great
purple grog-blossomed face and a huge paunch bulg-
ing over his breeches. But inside the fat man lurked a
sly, quick, clever one. Mr. Tarry often found his
deceptive appearance very useful. He first asked around
the village whether anyone who used to live there
had gone missing. The villagers closed ranks and
said that no one had left. They felt obscurely and in
their slow country way that they had been unjust to
Polly Jones. She was one of their community and
they had no intention of bringing trouble on her.

Mr. Tarry then took himself off to Meresly Manor.
Mr. Harry Sellen, the caretaker, took up a long and
weary hour of Mr. Tarry's time protesting his innocence. Mr. Tarry leaned back and folded his arms

over his massive stomach, closed his eyes, and to all appearances went to sleep. At last, as if the fact that Mr. Sellen had finished speaking had penetrated his dreams, he sat up and said, "And you saw no one, no fellow, skulking about?"

"Nary a one.'"

Mr. Tarry frowned. Perhaps the thief could be one of the earl's friends. Such things did happen in this age of gambling. "No member o' the Quality came around then?" he pursued.

"There was one," said Mr. Sellen. "A Mr. Pargeter. Friend o' her ladyship's." His eyes drooped in a wink. "If you take my meaning. But Pargeter's as rich as creases. Couldn't be him."

"He called when the earl and countess were not here?"

"That's right."

"Why?"

"Asking about some village girl. I told him I didn't have no truck with the hayseeds and that he should go into the village and ask."

"What was the name of this girl?"

"Bless me, can't call that to mind. Not as if it would ha' anything to do with the theft. Bit of petticoat he was arter, most like. Her ladyship gave him his marching orders."

Mr. Tarry heaved a sigh. He stood up and fished in a capacious pocket and pulled out a bottle of brandy. It was white brandy—moonshine, as smuggled French brandy was called. Mr. Sellen's eyes gleamed.

"Get us a couple o' glasses," said Mr. Tarry

expansively. "You must be weary with answering questions." Mr. Sellen produced two glasses from a sideboard and greedily watched Mr. Tarry fill them up.

The caretaker closed his eyes appreciatively at the first sip of the spirit, leaned back in his chair, and searched for some way to please the amiable Bow Street man.

All of a sudden, he seemed to be back on the step of the manor on a cold windy night. A girl was asking for . . . He closed his eyes tightly. Meg Jones, that was it. She wanted someone who knew Meg Jones.

"I call to mind," he said carefully, "that a girl called asking about a Meg Jones. I said I'd never heard of such a person and told her to go away."

"When was that?"

"Round last November, as I recall."

"Now, say this girl wanted to try her chances at thieving something, could she have waited and got into the house some way when you had gone?"

"No . . ." began Mr. Sellen, and then blushed.

"No?" echoed Mr. Tarry softly. He leaned forward and refilled Mr. Sellen's glass.

"Thankee. No, no way anyone could have got in," said Mr. Sellen in a strong, loud voice. "No way at all."

But Mr. Tarry had noticed that telltale blush. So the caretaker had left some window or door open that night.

Mr. Tarry returned to the village after having secured a description of the girl. Meg Jones, he learned, had been a wise woman, telling fortunes and dishing out herbal medicines. He did not want to ask directly about any young girl connected with this Meg, so Mr. Tarry pretended to have known her himself. Sensing she had been admired, he praised her remedies, while his mind wondered whether the girl had been some helper she had employed or a relative. But perhaps the girl had been just a cunning thief. She had gone to the manor to ask about a woman already dead.

He was seated in the tap room of The George, the small inn in the center of the village. Opposite him sat three of the local worthies.

Mr. Tarry paid for another round of drinks and sat down again. "Lovely eyes she had. Violet, they was," he said meditatively, looking at the ceiling, having picked out the most vivid part of Mr. Sellen's description of the girl.

"Ah," said one slowly. "Wild 'un, her were."

Mr. Tarry waited, being careful to show a marked lack of interest.

The silence seemed to drag on forever, and then one thickset man in a farmer's smock said, "We was a bit crool to her. 'Cause we knew'd her was no kin to Meg, being only a foundling. Vicar do say we drove her away, but was squire's bailiffs who was going to put 'er out, see. Her went arter they give 'er a week." *The name!* screamed an urgent voice inside Mr. Tarry's head, but his sleepy expression did not change.

Another long silence. "My boy, Charlie," vouchsafed one after what seemed like an hour, "was sweet on 'er. 'Twar Polly this and Polly that, I 'member.''

Polly Jones, thought Mr. Tarry. I am looking for a girl with violet eyes called Polly Jones. Where would she sell the stuff?

"Ain't no big towns hereabouts," he said.

The three chuckled and laughed and slapped their knees. The quick little man inside Mr. Tarry's fat carcass wanted to leap out and strangle these yokels.

He joined in the laughter. "Reckon I don't know much," he said.

"Reckon tha' don't," said the farmer, wiping his streaming eyes. "Hackminster's as big as Lunnon and be only a liddle bit away."

Soon Mr. Tarry was on the way to Hackminster. As he expected, it was only a small market town, but enormous to the likes of the inhabitants of Upper Batchett. He found two jeweller's shops in the back streets. He drew a blank at the first, but was lucky at the second. The jeweller, despite the dinginess of his stock, was an honest man. He had carefully recorded the items Polly had sold him in his book. He had believed her story.

"Now," thought Mr. Tarry when he stood outside the jeweller's shop again. "My bird, like all thieves, would try to go to London to hide." His enquiries at the Three Bells where the London stage called twice a week drew a blank. He checked livery stables, and then the sight of a waggoner's cart gave him the idea that she might have chosen this unobtrusive mode of transport.

He rode out to the London road and asked each

wagonner who passed if they had ever seen a girl of Polly's description. Mr. Tarry knew from the jeweller what clothes she had been wearing when she was in Hackminster.

At last, at the end of a weary day, a waggoner said he had seen Silas Brewer on the London road last November with a pretty girl in maid's dress sitting beside him.

Mr. Tarry heaved a sigh of relief.

The hunt was nearly over.

CHAPTER FIVE

BARNEY AND JAKE, DRIVEN ON BY THE LASH OF their mistress's tongue, grew weary of searching for the shop where Polly had sold the gown.

"Reckon she didn't sell it," grumbled Barney. "Reckon one o' the marquess's fine friends took her up. Stands to reason, a girl like that."

"Our Poll wouldn't ha' gone with no man," said Jake. "No, she'll ha' sold the gown and shoes and found work. Decent she was, despite her tales o' thieving."

It was a fine April day and their search had taken them into the City of London, that part which the fashionables had gradually left to merchants and commerce as they created an empire in the West End. They turned into a coffee house and called for chocolate and newspapers. As Jake put it, it was a fine thing to get away from being a whoremaster once in a while, although Barney said whoremaster was too grand a title, they being more in the way of whore-mistress's servants.

Both Barney and Jake had been brought up in an enlightened orphanage where they had been taught to read and write. Jake read every advertisement in the newspapers when he had the chance. He was sipping his chocolate and studying the lists of advertisements which contained interesting items such as: "Military gentleman willing to marry any Lady of Damaged Reputation for only a Small Sum. He promises that the Chains of Hymen will lie lightly." His eyes travelled down the page and then he let out a gasp and straightened up.

"Listen here," he said. *"For sale. Gown worn only once by a Lady of Quality. Of finest blue lute-string over blue quilted petticoat with white satin stomacher.* Ain't that Poll's gown? Look at that description Ma Blanchard gave you."

Barney pulled out a dirty and much-thumbed piece of paper. "Matches the description all right," he said. "Where does it say to enquire?"

"Barking's Pastry Shop, Pudding Lane. That's down by the Monument."

"What's a pastry shop doing selling gowns?"

"Let's go and find out."

Mr. Barking, the pastry cook, was in a great taking when he found himself being accused of trafficking in stolen goods. He protested he had bought the gown for his wife from a most worthy citizen. But Mrs. Barking had complained that the gown was too grand—and too tight—and so he had decided to sell it.

"Looks like you bought it honest," said Barney, leaning confidentially on the shop counter and picking his teeth with that implement in his pocket knife for taking stones out of horses' hooves. "See here, we'll go along and have a quiet word with this citizen and tell him the folly of his ways. What's his name?"

Mr. Barking looked nervously at the two men, at one-eyed Jake and squat and swarthy Barney. But then, he reflected in a cowardly way, if Silas Brewer was an honest man he had nothing to fear.

Armed with Silas's address, Jake and Barney set out for Shoreditch.

"He'd need to be honest to live here," sniffed Jake. "Either honest or a gin drinker," these being the only two types of people in Jake's experience who were condemned to live in poverty.

Silas was not at home. Instead, it was Mrs. Brewer who answered the door, a Mrs. Brewer supported by a neighbor and near fainting.

"Go along with you," said the neighbor when they asked for Silas. "Don't you see the pore thing has had enough, what with Bow Street men taking her husband away to show them where that girl worked?"

"What girl?" asked Jake sharply.

"Oh, poor, poor Polly. I can't believe it," wailed Mrs. Brewer.

"We're friends of Polly's—from the country," said Barney quickly. "If she's in need of help, you'd best tell us where to find her."

A little hope came into Mrs. Brewer's tear-washed eyes. "Polly is working for a merchant, a Mr. Gander at 350 Cheapside. Tell her . . ."

But Barney and Jake were off and running.

When they got as far as Mr. Gander's house, it was to find the pavement blocked with sightseers craning their necks. Barney and Jake roughly pushed their way to the front of the crowd.

And then the door of the mansion opened. Barney and Jake, recognizing an officer of the law, shrank back a bit and pulled their hats down over their eyes. When they looked up again it was to see Polly being dragged through the crowd. Someone had pulled her cap off, and the masses of her hair spilled about her shoulders. She was wearing a low-cut chintz gown with a frilly fichu about her shoulders—one of the outfits in which she delighted the lecherous eyes of Mr. Gander's guests.

"I knew she was a robber and slut!" screamed a massive woman from an upstairs window, her orange moustache bristling.

Polly was led away in the direction of Newgate. The crowd followed along. On the steps of Mr. Gander's house, Monsoor Petty sat crying his eyes out, the only member of the household to mourn Polly's going.

"Well, that's that," said Barney when the great doors of Newgate Prison closed in their faces. "She'll be hanged. One of the men said she'd stolen from a duke or something. Poor Poll. Tell you something, Ma Blanchard can fry in hell. I ain't going back." He turned and hurried off.

"Where you going?" screamed Jake.

"To get drunk!" yelled Barney over his shoulder.

"Wait for me," shouted Jake. "I'm going to get drunk, too!"

After a fortnight spent in Newgate, Polly's fetters were knocked off and she was taken to the courthouse in Old Bailey. The courthouse was a stark, forbidding building on the south side of the prison.

In the vast Justice Hall, the tall chair of the Court President dominated the silent and depressing scene. Above the chair was a statue of a particularly stern and unrelenting Justice looking toward the middle of the stone floor, where the prisoner's box stood.

Polly was already in this box when the officers of the court came into the Justice Hall: Sir Peter Devine, the Lord Mayor, followed by Sir Walter Browne, the Recorder, and Serjeant Pugg, the Recorder's Deputy. No attorney rose to introduce himself as counsel for the defense. A prisoner was not allowed a lawyer nor was he allowed to go into the witness box.

The Clerk of Arraigns read the indictment to the court and then the Old Bailey attorney rose to say, "May it please your lordship and you gentlemen of the jury, I am counsel for the King against the prisoner at the bar."

Mr. Tarry gave evidence and then the caretaker, Mr. Sellen. Mr. Paul Jenner, the earl's secretary, represented the earl, the earl of Meresly being considered too grand a personage to be summoned to court himself.

It was soon over. The jury did not even bother to

retire. Guilty. The judge picked up his black cap and put it solemnly on his head and pronounced sentence of death by hanging.

The condemned cell was a relief after the noise and squalor of the women's quarters where Polly had awaited her trial. She was now allowed exercise each day in a prison yard reserved for the condemned, and visited regularly by a chaplain, a determinedly cheerful man who tried to raise her spirits by telling her that the powers that be in their mercy would hang her on a Friday so that she would have the whole of Saturday free to make her journey to Heaven, arriving just in time for Sunday morning. Polly crossly asked him how the powers that be had managed to work out this absurd timetable and was reproved for blasphemy.

Silas Brewer came to see her, having used the money he had saved for her to bribe the jailor and to provide Polly with a clean bed and good food. When Polly admitted she was guilty of stealing from the earl of Meresly, Silas looked so wretched that Polly felt his look was more punishment than the judge and jury had inflicted. Honest Silas begged her to pray for her soul, but Polly's violet eyes hardened and glittered like jewels as she said she had no intention of praying to such an unmerciful God.

To Polly's surprise, she was given a hairbrush, pins, and rouge and powder. She was even given a change of clothes. Silas had told her the luxuries did not come from him. She reasoned that such treatment must be meted out to the condemned, and then immediately wondered why the other women in the condemned cells did not have such privileges.

Hanging day was to be the first of June. Unlike the other prisoners, Polly did not mark off the days on the wall of her cell. She lived in a vacuum, numb and devoid of feeling.

Unused to the ways of London, Polly did not know that a public hanging at Tyburn, up at the corner of Hyde Park, was a great event. Although prisoners were often hanged on the triangular gallows in batches, sometimes as many as seven on a side, Polly was still not aware that because of her beauty she was to have the "stage" all to herself.

It was Barney and Jake who broke the news to her. Barney had filched a gold watch from a gentleman's pocket on the very day he and Jake had decided to quit Mrs. Blanchard. News that tickets for Polly's execution were now changing hands among the gentry for as much as two hundred and fifty pounds had staggered them. Bribing their way in to see Polly, they sat before her and gazed at her in awe. "Never knew you'd be so famous," said Jake at last.

Polly tried to rouse herself from her lethargy. "Famous," she said in a dull, flat voice. "Why, there was ten condemned along o' me and one o' them stole *four sheep*!" A tinge of remembered awe crept into Polly's voice. She obviously thought the stealing of four whole sheep a much more dramatic crime than pilfering a few trinkets from the earl of Meresly.

"It's because you're beautiful, see," said Jake. He squinted with his one good eye at the brushes and rouge on the dressing table. "That's why they gave you the clothes and gee-gaws. Got a big crowd attending. That's why you got this cell to yourself 'stead o' being crammed in with the others."

"Since I'm to be hanged," said Polly with a shrug, "I don't care whether I hang alone or in company. What brought you buzzards here? The one consolation I got is that Mother Blanchard can no longer get her claws in me—unless she wants to sell my body to an anatomist."

"T'ain't that," said Barney restlessly. "We quit Ma Blanchard. You got kin, Polly?"

"No," said Polly.

"Well, see here, that's why we come. You get put on a cart and taken to Tyburn. The clergyman sits in the cart along o' you. Five minutes before you is topped, your relatives are allowed in the cart for a last word. Then the cart is driven off and leaves you hanging in midair. Takes a long time to die sometimes. So often the relatives pull at the prisoner's legs to end the agony quick. So me and Barney thought that if you could say we was your kin, we could swing on your legs. Break your neck in seconds."

"Thanks," said Polly grimly. "But I'll die alone."

Jake pushed back his greasy three-cornered hat and scratched his shaven head. "Don't be like that, Poll. We'd help if we could. Get you some poison."

Polly forced a smile. "I'm best left alone," she said. "I don't think about things much if I'm left alone. It's better that way."

In vain did Jake and Barney beg her to accept their help. Polly only relented enough to thank them for their visit.

She would have perhaps remained sunk in her peculiar state of numbness and lethargy had it not been for Miss Drusilla Gentle. Polly was standing in the exercise yard one morning near the end of May, rubbing her sore ankles where the leg irons had chafed them, when her attention was drawn to a huddled and weeping figure at the edge of the yard. Polly was used to weeping figures, but it was five in the morning, the time the cells were opened, and she knew she could normally depend on having the yard to herself. She had turned to go inside, but there was something so lost and desolate about that weeping.

Giving an impatient click of her tongue, she crossed the yard and shook the figure roughly by the shoulder. A woman gasped and turned a tear-stained face up to Polly. She was a faded creature, perhaps around thirty-five. She had sandy hair which still retained traces of powder. Her gown, stained and shabby, was of fine silk.

"It's no use crying," said Polly. "That don't help. It'll soon be over for all of us. What's your name?"

"Miss Gentle. Drusilla," said the lady, drying her eyes on a scrap of cambric. "I try hard to be brave, Miss . . ."

"Jones. Polly Jones. You can call me Polly."

"I try so hard to be brave, Polly, but I am in that cell over there with five coarse and rough women who jeer at me and torment me."

"Why should they be so unkind?" wondered Polly. "You'd think we'd all be sweet to each other, seeing the fix we're all in."

"Oh, they're horrid. Horrid!" said Drusilla passionately.

Her accent was pure, clear, distinctly aristocratic.

"You're a lady!" marvelled Polly. "Didn't reckon to see ladies in here. What did you do?"

"Nothing," wailed Drusilla, beginning to cry again.

"Now, look here," said Polly impatiently, "if you stop crying and pass the time for me by telling me your story, happen I'll get them to put you along o' me. I'm getting special treatment," added Polly grimly.

"Oh, that would be monstrous kind," said Drusilla. "Walk with me a little and I shall endeavour to be calm."

As they walked, Polly looked down at her smaller companion curiously. Miss Gentle had a thin, angular figure and a weak, trembling face, pale eyes as gentle as her name, and a large soft mouth. But her voice had fallen on Polly's ears like pure gold. All at once she remembered the marquess of Canonby's voice, seductive in its beauty and clarity. Despite her plain face and figure, Drusilla Gentle moved with grace.

At last, holding tightly onto Polly's arm, she told her story. She came from a country family, members of the untitled aristocracy fallen on hard times. She had obtained a post as companion to a certain Lady Comfrey. This Lady Comfrey was a widow who, despite the fact she took lovers, liked to maintain a genteel front and used Drusilla's patent respectability to supply that front. Her current lover had stolen a diamond brooch from her; Drusilla was sure he was the culprit. But Lady Comfrey was so enamored of this cicisbeo that she had accused Drusilla of theft, and so Drusilla was tried and sentenced to hang.

"Hard, very hard," said Polly, shaking her head. "Now I *did* steal things, but it still don't seem wrong to me. When some people have so much and some so little, it don't seem wrong to take a few things."

"But it is wrong. Very wrong," said Drusilla.

"It's wrong, very wrong," mimicked Polly, "to hang for something you did not do. There now, don't cry again. You can stay along o' me till we're topped." And with this gloomy consolation, she led Drusilla to her cell.

In the days that passed, Polly took the mad idea into her head to die a lady. She knew, like all the condemned, that she was to say a few words from the scaffold. She would quit this wicked world of London a lady. Drusilla, at first amazed at being begged to teach Polly how to move and speak like a lady, soon found the teaching made the weary days more pleasant. The odd couple became fast friends. And then, two days before the execution, a blow befell Polly. Lady Comfrey had tired of her lover and relented of her treatment of the companion who had supplied her with so much badly needed respectability. She bought another diamond brooch and claimed to have found the one that had been lost.

Poor Drusilla clung to Polly in farewell, torn between grief for her friend and joy at her own escape from death. "I'll pray for you, Polly," she said, before she was led away.

"Don't waste your breath," called Polly in her new, well-modulated voice. "There isn't anyone to hear you."

*   *   *

Mr. Barks was mincing along Bond Street, enduring all the agonies of tight lacing. But he knew he had to be laced tightly to show off the width of the skirts of his new whalebone-stiffened coat. In one hand he held a scented handkerchief and a bottle of smelling salts. A chicken-skin fan dangled from his wrist. In the other, he held a tall clouded cane embellished with scarlet ribbons at the top. He was feeling at ease in his mind, for Mrs. Barks had been stricken of the fever and could not leave the country . . . yet.

"Halloa!" Mr. Caldicott's voice in his ear made him jump.

"Don't startle a man so," wailed Mr. Barks, swaying back and forward on his high heels and trying to regain his balance. Mr. Caldicott caught him by the shoulder and steadied him.

"I have good news, my friend," said Mr. Caldicott. "Troth, but you will love me when you hear it. To St. James's. We must be comfortable."

It was only a short walk from the Bond Street Straits, as the narrow part in which they stood was called, to White's Club in St. James's Street. But Mr. Barks protested that his ankles were about to crack and he must be borne in a chair.

"I don't know why you insist on the heels of your shoes being made so high," grumbled Mr. Caldicott as he walked along beside the sedan chair. But secretly he was envious and planned to order a pair just the same.

"Never mind that," said Mr. Barks. "I saw Canonby t'other night and he gave me a half bow. Must be thawing."

"That man's a monster of ingratitude," said Mr. Caldicott. "But only wait until you hear what I have done for you. You will have Canonby eating out of your hand."

"Odso!" Mr. Barks felt quite dizzy with anticipation by the time he tittupped into the coffee room at the club.

"Now," said Mr. Caldicott, fishing in an embroidered pocket when they were seated. "I have here a present for you to give to Canonby."

He held up a piece of paper.

"What is it?" Mr. Barks's face had fallen in disappointment. He had been prepared to see some wonderfully chased and jewelled trifle.

"It is a ticket for a hanging. Best position. Right at the front under the gallows."

"A hanging," said Mr. Barks, pouting.

"This ticket," said Mr. Caldicott in slow, measured tones, "cost me two hundred and fifty pounds."

"Stap me!"

"Yaas," drawled Mr. Caldicott, enjoying the expression of amazement on his friend's face. "Have you not heard of this fabulous beauty who is to be topped?"

"I have heard gossip, yes."

"And do you know the name of the beauty?"

"Can't say as I do."

"Polly Jones."

"Polly Jones!" said Mr. Barks wrathfully. "Do you mean to tell that old abbess has had the gall to get the girl topped instead of handing her over to me?"

"Quietly. Our friend Miss Jones stole articles from Meresly. The law must take its course. But all London is fighting to see this hanging. Think on't. Canonby will be revenged on the strumpet who ran away from him. Only think how he will laugh to see her kicking her pretty legs in the air."

A slow smile lit up Mr. Barks's painted features. "You are a genius. Wait a bit. The body rightly belongs to me. I paid for her. Think I can grab her after she's cut down and sell her to the anatomists?"

"Not at this hanging, friend. The crowd would tear you to pieces."

"Let us go and see Canonby now," said Mr. Barks. "I cannot wait to see the look of pleasure on his face."

The marquess of Canonby was just preparing to go out when they arrived. His scarlet satin coat was worn open to reveal a long white silk waistcoat heavily encrusted with gold embroidery. Mr. Barks gawped enviously at that waistcoat and tried to console himself with the fact that the red heels of the marquess's shoes were only of moderate height.

"Gentlemen," the marquess said, giving them a half bow. He then stood impatiently as Barks and Caldicott made elaborate bows in return, their noses almost touching their knees, their scented handkerchiefs flourished in the air.

"Do you remember Polly Jones?" asked Mr. Barks when he had finally straightened up with a long scrape of his foot along the floor.

"I cannot remember her, since I am not aware of having ever known anyone of that name."

"She was the present I gave you."

"Ah, yes." The marquess took a delicate pinch of snuff, his face immobile. Then his gaze suddenly sharpened. "There is a Polly Jones who is to hang tomorrow. The same?"

"The same," laughed Mr. Barks.

"I never knew her name," said the marquess, half to himself. "How very beautiful she was."

"Indeed, indeed," chortled Mr. Caldicott, rubbing his hands. "And friend Barks here has a ticket for you to the hanging. Best view, I assure you."

The marquess frowned and the two friends stood shoulder to shoulder, watching him anxiously. "What is her crime?" he asked at last. "I mean, I know she is being hanged for theft. What did she steal?"

"She stole trinkets from the earl of Meresly. That hanging ticket cost all of two hundred and fifty pounds," added Mr. Barks desperately.

Meresly again, thought the marquess. Did this Polly take the stuff because she was one of Lady Lydia's family's bastards? But she had stolen from *him*. And yet . . .

"Thank you," he said, taking the ticket. "You are most kind."

"Not at all. Not at all, my lord," said Mr. Barks gleefully. "Now, if I may ask you . . . ?"

"I regret I have pressing business, gentlemen. I shall no doubt see you at the play this evening, where we may talk further."

"Yes, yes," said Mr. Caldicott. He tugged at Mr. Barks's sleeve.

"Best to play touchy coves like Canonby like a

fish,'' he explained as the couple walked round St. James's Square.

The marquess of Canonby did not go out. He went into his library and sat at his desk and thought about Polly Jones. A common thief. And yet, there had been a certain bravery and gallantry about the girl. The marquess detested hangings. His father had taken him to the hanging of a highwayman as a treat on his tenth birthday and the experience had made him ill. The highwayman had been cut down while he was still alive, his head had been shaved, he had been disembowelled and then plunged headlong into a barrel of boiling tar. Then his body had been hoisted up again on irons to hang as a warning to other presumptuous highwaymen.

He rang for his secretary, a middle-aged man called Mr. Peter Beauly. ''Mr. Beauly,'' said the marquess, ''here is a draft on my bank for two hundred and fifty pounds. You will no doubt find Mr. Barks in White's. Present my compliments and say I have decided to buy this ticket he was offering for sale. Then when you have done that, you are to find the direction of the public hangman and bring him to me. Bribe him to come, if necessary.''

''Yes, my lord,'' said Mr. Beauly, concealing his surprise.

''It's all your fault!'' wailed Mr. Barks half an hour later. ''You didn't say it was a present. Oh, dear. Oh, dear. We must go back to St. James's Square and explain.''

But when they returned, they were told the marquess was not at home. They tried again and again and at last took to waiting on the other side of the square until they saw him go in.

Mr. Beauly received them and said his master was not at home to anyone. The secretary refused to take back the draft. My lord, he said, would be furious if the money were not accepted. My lord did not like to be told he had been wrong about anything and had assumed Mr. Barks had been offering the ticket for sale.

"Well, that's that," said Mr. Barks gloomily. "Damn Polly Jones."

"It'll be a pleasure to see her swing," said Mr. Caldicott viciously. "I don't care what it costs. We are going. We owe ourselves the pleasure of watching that strumpet's last moments."

In the brothel in Covent Garden, Mrs. Blanchard had her maid clean and iron her best gown in preparation for the hanging. Mrs. Blanchard no longer mourned the loss of Jake and Barney or the money she had wasted on Polly. The joy of seeing that girl dance in the air would make up for anything.

"My sweet, do not cast me forth," begged Bertram Pargeter, down on one knee before Lady Lydia.

Lady Lydia looked at him impatiently. The earl was down at Meresly, fussing about repairs to that horrible old manor. He was growing oddly stubborn again, and Lady Lydia dreaded he might insist she live part of the year in the country. She took a sweetmeat from a dish on the table beside her and popped it into the mouth of the wheezing pug on her lap.

"You know I promised Meresly not to have anything more to do with you, Bertram. Besides, you know the rules of an *affaire*. Once it is over, it is no use kneeling there trying to blow life into cold ashes."

Bertram went slightly pale. "I am dying of ennui," went on Lady Lydia petulantly. "Every day is the same."

"I may be able to provide you with amusement," said Bertram.

"You?" mocked Lady Lydia, and Bertram flinched. When she had lain under him, moaning with passion, he had never dreamed that the day would come when she would behave as coldly as this.

"I have reserved a place for my carriage next to the scaffold at Tyburn tomorrow for this famous hanging," said Bertram.

"I only heard about it this morning," said Lady Lydia with marked interest. "As you know, I have had the vapors, and am behindhand with the news. It is some vastly beautiful girl, I believe."

"As beautiful as you are yourself."

"Then I shall go with you," said Lady Lydia, giving him a bewitching smile. He tried to bury his face in her lap, but had forgotten about the pug, which snarled and bit him on the nose. Lady Lydia laughed and laughed. "I declare I am grateful to you, Bertram. I have not laughed this age. Come, you shall have your reward."

She rang the bell and, when a footman came in, handed him the pug.

When they were alone again, Bertram lifted her in his arms to carry her to the bedroom. "Put me down," said Lady Lydia. "We must stay here. The maids are cleaning the bedroom."

"Very well, my love," said Bertram huskily. He set her gently on the sofa and then reached out to unlace her stomacher. Lady Lydia slapped his hand away. "Can't you just raise my skirts," she said crossly. "It took the maid simply hours to lace me in."

What followed might have looked like rape to any onlooker, had there been one, as Bertram released himself of all his pent-up passion and rage and humiliation, going on and on and on, deaf to her pleas for him to stop. At last, spent and exhausted and sick at heart, Bertram looked down at her, his eyes pleading for some sign of love, but the beautiful, violet eyes that looked up at him had a sated, animal glaze. Despite her pleas for mercy, Lady Lydia had obviously enjoyed his savage lovemaking more than any of his former tenderness and delicacy.

"What is her name?" asked Lady Lydia sleepily.

"Who?"

"This girl who is to hang tomorrow."

"I can't remember," lied Bertram. The pain eased at his heart as he thought of what his cruel mistress's reaction would be when she saw that girl Polly, who looked so amazingly like her, on the scaffold.

CHAPTER SIX

OLLY MISSED THE COMPANY OF DRUSILLA QUITE dreadfully. In keeping Drusilla's spirits up, she had managed to forget her own plight. Now, on the eve of her execution, she sat in the "condemned pew" with eighteen others who had been sentenced to death, listening to the chaplain begging them to repent of their sins. To remind them of the gravity of the situation, a coffin had been placed in the condemned pew alongside them. The condemned pew in the prison chapel was more like a pen at a cattle auction, being square and surrounded by high wooden spike-topped walls over which spectators gawped at the prisoners.

The chapel was open to the public on these occasions and the congregation, boisterous and profane, shoved and pushed to catch a glimpse of Polly.

The other prisoners were drunk, Polly noticed. She

herself intended to maintain as much of her dignity as
she could. She did not know that the other prisoners
were numbing themselves with gin for the very ordeal of being borne to the gallows. If the mob did not
like a prisoner's appearance, he or she could be
stoned half to death before Tyburn Tree was reached.

There was the last long night before the execution
still to be endured, a night where the sexton went
along in front of the condemned cells clanging a bell
and reciting a mournful poem about their impending
doom:

"All you that in the Condemned Hold do lie,
Prepare you, for tomorrow you shall die;
Watch all and pray; the hour is drawing near
That you before the Almighty must appear;
Examine well yourselves; in time repent;
That you may not to eternal flames be sent.
And when St. Sepulchre's bell tomorrow tolls,
The Lord above have mercy on your souls!"

Although Polly continued to defy the chaplain by
refusing to pray for repentance, she nonetheless took
the little Bible Silas had given her from under her
mattress and held it in her hand throughout that long
and sleepless night.

The first of June dawned a perfect day. Polly
refused to eat breakfast, although she could, like the
others, have ordered what she wanted. She brushed
her hair until it shone and let it hang loose on her
shoulders. She smoothed the folds of her apple-green-
and-yellow chintz gown and tied a lace fichu across
her bosom.

The great bell of St. Sepulchre's was tolling its

dark message across the sunny city. Each great *boom* seemed to send a shudder down through the very stones of the prison.

Polly was taken to the Press Yard, where the under sheriff, Mr. Blackstone, made the customary demand for the condemned woman to be handed to his custody, giving, as if Polly were already dead, a formal receipt for her body. Then she was taken to the smith, who hammered off her fetters and unlocked her handcuffs.

The Knight of the Halter then tied the rope which was to hang her round and round her waist. As this was taking place, the city marshal was forming outside the prison gates the procession which was to accompany Polly to Tyburn.

Polly's step faltered slightly when she was led to the cart and saw the hangman seated on a coffin in the front of it. Eager hands helped her to mount. The chaplain took his place in the cart behind her.

Slowly the great wooden doors of Newgate Prison were opened, and the noise of the mob rushed in to strike Polly like a hammer blow. Slowly the cart moved forward. Polly stood very straight, head up, looking over the staring, greedy, curious faces. The great pulsing boom of the bell went on and on. The streets about Newgate were jammed with people. Down on the river, sailors clung to the top of their ships' masts to try to get a glimpse of Polly.

Then a great silence fell, as the crowd stared at Polly high up on the cart. The sunlight glinted on the gold threads in her chestnut hair. *I have only this short time to live. I may as well go bravely to my death,* thought Polly. She looked down and about the crowd, waved her hand and gave a radiant smile.

They cheered her to the echo. Women tossed bunches of flowers into the cart. Men blew kisses. Had Polly appeared in the least afraid, had she cried, then the crowd would have stoned her. But bravery was practically worshipped. The chaplain sighed with relief. He would not have to protect himself from missiles on this journey.

A contingent of peace officers led the way. Behind them marched the city marshal, followed by the under sheriff and a posse of constables. Then came the cart with Polly and hangman and chaplain. Behind was a troop of soldiers in red coats and tricornes, carrying pikes. Lastly came a second posse of constables on horseback.

The parade came to a shambling halt opposite the steps leading to the porch of the church of St. Sepulchre. The sexton who had rung the bell outside the condemned hold the night before stood with bell in hand behind the church wall and rang it in the intervals between the deep booms from the great bell in the belfry above, intoning a gloomy speech for the comfort of the convict:

"You, that are condemned to die, repent with lamentable tears; ask mercy of the Lord for the salvation of your own soul, through the merits, death and passion of Jesus Christ, who now sits at the right hand of God, to make intercession for as many as penitently return to Him.

"Lord have mercy upon you
Christ have mercy upon you

Lord have mercy upon you
Christ have mercy upon you."

As was the custom, Polly was then showered with flower petals and bits of colored paper.

The parade moved on, down Snow Hill and over the Fleet River by a narrow stone bridge, up Holborn Hill and past the church of St. Andrew's, where even the roof was covered with people who stared giddily down from behind the narrow safety of the parapet wall.

The procession stopped at St. Giles, where the customary bowl of ale was handed to the prisoner. Polly smiled at the crowd and drained it in one go. And although she smiled and waved, behind her the great bell of St. Sepulchre's continued to thud and reverberate on the air like some terrible monstrous iron heartbeat.

They were just moving into the Oxford Road when a gentleman on horseback, using his whip, forced his way through the crowd and began to ride alongside the cart.

Polly glanced down and found herself staring at the handsome profile of the marquess of Canonby. How odd to feel so disappointed in one man, thought Polly bleakly, as if anyone mattered on the road to the scaffold. But the sight of him made her legs tremble. She had thought of him from time to time in a confused way. But she never would have believed him capable of such vulgar behavior.

It was as if after all the long weary weeks of numbness, she had suddenly come to life. I am going to die, she thought. It is sunny, and the whole of

London is happy and joyous because I am going to die. Even the great marquess had come to enjoy the show.

She clutched Silas's Bible tightly to her. Ahead of her rose the gallows of Tyburn. Stands had been erected next to it so that the Quality could get a fine view. It was like a great fair. Jugglers were performing, vendors were hawking various forms of her supposed last confession, the gingerbread man in his gold-laced hat was calling, "Tiddy-dol. Tiddy-dol."

The cart came to a halt. Barney and Jake clambered on to it. "Said we was your cousins," whispered Jake. "Better if we pull your legs."

Polly sighed and nodded. Now that she was here, the idea of a quick death seemed sane and logical. The clergyman read a prayer. The marquess had dismounted and was standing beside the cart. Because of his great rank, no one ordered him to leave.

"Speech! Speech!" roared the crowd.

Lady Lydia, standing on top of Bertram Pargeter's carriage, clutched his arm. "Get me away from here," she said savagely.

Bertram seized her hand and kissed it. "Alas, my love, there is no way through the crowd. I shall support you." He put an arm like a band of iron around Lady Lydia's slender waist, holding her firmly so that she was forced to face the scaffold.

Ashen-faced, Lady Lydia muttered, "What is her crime?"

"She stole from Meresly Manor," said Bertram, avidly watching her face. "Did you not know?"

Lady Lydia numbly shook her head. The earl had

said nothing of the matter, but then he rarely discussed anything at all with her. Possibly he had forgotten about the whole business once the girl was arrested.

"If she survives the hanging," muttered Lady Lydia, "then she is cut down and allowed to go free, is she not?"

"Yes, but it will not happen," said Bertram, who had bent his head to catch the words. "Only look at that fair white neck of hers! The ones who survive have stout neckties and there's precious few of them—about one in every ten years. Shhh! Our fair prisoner is about to speak."

Polly had prepared quite a grandiloquent speech. But as she glanced down at the rows of spectators in the stands in front of her, she saw Mrs. Blanchard, and Mrs. Blanchard gave her a slow smile.

Polly raised her hands and the crowd fell silent.

"My lords, ladies and gentlemen," said Polly. "I had prepared a long speech for you. Instead, I would prefer to leave you with one question. Why is it that such as I, who am poor and have nothing, should hang for a petty theft when such as she—" here Polly pointed straight at Mrs. Blanchard— "Mrs. Blanchard, that abbess of Covent Garden, can commit murder on the souls of innocent country girls over and over again, and yet go free. I bid you good day, my friends. We shall meet again. For you who enjoy a spectacle such as this will surely roast in hell!"

She dropped a mocking curtsy to the crowd.

The hangman approached Polly, stood on the cart

and arranged the noose about her neck. He fumbled and fumbled, taking a long time about it. Then Polly realized he was whispering in her ear. "I put a wire down your dress and hooked it on your bodice. It's black and I hopes they don't see it. It'll hold you enough though your neck will hurt for I must make it look real. Pretend to die or it'll be my neck as well as yours. Nod if you understand."

Polly nodded, her heart beginning to race.

The hangman climbed back on the scaffold. Barney and Jake crouched ready in the cart. Polly suddenly thought frantically, "What if they pull my legs!" She raised her hands again. Again the crowd fell silent.

"My kinsmen here," she said, "plan to pull my legs to shorten my agony. But let's have some sport!"

This was greeted with a roar of approval while Barney and Jake stared at her in dismay as they were hustled off the cart.

The hangman gave the signal. The chaplain prayed louder and louder, the cart jerked forward and Polly found herself dancing in the air. The pain and wrenching at her neck was so great that she thought the hangman had tricked her, but then she felt the strong pull of the wire hooked into her bodice. She kicked wildly and struggled and then let her head drop to one side and hang still. Her dress floated about her body in the lightest of summer breezes.

"Let's get that old beldame she was talking about and hang her!" yelled one voice. Jake and Barney looked toward where Mrs. Blanchard had been sitting—but that lady had gone. As soon as she had heard Polly's words, she knew what was in store for her. She had dropped to her knees and crawled away under the benches while everyone was watching the hanging.

Lady Lydia let out a long shuddering sigh and some faint color returned to her pale cheeks. "It is over," she said in a flat voice. She turned to Bertram, who was watching her face, and laughed, "What a tedious entertainment. You weary me, Bertram. Too, too provincial in your amusements."

Baffled and furious, Bertram helped her down from the coach. He had been so sure that that girl on the scaffold had been Lady Lydia's illegitimate daughter. So very sure.

The hangman cut Polly down and she fell unconscious at the foot of the scaffold. The crowd began to press close, each anxious to snatch a piece of her gown as a souvenir.

"Here!" called the marquess of Canonby urgently. He was once more on horseback. The hangman seized Polly and threw her body over the saddle in front of the marquess. He turned about and rode away behind the scaffold, followed by the roar of pursuit. He urged his horse toward Hyde Park and, holding Polly firmly with one hand, dug in his spurs. The horse cleared a hedge at one bound. Then he galloped away through the park toward Kensington, through Brompton, and then headlong back through the streets to his home.

The carts containing the prisoners for the mass hanging were entertaining the crowds at Tyburn, and St. James's Square was deserted as he lifted Polly gently down and carried her into his house.

His servants were too well trained to show any surprise. He told his butler to summon the housekeeper and maids and put his injured guest, Miss . . . er . . . Peterson, in one of the guest bedchambers. The marquess did not want his servants to know yet that this guest was none other than the notorious Polly Jones.

He waited outside the door until he was informed that she was in bed and recovering consciousness. He went in quickly and dismissed the housekeeper and maids. He was frightened Polly might say something to betray herself.

She was wearing a pretty lawn nightgown. The marquess did not wonder where his efficient servants had found it. He had trained them so well that he expected them to rise to any occasion. Ugly red marks where the cruel rope had bit marred the white skin of her neck.

She stirred and mumbled and then her eyelids rose and she looked up at him. "Oh, it's you," she sighed. "Did you plan to sell me to the anatomist? Tis a pity I did not die."

"I saved you that fate."

"*You!* I thought that was Barney and Jake."

"Your relatives."

"No relatives of mine. They worked for Mrs. Blanchard, but have left her. They tried to be kind. How did you persuade the hangman to fake it?"

"A monstrous amount of money."

Polly heaved a great sigh.

"And you will want my favors in return." It was a statement, not a question.

"No, not I. Lie quietly now."

"What will you do with me?" Polly tried to struggle up, but he pushed her down with a firm hand.

"Gently, child. We will worry about that later." He saw the restlessness in her eyes and asked, "What ails you now? You are safe. No one shall touch you here."

"I am hungry, my lord. I could have had anything I wanted for breakfast, but I could not eat."

He burst out laughing. "What wonderful powers of recovery! You shall be fed. While I remember, your name in this house is Miss Peterson. Can you remember that?"

"Yes, my lord."

His gaze sharpened. "You have acquired the speech and manners of a lady, Polly. How came you by them?"

Polly thought of Drusilla and blinked hard. She would cry later, but not now. Funny how the kind people of the world make you feel weak and helpless, thought Polly. "It was a lady I met in prison," she said wearily. "I liked her ways and learned from her. Now, may I eat?"

"Yes, you may eat." He rang the bell. "Anything else?"

"I would like something to read."

"Very well. Anything further?"

"Don't leave me," said Polly, catching hold of his hand. "Don't leave me to strangers."

The pathos of her gesture moved him more than her beauty ever could have done. "I shall not leave you, child," he said gently. "I shall be close by. All you have to do is call, or send one of the servants. My servants will not question you. They will take you for a lady. Do not be afraid of them. They may wonder about the marks on your neck and they will read in the newspapers tomorrow that I snatched you away from Tyburn. They will know then who you are, but by that time I shall have sworn them to secrecy. They will continue to call you Miss Peterson, however. Knowledge of your presence here must not go beyond the front door of this house.''

He gave her a slight bow and left.

Polly sighed and stroked the silken coverlet of the bed and then looked in wonder at the rich hangings. The house was very still and quiet. She heard a rattling of china and glass and stiffened. Two footmen entered carrying a large tray. Polly struggled up. They set it on the bed and asked her in deferential tones if she wished anything further. There was wine and cold meat and salad, white bread and butter, and a pudding in a glass bowl.

Polly shook her head and they bowed and left.

She ate ravenously, marvelling at the taste of the white bread and then at the delicate flavor of the pudding. At last, she had finished. She made a move to get out of bed and carry the tray to a table, and then realized a lady would ring the bell for the servants to take it away. There was a long bell rope beside the bed. Timidly, Polly gave it a tug and winced as she heard it sound far below her in the house. The door opened almost immediately and the same two footmen came in followed by two housemaids. The tray was removed and Polly's hands and

face were sponged in warm water scented with co-
logne. Then the butler came in and solemnly handed
her a book with the marquess's compliments. Polly
remained rigid in the bed until they had all left. Then
she settled back against the pillows and picked up the
book. The pleasant moments in life, Polly had quickly
learned, had to be savored when they came. Tomorrow could take care of itself. She opened the book,
read the first sentence, and plunged headlong into a
deep sleep.

Later that day, Barney and Jake walked up and
down St. James's Square on the opposite side from
the marquess's house.

They had tried all the hospitals, sure that the marquess had run mad and snatched the body to sell to
the anatomists, but no hospital reported receiving the
body.

"Calm down, Jake," said Barney wearily. "Look
at it this way. Look at all that money Canonby has.
He don't need to sell bodies. And why wouldn't she
let us pull her legs? You know what I think?"

"No," said Jake, moodily kicking a pebble.

"I think Polly's alive!"

"What!"

"Alive. I think she took his fancy that night she
was taken from Ma Blanchard's. He could've bribed
the hangman to fiddle something. A dead girl ain't
no use to him. But a pretty one, alive and kicking,
that's another matter."

"Can't be!"

"Can. He ain't seeing no one. All callers have
been turned away."

"Well, we can't stand here all day and night. What d'you suppose we do?"

"Find out which tavern the servants go to when they gets any time off, that's what. Follow 'em and try to find out something."

"That'll take money."

"Right. So let's go and steal something, but be careful. One hanging's enough for one day!"

Three hours later, Polly awoke from her sleep, screaming with fright. She had been dreaming she was hanging over a pit, about to be dropped down into a crowd at the bottom who were waiting to tear her to pieces. She was running a high fever. The marquess sent for a physician and then sat by the bed, holding her hands and talking quietly, hoping the sound of his voice would penetrate the fevered madness which now seemed to grip her.

The physician came and bled her and then recommended bleeding again on the morrow, but the marquess, alarmed by Polly's weak state, sent him packing. By morning, tired and aching with exhaustion, he at last fell asleep in a chair beside the bed.

Like a great receding wave, the tumult of Polly's fever left her. She lay against the pillows, weak and dazed. Then she glanced sideways and found the marquess fast asleep. He had torn off his necktie, and the lace collar of his shirt lay open exposing the strong column of his throat. Stubble darkened his chin. His hair was brushed free of powder. It was cut close to his head, shiny and as black as a raven's wing. His face looked younger in sleep. His coat lay discarded on the floor beside his chair and his long waistcoat was unbuttoned. His powerful legs in their silk knee breeches and clocked stockings were crossed at the ankles.

As she watched, he came awake and started up. He got to his feet and bent solicitously over her. He put a cool hand on her forehead and smiled his relief. "You are recovered," he said. "Go back to sleep. You are still weak."

Polly smiled up at him mistily. Slowly her lids drooped over her eyes.

The marquess waited, hearing the regular breathing, listening to make sure there was no change. At last he took himself off to his own bedchamber. "Now," he said, as he undressed and climbed into his bed, "what on earth am I to do with you, Polly Jones?"

Banished again from Lady Lydia's side, Bertram Pargeter contented himself with going to balls and ridottos and in general leading the life of a carefree young rococo man about town. He felt cured of her. He felt as if a great sickness had left him.

She was much too old, he told himself, as he wondered over the sickness and madness that had possessed him. He, on the other hand, was young, rich and unmarried. Lady Lydia, it was rumored, was thirty-eight. Middle-aged!

All went perfectly splendidly until a week after the hanging. He went to the playhouse and there in a side box near the stage sat Lady Lydia. She had what appeared to be a new inamorata with her, a man of about thirty whom Bertram did not recognize. She looked radiant, her powdered hair worn in tight curls, a black patch on her face highlighting the whiteness of her skin and the full redness of her mouth. All the torment came rushing back and Bertram actually groaned aloud. He could not bear to sit any longer in the theatre. Oblivious to the stares of surprise as he pushed his way out of the pit, he made his way out of the theatre and to the nearest coffee house where he called for coffee, cancelled the order, and changed it to a request for a bottle of Lisbon. But the wine, instead of dulling his renewed passion, seemed to inflame it.

Gradually he began to wonder again about that girl called Polly. Her resemblance to Lady Lydia had been striking. Pity she was dead.

"Is she?" suddenly nagged a little voice in his head. "Is she *really*?"

He poured himself another drink and for the first time began to think about the strange behavior of the marquess of Canonby. People had ceased to talk about it. Canonby had laughed and said he had snatched away the dead girl for a bet. He had given her a decent burial, he said, which is more than she would have had, had he left her to the tender mercies of the authorities.

But such behavior was completely out of character for a man like Canonby, who was as punctilious and fastidious as a cat. What would he want with a dead girl? Could Polly have miraculously escaped death? Then he remembered that sickening jerk of her neck and how her body had swung lifelessly in the sunny air.

He finished his wine and got up and went out and wandered aimlessly through the streets. Somehow, he found himself in St. James's Square. He stepped aside to let a chair bearing some Exquisite go past. The gentleman in the chair was guarded on either side by liveried servants carrying blazing flambeaux. And then, in the light of their torches, two faces seemed to leap out of the dark night at Bertram. One man was squat and swarthy and the other had only one eye.

His heart beat hard. Those two men were the ones who had been in the cart with Polly, so they must be her relatives. He moved back into the shadows and waited. As his eyes became accustomed to the dimness, he could make them out. They were standing, like him, in the shadows, away from the weak light of the parish lamp at the south corner of the square. They were looking at the marquess of Canonby's house.

Bertram turned his own gaze on the marquess's house. As he watched, a figure came up the area steps and headed toward him. He felt, rather than saw, Polly's two "relatives" stiffen and become alert. The figure came closer, passed under the lamp, and was revealed to be that of a man in butler's livery. The two men let him go past and then started to follow him. Intrigued, Bertram followed the two men.

The butler turned into a tavern in one of the lanes leading off St. James's Street. The two men waited a few moments and went in after him. Bertram gave it only a minute before going in himself.

The tavern was full of liveried servants—butlers

who were often allowed a little time off in the evening, running footmen in their divided skirts who were, according to their masters, supposed to be out on errands, black pages, coachmen and grooms.

The butler had joined some friends at a table in the corner. Barney and Jake stood baffled for a moment and then crammed into chairs at a table nearby. Bertram called for a bottle of wine and sat at a table near theirs.

Then the butler's friends said something and got up to take their leave. Barney and Jake quickly moved over and sat at the table next to the butler.

Bertram moved to their table so that he could hear what was being said.

"A fine evening," Bertram heard the thickset man say. "May we present ourselves. I am Mr. Barney . . . hem . . . Smith and this is Mr. Jake Smith."

The butler was a large, pompous man. He looked coldly at Jake's one-eyed face and then at Barney's unshaven one and buried his nose in his tankard.

"I'm sure you would like another drink," Bertram heard the man called Jake say.

The butler visibly thawed. "Very kind of you, gentlemen," he said. "I am Mr. Durrell."

"And what is your pleasure, Mr. Durrell?"

"Another tankard of Dog's Nose."

"Dog's Nose it is," said Barney jovially. "Me and my friend here will join you. We're still feeling a bit poorly. Bad shock we had last week."

"Indeed?" said Mr. Durrell politely. "I am sorry to hear that."

The drinks were brought by a serving girl. Barney

and Jake exchanged a glance and then Barney said, "Yes, quite a shock we had. Poor Polly."

The listening Bertram felt such a rush of excitement that he nearly fell off his chair.

"Is this Polly a relative of yours?" asked the butler.

"In a way," sighed Jake. "Poor, poor Poll."

"Sickness?" asked Mr. Durrell.

"Hanged at Tyburn," said Barney lugubriously.

Something flickered across the butler's eyes and was gone in an instant.

He rose to his feet. "You must excuse me, gentlemen," he said hurriedly. "My master does not know I am out. Pray forgive me. Should I have the fortune to meet you on another occasion, I will gladly repay your hospitality."

Barney opened his mouth to protest, but the butler had slid off through the tables and company to the door with amazing speed.

"Clumsy," said Jake, shaking his head. "Very clumsy, Barney. Shouldn't ha' mentioned hanging at all. Now we'll never know. He could've shied off on hearing we was the sort whose relatives get topped. Should've asked about his job and who was in the house and so forth."

"Well, if you're so poxy clever, you punk, ask yourself the next time," raged Barney. "You wasn't much help with your poor, poor Pollys."

"Good evening to you, my friends." Barney and Jake looked suspiciously up at the newcomer. Here was no servant. Bertram had thrown back his cloak to reveal his coat of gold satin and long embroidered waistcoat. The tavern light glinted on the jewelled hilt of his dress sword. His hair was powdered gold to match his coat, and instead of a patch, he wore a gold spangle next to his thin rouged mouth.

A tinge of fear came into Barney's eyes. Young men who frequented servants' taverns were usually of the sort who belonged to the Mohawks, those gangs of rich idlers who roamed the streets at night, raping young girls, tormenting old women, and torturing such as Barney and Jake if they happened to come across them alone and unprotected.

"I heard you talk about a girl, Polly, hanged at Tyburn," said Bertram, fastidiously dusting the chair with a lace handkerchief before sitting down.

"Wot if we did?" said Jake, turning the scarred side of his face to Bertram.

"Well, you see, my friends, I have an interest in the late Polly Jones . . . or shall we say, the present Polly Jones? Do not sit with your mouths hanging open, gentlemen, or your souls may fly out and be lost to you. Now, a bottle of the best sack and then I think we will find we have much in common. . . ."

CHAPTER SEVEN

At FIRST POLLY WAS CONTENT TO LIVE IN THE dream-world of the marquess of Canonby's town house. She savored every moment of her new freedom, every delicious meal and every fascinating book and magazine. Despite her fears, the servants had not changed in their attitude toward her.

New gowns appeared as if by magic, new shoes, new stockings.

But by the end of a week, a restlessness began to possess her and she regretted her healthy country-bred constitution which had put her back on her feet so very quickly. For as soon as he saw that she was recovered, the marquess had gone about his own affairs and she barely saw him. Her meals were served to her in a little drawing room off her bedroom. The silent servants came and went like clockwork toys, and Polly, much as she longed for some conversation, was frightened that if she became familiar with the servants, they might begin to despise her.

The evenings were the hardest to bear when the marquess entertained friends. Sometimes she stole to the top of the stairs and looked down at the fine gowns and glittering jewels, heard the laughter and music, and longed to be a part of it. But for Polly it was rather like that little scene with the man and woman she had witnessed in the Strand before the brothel had swallowed her up—pretty and perfect, but belonging to a world from which her low origins barred her for all time.

Just when she was beginning to think the marquess had forgotten her very existence, he came to her drawing room one evening. He was dressed to go out to the opera, in black velvet and silver lace. Diamond buttons ornamented his long waistcoat and flashed on the buckles of his shoes.

Polly was wearing a simple sack gown with Watteau pleats at the back. It was made of pale green silk but without elaborate sleeves or quilted petticoat, the petticoat being of plain white silk without trimming. Her unpowdered hair was brushed until it shone and piled in a careless knot on the top of her head.

How incredibly innocent she looks, he thought. What is to become of her? And yet she is a thief. It is a miracle she has not yet stolen anything from me. Aloud, he said courteously, "I am come to see how you go on."

"Very well, my lord," said Polly. "I am become anxious as to my future, nonetheless. I cannot remain mewed up here."

"No more you can," he said. "Give me a little more time and I shall hit on something." He hesitated, wondering whether to tell her that her two companions, Barney and Jake, had been seen watching the house and had questioned his butler, and then decided against it. The sooner she forgot about her past life the better.

"Are those *real* diamonds?" asked Polly, and then flushed. She felt sure Drusilla would have told her that such a question was vulgar. But he looked amused and said, "Yes, my sweeting. Every one. Now, I bid you good eve. I am expected at the opera."

Polly's face fell. "I had . . . I hoped you might stay and talk to me a little," she said. "I see no one."

He frowned, and then said, "I shall tell my servants to summon you to breakfast. We shall talk then."

Polly's eyes were like stars at the promised treat, and he felt worried and guilty when he left her. He should never have rescued her . . . but on the other hand, he could not let her die.

Polly tossed and turned all night, frightened she would oversleep, frightened he might forget or the servants might forget.

She fell into a heavy sleep at dawn and jumped out of bed in alarm when a servant awakened her at eleven in the morning.

"He will already have breakfasted. He must have breakfasted," wailed Polly.

"No, miss," said the chambermaid. "My lord hardly ever sits down to breakfast before eleven when he is in Town."

Feeling as if she were setting out on an adventure, as soon as she was dressed Polly followed a footman down the main staircase to the first floor. The footman held open a door and Polly walked in.

She found herself, not in the great dining room she had expected, but in a little morning room with sun flooding in through the windows.

The marquess put down his newspaper and smiled at her. He was wrapped in a thick banyan of gold damask. His black hair had grown longer and was confined at the nape of his neck with a black silk ribbon. His undress somehow made him look more formidable than ever.

"What is your pleasure, Miss Peterson?" he asked.

Polly seated herself at the small round table and cast a dismal glance at the butler and two footmen in attendance. She had hoped to be alone with him.

"What are you having, my lord?" she asked.

"Steak and small beer."

"Very well. I shall have the same."

When her breakfast arrived, Polly wished she had asked for something simple, like bread and cheese, for his presence was making her nervous.

There was an ache in the pit of her stomach as she looked at him. She felt the insecurity of her own position. She longed to be on equal terms with him. At last he dismissed the servants, finished his breakfast, and said, "You do not eat."

Polly had cut up her steak into little pieces in the hope it might look as if she had at least eaten some of it.

"I am worried," she said candidly.

"Yes, about your future. I must tell you what I have decided . . ."

At that moment, there was a commotion outside. The door burst open and a tall man in scarlet regimentals strode into the room and stopped short at the sight of Polly.

"Colonel Anderson would not listen when I told him you were not to be disturbed," said the butler from the doorway.

The marquess flashed a warning look at Polly and said smoothly, "Sit down, Guy. Miss Peterson was just leaving."

Polly bobbed a curtsy in the direction of the tall colonel and made her escape. The butler closed the door behind her.

Polly stood in the hall, reluctant to return to her expensive "prison" abovestairs. And then she heard the colonel say, "Who was that dazzler you were entertaining?"

Polly heard the marquess sigh. Then he said, "You are just returned to London and have no doubt missed reading of my adventure at Tyburn."

"On the contrary, I heard all about it on the road to Town."

"The girl did not die. That was Miss Polly Jones who just left the room."

"Bedad, my friend, I am come most opportunely. You have run mad. She is extraordinarily beautiful, but you can have your pick of the charmers without snatching them from Tyburn Tree. Is she your mistress?"

"No, nor shall be."

"Then what is your interest in her?"

The marquess found that too hard to explain, since he did not really know himself. So he shrugged and kept to the lie he had already given about. "I did it for a wager."

"And so what do you plan to do with your wager now?"

"I have made up my mind to send her to the country, where my housekeeper may be able to train her as some sort of upper servant."

There was a long silence. Polly glanced about the hall, frightened of being caught listening but desperate to hear more.

Then the colonel's voice sounded again. "She was, if I remember, charged with theft. Was she then innocent?"

"No. I know her to be a thief."

Polly's face flamed.

"Then turn her out immediately," said the colonel harshly. "It is unlike you to be gulled by a pretty face. She will go to that palace of yours in Shropshire and immediately resort to her old ways. Throw the slut out!"

There was the sound of the door opening from the servants' quarters at the back of the hall. Polly gathered up her skirts and ran up the stairs.

All Polly knew that she was hurt beyond measure. And yet the marquess had only spoken the truth. She thought of his kindness to her but then hardened her heart. It was easy for such as he to sit surrounded by wealth and servants and never know what it was to be poor and hungry. All his seeming bravery and

gallantry in saving her life had been caused by a
mere bet and not by any higher feelings. She would
need to leave. Her pride would not let her be a
burden on him further. She realized she had come to
hope that he might care for her a little, not as a lover,
but as a friend.

She went to a tall wardrobe, took out the gown in
which she had arrived and changed into it. She crossed
to the window and looked out. She would wait until
he had left and then make her escape. She was sure
the servants had no instructions to stop her. As she
looked down into the square, she saw a couple of
familiar figures slowly walking up and down. Barney
and Jake! She shrank back, wondering if they knew
she was still alive, wondering whether they were
waiting to take her back to Mrs. Blanchard. And then
she remembered their kindness to her in prison, how
they said they had left the brothel, and how they had
tried to save her from prolonged death agonies. They
were her kind, her class. They could not look down
on her, for in their way they were lower than she was
herself.

And then she heard the street door open. The
marquess and the colonel emerged. They strolled off
across the square arm in arm, chatting like the old
friends they obviously were. The tall colonel looked
grand in his regimentals and yet was outshone by the
marquess's greater height and elegance.

She half-lifted her hand in farewell, although she
knew they could not see her. Then, as soon as they
had vanished from sight, she ran from the room and
down the stairs, deaf to the startled shout of Durrell,

the butler, and straight out of the door and into the square.

"Quickly," she cried, as she came up to Barney and Jake, "or they might come after me." The three hurried off, keeping to the back streets until they were sure there was no sound of pursuit behind them.

They said not a word until Barney discovered a sleazy tavern and led them inside and found a table in the corner.

"We knew'd you was alive, Polly," he said triumphantly. "We've bin waiting and watching for days."

"Why?" asked Polly in a flat voice.

Barney shrugged and Jake looked at the sawdust on the floor as if it were the most interesting thing he had ever seen.

"Thought you might be in need of help," said Barney at last in a gruff voice. "Besides, a grand gentleman was trying to help us as well. He was going to call at the house today to see if you was there."

Polly looked alarmed. "Who could that be? Everyone else thinks I am dead. What was his name?"

"A Mr. Pargeter."

"And what is his interest in me?"

"Didn't say. We was glad of his offer, us not being able to call at the house ourselves."

"Well, we'll talk about him later," said Polly. "I am glad of your offer of help. I have only got these clothes I stand up in."

"Thought you might have lifted a few gee-gaws from his lordship," said Jake. "Seems like common sense to me."

"I couldn't do that," said Polly fiercely. "I would never steal from him!"

"Like him, do you?" said Barney with a leer.

"There was nothing like that between us. Nothing," said Polly haughtily.

"Very well, m' lady," said Barney. "Now Jake and me, we's calling ourselves Mr. and Mr. Smith, the brothers Smith, and we've got a cozy lodging down in Westminster near the Abbey. We've managed to thieve a few bits and bobs to keep us going. You can stay along o' us."

"It is a terrible risk," murmured Polly. "Picking pockets, I mean."

"Ho! What would you do, pretty miss?" sneered Jake, his one eye gleaming with contempt. "Walk into a grand house, say excuse me, fill up a sack and walk out?"

There was a long silence, and then Polly threw back her head and laughed. "It's possible," she said. She rested her dimpled elbows on the table and leaned forward.

"Look here: when I was at Canonby's, he gave parties of an evening. Now the latest fashion is for ridottos. Everyone goes masked and in fancy dress. I used to watch from the top of the stairs. And do you know what I thought? I thought to myself that if I were masked and finely gowned, no one would know I was not a guest. I could have a gown with deep pockets in the petticoat. Then I could creep away from the main room and drop a few objects into these pockets and slip out. No one would notice there was anything missing for days."

Barney and Jake stared at her in amazement. "Seems wrong," said Barney at last. "If you're caught picking pockets for wipes and timepieces, you might just get burned on the hand. You take so much as a patch from a nobleman's house, and it's back to Tyburn Tree again."

Polly shuddered. She took a drink of ale and then said, "The way I see it, if I took a purse or something from someone on the street, I would never know whether or not it was their last farthing or some brooch or watch that meant a great deal to them. But if I took from a grand house, that would not be wrong. I need the money, and they would not miss it."

"You talk very fine, Poll," said Jake, "and you looks and sounds like a lady now. But it'd never work. You'd need an escort, and fancy dress or no fancy dress, the servants would catch one glimpse of me and Barney and howl for the watch."

"But I saw some great ladies arriving alone," said Polly eagerly. "I watched from the top of the stairs."

"You've got to carry a card, saying as how you's invited," pointed out Barney.

"Yes, but on some occasions, the lady would search about for her card and find she had forgotten it, give her name to the butler and he would usher her in nonetheless. One only has to look the part!"

"Drink up," said Barney, "and we'll take you to our place and talk further. And you'd better dirty yourself up a bit and cover your hair when you're living with us or people'll wonder what a lady's doing living in a slum."

"I thought you said it was a cozy little place," said Polly sharply.

"Beggars can't be choosers," said Barney sourly.

"Oh, yes they can!" said Polly Jones.

"So," said the marquess of Canonby as he returned with the colonel to St. James's Square, "there you have it. Although all evidence points to the contrary, I am convinced that Polly Jones is basically a sweet and innocent girl who has been a victim of circumstances."

"And though you call her Miss Peterson, your servants must be well aware of her true identity," said the colonel.

"Yes, I told them myself and swore them to secrecy."

"Too big a secret by half," said the colonel. "It will come out sooner or later."

"By which time Miss Polly Jones will be leading a blameless life in the country," said the marquess patiently. "But you shall talk to her and judge her character for yourself."

They were met by Durrell, the butler, who burst out with, "She's gone, my lord!"

"Miss Peterson?" demanded the marquess sharply.

"Yes, my lord. She ran past me and out of the house. You gave me no instructions to stop her. I did not know what to do, my lord."

"Did she take anything with her? Her clothes?"

"No, nothing, my lord. Miss Peterson was wearing the gown she wore when she first arrived here."

"Better check the silver," laughed the colonel.

"Who has gone? Someone missing from your household?" came a silky voice from behind them.

The marquess swung round. "Pargeter! What are you doing here?"

Lady Lydia's Exquisite stood framed in the open doorway.

"I came to call on you, Canonby," said Bertram plaintively. "A social call. Now it appears you have lost someone."

"I am very busy, Pargeter," said the marquess acidly, "and must bid you good day. Who or what I have lost is my affair."

Bertram gave a light laugh. "Such ungrateful behavior, considering you saved her from the scaffold."

The marquess looked at him stonily, but Bertram's eyes had flicked quickly to the colonel's face and surprised a look of consternation.

"Get out, Pargeter," said the marquess, "and shut the door behind you."

With many sweet smiles, apologies and bows and flourishes, Bertram backed out just as the marquess slammed the door in his face.

He stood for a moment on the step, drawing on his gloves. Polly had been there, he was sure of that. Just as certain was the fact she had run away. He was supposed to meet those two ruffians, Jake and Barney, in the servants' tavern in a few moments to report his progress. He made his way there, picking his way through the dirt of the rainy streets on his high heels.

He waited and waited in the tavern, a conspicuous figure among the liveried servants, but Jake and Barney did not appear.

I must find this Polly Jones, thought Bertram. She must be somewhere in London. Lydia took the hanging coolly, but it was almost as if she were glad a chapter was closed, that some worry had been removed from her life. But I cannot scour London by myself.

He minced out of the tavern, the silken skirts of his coat swishing against the tables as he went. He made his way to White's Club and searched the rooms but the couple he was hunting for were absent. He went out and called for a chair and went from coffee house to coffee house until he ran them to earth close by at the Cocoa Tree—Mr. Barks and Mr. Caldicott.

Mr. Barks had a large quizzing glass raised to one eye and was scowling fiercely at a letter. "Oh, it's you, Pargeter," he said, lowering the letter as that gentleman sat down next to him.

"Bad news?" asked Bertram sweetly. "From home?" Everyone knew of Mrs. Barks's ambitions to be presented at court.

Mr. Barks crumpled the letter. "Very bad," he said. "Let's talk of something else."

"By all means." Bertram took out an enamelled snuffbox, helped himself to a delicate pinch, and sighed, "Such a pity your beautiful present to Canonby ended up on the scaffold."

"Serves her right," said Mr. Caldicott, tossing his head and then letting out a yelp of anguish, for the sharp movement had hurt, his hair being a solid mass of flour and pomatum, not to mention a small cushion over which it was backcombed, piled up and topped with a tiny three-cornered hat.

"And yet," said Bertram, "it was most strange that Canonby should snatch the body."

"Did it for a bet," said Mr. Barks. "Told everyone."

Bertram leaned forward. "What would you say, gentlemen, if I told you I had reason to believe that Polly Jones was still alive when she was cut down, still alive when she was taken to Canonby's house, and still alive when she escaped today?"

"You've been seeing too many plays," said Mr. Caldicott.

"Not I. I swear she is alive."

"Then we'll find her and hang her ourselves," growled Mr. Barks.

"A waste of a pretty neck. Only think how grateful Canonby would be to get the jade back. I' faith, Barks, that wife of yours could make her curtsy in the royal drawing room any time she chose to do so!"

"So if you know she is alive, where is she?"

"That is where I need your help. I cannot comb London looking for her myself."

"And what is *your* interest in her, Pargeter?" asked Mr. Caldicott.

'I would find her for a whim," said Bertram carelessly.

Mr. Caldicott laughed. "That whim being that the jade bears a striking resemblance to Lady Lydia."

"You noticed? Do you not find such a resemblance strange?" Bertram looked eagerly from one to the other.

"Hardly strange," said Mr. Caldicott, "when you

consider she has three brothers who must have fathered a deal of bastards about the length and breadth
of England. Lady Lydia's from the Berkeley family
and they're all wild to a fault.''

Bertram's face fell. If that were indeed the case,
he would have no hold over Lady Lydia. And yet the
girl, Polly, had frightened her, that he knew. ''Are
you interested in finding her or not?'' he asked sharply.

''Oh, very interested,'' said Mr. Barks. ''We'd
best enlist Mother Blanchard. For wherever Polly
Jones is now, it's bound to be in some low-life ken.''

Polly looked around the room near Tothill Fields
in Westminster which was home to Barney and Jake.
It boasted two truckle beds, one table covered in
dirty dishes, four chairs, and dirt everywhere. ''I
cannot live here!'' she cried.

Jake shrugged. ''Picked up some grand ideas at
Canonby's, ain't you? So where else you going to
go?''

Polly bit her lip. She thought longingly of the
Brewers, and yet felt she could never go back there.
Silas would no doubt try to find her work, but she
had no right, notorious as she had become, to inflict
herself on such a decent family.

''Oh, go away somewhere, the pair of you,'' she
snapped, ''and don't come back until I have had time
to scrub this place.''

In the days that passed, a little home slowly grew
up about the ill-assorted threesome. A bed was found
for Polly and curtains for the windows. She cooked
over a wood-burning stove in the corner of the room,

producing some of the dishes she had learned to prepare at the merchant's home. At first she had been wary of Barney and Jake's friendship, for after all they were men, and the first few nights she slept uneasily, a rolling pin under her pillow. But they seemed to have adopted her as a sort of sister, a talisman. Her very beauty kept them at bay. Barney and Jake were enjoying all this new domesticity and pleaded time after time with Polly to give up her mad idea of masquerading as a lady and stealing from a grand house.

But Polly was adamant. If they were going to be thieves, then they would be thieves on a grand scale. So Barney and Jake, falling more and more under her influence, stole more and more bits and pieces, sold them, and saved the money to buy material to make Polly a grand enough gown. Polly had been taught by old Meg how to sew and make clothes. She also studied the social columns in every newspaper, waiting for an announcement of some ridotto where she could make her debut. The tedious, hot days of summer dragged past, and then autumn came, bringing the Little Season and society back to Town.

She felt uneasy over the things that Barney and Jake stole, but comforted herself with the doubtful piece of logic that once her own thieving days had begun, they need not steal anything from people who might not be able to bear the loss.

Polly had created a splendid outfit for herself. She had decided to avoid fancy dress, preparing herself a grand ensemble and a mask. Hoops were coming into fashion, and so Polly finally learned how to construct one from a wicker frame and pads of horse hair. The new hoops were flat at the front and back, stretching out on either side, which gave the impression that the wearer was standing behind a sort of embroidered silk wall.

Finally, the outfit was ready. It had to be strung up to the ceiling on a pulley to leave space in the room below for the occupants.

'This is it!'' said Polly one morning. ''A ridotto at my lord Hallsworthy's. It is time to begin.''

"Feel it's all wrong, Poll,'' said Barney uneasily. "Feel it's wrong for you. Wasting your life. Forgit about the whole thing. Let me and Jake save a bit more, then maybe we'll find a place in the country and turn ourselves into respectable folks.''

Polly felt a sharp jab of conscience. Aunt Meg would have been horrified—poor Meg, so decent, so wise and so honest. Then she clamped down on these weak thoughts. It was a cruel, unfair world, and all she was going to do was even up the balance a little in her favor by taking a few trinkets from people who had more money than they knew what to do with. And without money, she could not afford the luxury of searching to find out what had happened to Meg on the last day of the old woman's life.

CHAPTER EIGHT

OLLY HAD NOT ANTICIPATED THAT FASHION might keep her trapped in the room in Westminster.

Certainly she made a breathtaking picture as she stood ready to go. Her gown was of salmon damask embroidered with gold and opening over a gold ruffled petticoat ornamented with knots of gold and salmon ribbons. It was cut very low at the bosom and the long-laced stomacher showed Polly's tiny waist to advantage. There were ten ruffles on each elbow-length sleeve. Polly had powdered her hair and it was piled up over a cushion on her head to a great height, decorated with a long faux-diamond necklace wound in and out the powdery curls. One long ringlet fell to her white shoulders. Her face was covered with a white velvet mask ornamented with gold sequins. As well as the pockets in her petticoat, she carried an etui hanging at her waist, that indispensable ornamental bag in which the fashionable lady carried her needles and thread, her scissors and her pomadour. Polly's was empty. She planned to fill it with more exciting trifles.

After Jake and Barney had duly admired the effect, Polly draped herself in a long black cloak to hide all this magnificence from their unsavory neighbors.

She just managed to get out of the room by edging sideways, and then found the size of her hoop would not allow her to go down the twisting, broken staircase which led to the street.

"Better give up the idea," said Jake with relief, for he and Barney were secretly sure that if Polly went through with her mad scheme, they would find themselves spectators at her hanging once more.

"No!" said Polly fiercely.

She looked around the room and then her eye fell on the discarded pulley.

"You could lower me from the window," she said slowly. The window had once been a door high up in the wall for loading and unloading goods, and the bottom of it still consisted of two thin double doors which opened out. Above was the actual window of two grimy panes of glass.

"And have the whole street come running!" exclaimed Jake.

"Let me see," said Polly, thinking hard. "You, Jake, go down to the end of the street and create a diversion. Then when the street is empty, Barney can lower me down."

Jake argued for a few moments and then finally caved in before the force of Polly's stronger personality.

When Jake had left, Barney opened the window and looked out. Then he saw everyone beginning to run toward the end of the street. He fixed the pulley back on its hook in the ceiling, Polly tied the rope firmly about her waist, and then Barney draped her cloak over her and pulled the hood gently up over her head.

As Polly was lowered down into the street, she was momentarily overcome with dizziness. The whole experience was so reminiscent of that terrible hanging. But she landed safely on the ground. Barney hurtled down the stairs and Jake came running down the street at the same time. "Quickly," he said. "I told them there was a two-headed man and they're busy searching, but they'll soon give up."

One on either side of Polly, they hustled her through the streets. It had been planned to find a chair for Polly as soon as they reached the more salubrious neighborhood of Whitehall, but that wretched inflexible hoop would not allow her to get into a chair. Fortunately, Lord Hallworthy's house was in the Haymarket so they had not very far to walk. Polly was wearing pattens over her shoes to protect them from the mud, and the iron rings on their soles made a sharp clatter as she hurried over the cobbles.

"I cannot arrive on foot," she said breathlessly. "I must think of something."

"There's the house," said Barney gloomily. "You'll never manage it, Poll."

But Polly had come so far and was not going to turn back. A line of footmen in green-and-gold livery, gold swords hanging at their sides, flanked either side of the entrance. Carriages were driving up, their coachmen fighting and jostling for space.

"At the back of the carriages . . . quick!" said Polly urgently.

She waited until an aristocratic family had just alighted from their coach, swung off her cloak and thrust it at Barney and Jake along with her pattens and, to their horror, opened the carriage door at the far side and then made her exit through the other carriage door in front of the house. The footman, who had been about to shut the door, held it open again and assisted her down in a bemused way. He wondered why he had not noticed her earlier with his master's party but the richness of her dress silenced him.

Barney and Jake clutched each other in the shadows and watched tensely.

Polly had learned from Drusilla that there was a separate etiquette for entering a grand house. It was known as "bridling." A lady kept her head high and her chin tucked well in, stared straight in front of her and did not even deign to look at the servant as she proffered her card. If she had forgotten her card, then she gave her name in a clear voice and continued walking in the direction of the ballroom.

"What name will she give?" asked Jake. The door was open and they could see Polly standing up in the entrance hall.

"Don't know," said Barney. "Let's hope she don't say she's Polly Jones."

"I have forgot my card," Polly was saying. "I am Lady Mary Peters."

And then, without waiting to see how this was being received, she walked slowly up the staircase to the ballroom on the floor above.

"That's that! She's in!" Barney clutched Jake in his excitement. "Now we've got to wait here with 'er cloak ready till she comes out, for she can't walk home to Tothill Fields in that rig."

Inside, Polly almost made the mistake of curtsying to the major-domo, he looked so grand and so proud. But she rallied quickly, and looking straight ahead, glad of her mask, she said firmly, "Lady Mary Peters."

"Lady Mary Peters!" roared the major-domo. Polly stepped past him and sank into a low curtsy before Lord and Lady Hallworthy. They were both in Elizabethan costume. Polly's name meant nothing to them. They had barely heard it. Their secretary was responsible for the invitations.

"Welcome," said Lord Hallworthy. Lady Hallworthy murmured something, but their eyes were already straying past Polly to the next newcomer. Polly walked into the ballroom, under a blaze of hundreds of candles. Masked and costumed figues circulated about. Two pairs of dancers were performing the minuet.

It was only then that Polly's feeling of triumph began to ebb. She could not dance. She could not sit down because her wicker hoop would not bend.

Then her courage returned. She had to thieve something, anything, and that something or anything would go to pay for a quilted petticoat with one of the new hoops sewn onto it, one of those hoops which folded up like wings when you got into a sedan chair.

The music of the minuet stopped. A country dance was announced. Polly saw Lord Hallworthy approaching her and her heart sank. Why couldn't he stay at his position at the door? But her arrival had been late and most of the guests had already been there by the time she made her entrance.

"May I present Colonel Anderson, Lady Potters," said Lord Hallworthy. "He is desirous of a dance."

Polly had not the courage to refuse. She miserably allowed the colonel to lead her into a set. The colonel, of all people! "Are you newly come to Town, Lady Potters?" she heard the colonel ask.

"Peters," corrected Polly, while inside she wildly wondered what on earth it mattered *what* he called her.

"My apologies," said the colonel. "Old Hallworthy can barely remember his own name, let alone that of his guests. Are you newly come to Town?"

"Yes."

"From far?"

"Very far."

"How far?"

"Miles and miles," said Polly repressively.

The music struck up. What am I going to do? thought Polly desperately. Then, giddy with relief, she realized the country dance was one she had been taught to perform at the parish school. Her capacity for living in the minute took over, and soon she was flying down the set with the colonel, briefly forgetting she was a thief and imposter, and enjoying all the heady delight of wearing an expensive-looking gown and dancing with a handsome man. For the colonel *was* handsome, she thought, even though his face was hidden with a black mask. He had good shoulders and fine legs and danced beautifully.

The country dance lasted half an hour, half an hour in which Polly Jones briefly became Lady Peters inside as well as out. What dresses there were and what jewels! Everything glittered and shone and sparkled.

And then two things happened to shatter the dream. The music ended, and the marquess of Canonby entered the ballroom. He was wearing a gold mask, and his hair was powdered, but Polly would have known him anywhere. In a daze, she realized her partner had also recognized the marquess and was waggling his fingers in his direction in that irritating way society had of signalling to their friends across the room.

"I say, Lady Peters," said the colonel enthusiastically, "you must meet my friend, Canonby. Lady Peters?" But his fair companion had melted away into the crowd.

Polly's heart beat hard. She must do the work she came to do and then leave. She was worried in case the marquess might recognize her.

She glanced around the ballroom. There was a supper room to one side and a card room to the other, neither of them good places for a thieving expedition. There was bound to be a room off the hall where the ladies repaired their toilette and left their cloaks. That was it! Perhaps there were some china knickknacks on the mantel. She went slowly down the staircase, her head held high, her face rigid with hauteur. An impressed footman showed her to the room reserved for the ladies, and then bowed his way off backward.

Polly went in and looked about. No one. There were rich, fur-trimmed cloaks and mantles piled on a table. Just one of those would do. But, thought Polly, what if the owner of one of those cloaks was not very rich and would miss it badly? That would be cruel. Taking the cloak from the marquess's house had been another matter. She had been desperate then. There were bowls of powder on the toilet table, and little dishes of bone pins. But Polly had not come so far to steal items which would fetch so very little. There was nothing on the mantel or near the fireplace but the fire irons and coal scuttle.

She was about to leave and try her luck in one of the other rooms when a low groaning coming from behind a lacquered screen in the corner of the room made her stop. "I cannot bear it," said an elderly voice suddenly. "Oh, the shame!"

Polly went forward and peeped round the screen. A massive lady was sitting on a closed stool, her wig askew and her face scarlet.

"Your pardon, ma'am," gasped Polly and made to retreat.

"Don't go, child," wailed the elderly lady. "Now you have seen my predicament, I must beg for help."

"Have you trouble with your bowels?" asked Polly delicately.

"A pox on my bowels," said the old lady. "I'm stuck."

"Stuck!"

"Yes, stuck fast, my child, and too embarrassed to

have one of these footmen come snickering around me.''

"Then you must let me help you," said Polly, trying not to giggle. What an odd beginning to her life of crime! So far she had not stolen one trinket, and now she was going to have to waste precious time by extricating this dowager's bottom.

She put her arms round the old woman's waist, or where her waist used to be, and with her strong country arms she gave a mighty heave. Just when Polly thought her muscles would crack, there came an odd smacking plop like a massive spongy cork being removed from a bottle and the old lady fell forward against her.

"Free at last!" crowed the dowager. She straightened up and smoothed her crushed skirts. "Odd's fish, you have the strength of Samson, my child. What is thy name?"

"Lady Mary Peters."

"And I am Mrs. Worthington." She leant on Polly's arm and allowed her to help her round the screen.

"La! We seem to be walking on firewood," exclaimed the old lady.

Polly looked down and stifled a groan of dismay. Her strenuous efforts in freeing Mrs. Worthington had shattered Polly's fragile wicker petticoat, and little bits of wood fell to the floor with every movement.

Her face flaming scarlet, Polly tried to laugh. "It is my petticoat, ma'am. A new invention. I made it myself out of wickerwork for a whim."

Old Mrs. Worthington began to laugh, a deep

sound which started somewhere inside her capacious body and then surfaced in a full-blooded roar of merriment. "What a pair we are!" gasped Mrs. Worthington when she could. "Me stuck in a closed stool and you with your shattered petticoat. Lor'! When did I last laugh like that? Here child, my husband will be waiting for me. Take this trifle with an old woman's thanks." She thrust something into Polly's hand and rolled from the room, still chortling, her great sides shaking with mirth.

Polly opened her hand which she had automatically closed around the object and stared at it. It was a huge emerald and diamond ring, the stones set in a hoop of heavy gold.

She sat down suddenly and the remains of her petticoat dug into her, making her jump up again with a yelp.

In a dazed way, Polly made her way out. Two footmen leapt to open the street door for her which had been closed after Lord Hallworthy had decided to join the dancers.

"May I fetch you a chair?" asked one footman.

"No," said Polly. "I shall walk."

Foxed, thought the footman. I told them the claret punch was too strong for the ladies. He bowed again and closed the door behind Polly.

Polly walked off down the street in a dream. Jake and Barney came hurrying up, Barney swinging the cloak about Polly's shoulders to hide her gown. "Put your hood up," hissed Jake. "Who's to know the diamonds in your hair ain't real?"

Dreamy Polly said hardly a word on the road home

and her henchmen tactfully remained silent. They were sure she had failed to steal anything. Polly had her skirt looped over her arm to hold the extra material that had been supported by her enormous hoop before it broke.

"Put on your pattens," fussed Jake, breaking the silence. "You're fair ruining those shoes in the mud."

But Polly walked on in a daze of relief. She had not stolen anything and yet she had the ring.

It was only when they were safely back in their stuffy room that she showed it to them, listening to their gasps of awe.

"How on earth did you come by it?" asked Barney at last.

"An old dowager gave it to me," said Polly. "I didn't steal it. I mended a tear in her gown." Polly had no intention of telling Barney and Jake Mrs. Worthington's real predicament. "So we can sell it fair and square and get a good price for it."

"It's your money," said Barney. "What you going to do with it, Poll?"

"It's *our* money," said Polly, "and the first thing we're going to do is find us a decent place to live."

Which all went to show it really was Polly's money, for left to themselves Barney and Jake would have drunk and gambled it all away. But they were weak men, and the very strength and energy of Polly's personality made her appear almost sexless in their eyes. It was much easier to go along with what Polly wanted than to try to stand up to her.

"I am tired of searching and searching for this

beauty of yours,'' said the marquess of Canonby crossly. ''Are you sure you did not imagine her?''

''Not I,'' said the colonel. ''One minute she was by me, the next she was gone.''

''You have been seduced by a pretty figure,'' said the marquess. ''The reason she fled is probably that the unmasking at midnight would have revealed a pockmarked face.''

''She had such grace, such delicacy,'' said the colonel, kissing his fingers. ''And those eyes. Like jewels.''

''Rubies?'' said the marquess nastily.

''No, amethysts. But lighter. Violet. Odd color.''

The marquess went very still. Then he visibly relaxed. ''My dear friend, you have been flirting with none other than Lady Lydia Meresly. Look! There she is over there, affecting not to see that idiot Pargeter who wanders after her like a shadow.''

He waved across the room with his quizzing glass. The colonel looked eagerly and then said, ''No, that is not she. Lady Lydia is dressed as a Greek goddess and her hair is unpowdered. My goddess was not in fancy dress, her hair was powdered, and she wore a mask of white velvet.''

The marquess frowned. Surely there was only one other female in London with such eyes. But it could hardly be Polly Jones. And he was certainly not going to remind Colonel Anderson of her existence, for the colonel was apt to tease and refer to his friend's dramatic Tyburn rescue as ''Canonby's Folly.'' One of the marquess's servants reported that he had seen ''Miss Peterson'' cross the square and move off in the company of two unsavory characters, one of whom had had only one eye. Polly had obviously left him to go back to those villains from Mrs. Blanchard's. If they had indeed left the brothel, then they were no doubt engaged in some other criminal activity and would drag Polly down with them. That fop, Pargeter, obviously suspected Polly was still alive, but Pargeter was nothing more than an idle gossip and mischief-maker.

Just then, the colonel slapped his brow. "She gave me her name! I remember. Lady Mary Peters. And it was Hallworthy himself who introduced us."

"Then we shall ask Hallworthy," said the marquess, feeling obscurely disappointed that he had been right and that the unknown could not have been Polly Jones.

But Lord Hallworthy claimed he had never seen the lady before that evening. He sent for his secretary who pointed out that no such person had been invited.

To the marquess's relief, the colonel gave up the pursuit. It was best to forget about Polly Jones, who had run away from his household without even stopping to say goodbye. But he danced and flirted absentmindedly for the rest of the night, trying to banish a little image of Polly from his mind.

When he finally left the Hallworthys' to walk home, the whole of London still seemed to be riotously awake despite the fact that it was four in the morning: a London of pleasure and gambling and vice, strung up from morning to night with a hectic air. And somewhere in its teeming streets was Polly Jones.

"Forget her," said the marquess aloud. "In such company, she will not live long."

Some three weeks after the ridotto, Miss Smith and her two brothers took up residence in Biddeford Row in Bloomsbury in a snug apartment which boasted a minuscule hall, parlor, a cupboard of a kitchen and two bedrooms. Polly still did not know the surnames of her two companions; she had agreed to adopt their alias of Smith. The days were cozy and pleasant. They had plenty of money for coal and food. Before she started to furnish the apartment to her taste, Polly had refurnished both Barney and Jake, deaf to their wails of protest. Jake now boasted a smart black silk patch over his missing eye. Both men were soberly attired in the garb of city merchants: plain good dark coats, knee breeches, clean linen, buckled shoes, wigs and three-cornered hats.

Polly had pointed out that as they had enough money for the moment it was dangerous for them to waste their time in petty thieving and risk getting caught. She herself spent most of her time stitching and sewing an elaborate ensemble where the quilted petticoat was stitched onto a flexible hoop. They had one servant, a grumpy woman who did not live in but came daily to wash their clothes and clean the rooms.

Jake settled quickly into this new life of ease, passing his time drinking and playing skittles in the local tavern. Barney, on the other hand, missed the danger and excitement of the underworld. He felt bored and restless and went for long walks.

One day he was strolling through the city when a

sedan chair passed quite close; and in the sedan chair was Mrs. Blanchard. She looked at him in an unseeing way, but Barney, not knowing she would hardly recognize him in his new respectable clothes and wig, dived into a coffee house for shelter. It was full of merchants and lawyers and men from the stock exchange. Everyone seemed to be haggling and dealing as if at a horse fair.

Although they were obviously not criminals, there was something familiar in the air to Barney, a hectic feeling of perilous living. He found himself a chair and ordered a tankard of mulled wine, for the day was cold.

The man next to him seemed a little island of calm among all this business trading as he smoked his long churchwarden and read the newspaper.

At last he put down the paper and said to Barney, "Monstrous cold, is it not?"

"Yes, sir," agreed Barney politely.

"My name is White," said the gentleman. "I have a feeling we have met before."

"No, not possible," said Barney, wondering all the while whether he had at one time picked this gentleman's pocket.

"And yet your face looks familiar. Do you work in the city, Mr. . . . er . . . ?"

"Smith," said Barney, wishing he could escape. "No, I'm a gentleman o' leisure at the moment."

"You are fortunate, Mr. Smith, and yet I would not like a life of idleness. I am a tea merchant. I have spent a weary morning here interviewing applicants for a clerking job. I am having an amazing hard time

finding someone who can add up sums. For example,
I start with an easy question . . . what is eight and
eight?''

"Sixteen," said Barney automatically.

"And another sixteen?"

"Thirty-two."

"And subtract nine?"

"Twenty-one."

"And multiply by seven?"

"A hundred and forty-seven," said Barney.

"Oh, bravo, Mr. Smith. But how unfortunate I
am. Here I am prepared to pay a goodly sum for
someone to keep my books, and the only person who
seems to know the first thing about mathematics is a
gentleman of leisure."

"Frankly," said Barney, beginning to feel at ease
for he had enjoyed showing off his ability, "I am not
a gentleman. I jist don't work."

Mr. White hitched his chair forward. "Could I not
persuade you to work for me for a little, just until I
find someone suitable?"

"Wot? Adding and subtracting, like?"

"Yes, keeping the books."

"I couldn't do that," said Barney. "Never kept no
books before."

"My counting house is only a little way away, Mr.
Smith. Perhaps you could just step along and look at
the books. But then, perhaps you are too busy."

Barney thought of the long, empty day stretching
ahead—another long, empty day. "Don't mind," he
said. "No harm in taking a look."

Two hours later, Mr. Barney Smith found himself

employed as bookkeeper in the tea merchant's business. He himself couldn't see what Mr. White was making such a fuss about. Barney could add and subtract sums in his sleep. He had to admit he was tickled at the idea of having a job. A clerk had called him "Mr. Smith, sir," as he had served him with a cup of tea.

But I daren't tell Polly, thought Barney. Whatever would she say if she knew'd I'd turned respectable!

CHAPTER NINE

AS WINTER FINALLY GAVE WAY TO SPRING, POLLY led a life which would have driven any other resident of that hectic city mad with boredom. But Polly had not become so accustomed to the luxuries of security, food, and peace to want change. Jake had been spending a great deal on gambling and she herself had expended a lot of money on books and material for gowns. Soon, she would have to return to a life of crime.

She was often alone. Barney had grown very silent and taciturn and would not say where he went. Jake spent all his time in the taverns.

It was Jake who eventually found out Barney's secret. He followed him one morning and saw him turn in at the respectable doors of a city tea merchant's establishment. Jake waited and waited, curiosity mounting, as Barney did not reappear.

After two hours, he had just decided that Barney had known he was being followed and had escaped into this building only to exit by the back door, when Barney came out, accompanied by three clerks. He did not see Jake, who followed the four men until they entered a coffee house.

After some hesitation, he pushed open the door and went in. Barney and his companions were deep in animated discussion over the coffee cups. Jake could hear Barney's voice, which had taken on an oddly refined cadence. "I said to Mr. White, I said, if you invest in limes, you'll make a killing," Barney was saying. "Seems they stop the sailors' scurvy on the long voyages. Of course, most of the captains pooh-pooh the idea, but I says it makes sense. I . . ."

Barney broke off as he suddenly saw Jake. He muttered an excuse, rose and crossed the room to where Jake was standing by the door. "So now you know," hissed Barney. "You tell Poll, and I'll murder you."

"Tell 'er what?" said Jake. "What you a-doing of?"

Barney sighed. "I got a job. I keep the books at a tea merchant's."

"Work!" exclaimed Jake, appalled.

"Why not?" said Barney. "Passes the time and you gets paid for it. Get along with you, Jake. We'll talk this evening."

But Barney should have guessed that Jake was too much in awe of Polly to keep his secret. When he returned that evening, it was to find that Polly knew all about it.

"I think it is wonderful," said Polly, cutting through his excuses.

"Never thought you'd take it that way," said Barney. "But you see what it means? I can keep the lot o' us, if Jake here'll stop blowing all the money on bets."

"Oh, but it is your money, Barney," said Polly. "I have been reading the newspapers again. Soon Ranelagh and Vauxhall will be open again, and the Season will begin. I only need to take a few things and I can be set for a while."

"Stealing's wrong!" Barney burst out and then turned brick-red with embarrassment.

"Don't you listen to him, Poll," said Jake hotly. "Betraying our way of life, that's what he's doing."

"I think it is wrong to steal from people who cannot afford to lose what you take," said Polly. "But I do not see there is anything wrong in relieving the rich aristocracy of a few of their favors. But tell me about your job."

Barney plunged in, bragging about his mathematical ability and how he was valued, the fun they had in the City, and cozy suppers after work. "And we're all taking a barge on the river next Monday and we can bring our families," he ended. "Say you'll come, Polly, you and Jake."

Polly hesitated. "I go in fear that someone might recognize me."

"Stuff," said Barney. "Polly Jones is dead. Most of the crowd that was at Tyburn that day saw you as a little figure miles away on the scaffold. You powder your hair and put on a fine gown and no one's going to recognize you.''

Polly would have refused had the days suddenly not become warmer. And with the warmth came langorous female dreams of falling in love. Polly dreamt of some strong man who would marry her and look after her and protect her from the world. And though she knew they were only dreams and that she would probably always have to fend for herself, they made her restless. The marquess of Canonby and Drusilla had made her long for a man from the class from which her birth excluded her.

So when Monday dawned a perfect day, Polly agreed to go. She put on her new quilted petticoat over a modest round hoop. The petticoat was a miracle of embroidery. Green leaves and flowers of nasturtium, periwinkle and honeysuckle twined in an embroidered riot over the white silk. Over it, she wore an apple-green damask sack gown with a thin edging of lace at the low square neckline and foaming lace at the ends of the three-quarter-length sleeves. Her powdered hair was dressed *a la mouton,* that is, short tight curls at the back of her head and longer rolled curls at the front and sides.

Barney was resplendent in a light-colored broadcloth coat with pearl buttons, breeches of black satin, swansdown vest, muslin undervest, black silk hose, and silver-buckled shoes with high heels. He had painted his face white through which the darkness of his ever-incipient beard loomed like a thundercloud. Jake, at first taken aback with all this magnificence, threw himself into the spirit of the party and had

Polly stitch gold braid onto his tricorne and ran out
and bought himself a long walking cane which he
embellished with gold ribbons.

Work had changed Barney, thought Polly. The
brutishness of his appearance had gone and he looked
more and more like a prosperous city gentleman.
Jake, however, appeared like a villain masquerading
as a city gentleman.

"I just heard of a good lay, Polly," muttered Jake
as they were setting out. "I dress as a porter and hire
one of them little street urchins to hide in the basket
on my head. When we passes a gent with a good wig
on, I raps the basket and the imp leans down and
snatches the wig, but when the gent looks round,
there's nothing but me with a basket on me head."

"No," said Polly firmly. "We do not take even a
handkerchief from people unless we know they are
vastly rich. I plan to make one more foray and find
enough to set us up for a few years."

"But I'm getting tired of doing nothing," wailed
Jake.

"Then get a job like Barney."

"You need your mouth washed out with soap,
Polly," said Jake huffily. "Why don't you get a job
yourself?"

"Because I'm a woman, that's why," said Polly
fiercely. "And what is there for me but to work and
slave in some household for the rest of my days."

"If you're a thief, you're a thief, and that's all,"
protested Jake.

"No, it is not all. I am not really a thief," said

Polly. "I am simply righting the balance in an unfair world."

"Don't argue," pleaded Barney. "It's such a lovely day."

They hired a sedan chair for Polly and Barney and Jake walked along beside it until they reached the steps leading down to the river below. They were late in arriving, and most of the party were already seated in the barge. The wives and daughters stared open-mouthed at Polly, and she looked at their more sober gowns and unpowdered hair and realized she had dressed for the aristocracy and not for the working city classes.

Polly and Jake were introduced to Mr. White. His open admiration of her made Polly feel more at ease, and for a minute she felt she really was Barney's sister; she glowed with pride when Mr. White enthused over his employee's amazing gift of mathematical ability. Seeing that the head of the firm was delighted with Polly, the other men urged their wives to court her company, and soon Polly was happily sipping the claret cup and talking about delightfully safe things like dressmaking and housework. When the ladies learned she had embroidered the petticoat herself, the last barrier came down.

But Polly was in for a surprise. She was just basking in the sheer ordinariness and respectability of her company when she received a rude shock.

The river was full of pleasure craft. A feature of London life on the river was the surprising flow of insult between the watermen and passengers of one boat to another. Polly was to learn later that even the

royal family when they came on the River Thames
were abused with insults which would have landed
the perpetrators in prison had they shouted such abuse
at royalty on the streets.

Her first introduction to this strange custom happened as a boatload of young men and women passed
near them on the water. One young man stood up and
pointed at Mr. White and yelled, "Look at that queer
old putt. Isn't he ashamed to go wenching at his
years?"

To Polly's amazement, a city clerk's wife—Mrs.
Tally, a small and faded lady of great gentility—
immediately broke off a discussion with Polly about
the best way to clean silver, jumped to her feet,
puffed out her meager chest and began to bellow:
"You treacherous sons of Bridewell bastards who are
pimps to your own mothers and cock-bawds to the
rest of your relations, who were begot by huffling
and christened out of a piss pot, how dare you show
your ugly faces on the River Thames!"

Both boatloads cheered this tremendous perfor-
mance. Mrs. Tally sat down, cleared her throat with
a delicate cough and leaned toward Polly. "As I was
saying, Miss Smith, I really do think jeweller's rouge
is the best cleaning agent for silver."

Soon Polly learned to turn a deaf ear to the verbal
battles. The soft warm wind was pleasant. The company, leaving their waterman to continue the verbal
onslaught alone, settled down to a picnic of wine,
cold roasted stuffed pigeons, wine-roasted gammon,
garnished turbot, and a dessert of buttered meringue
a la Pompadour.

Their waterman had been drinking well and deep to lubricate his vocal cords. Polly glanced up and saw a boatload of richly dressed people approaching. They were being slowly borne forward on a decorated barge covered with a canopy of gold and silver. An orchestra was playing and the scent of musk drifted across the water.

Mr. White saw the waterman opening his mouth and jumped up with an alarmed cry of, "Be quiet, fellow."

Royalty might pretend not to hear insults but aristocrats such as these often drew blood in revenge. But as the barge full of the aristocracy came alongside, the waterman launched forth with a glad cry of: "You dirty creeping brood of night-walkers and shoplifters. Have a care of your cheeks, you whores, we shall have you branded at the next sessions that the world may see your trade in your faces. You are lately come from the hemp and hammer. You lousy starved crew of worm-pickers and snail-catchers. You offspring of a dunghill and brothers to a pumpkin. You . . ."

That was as far as he got. A richly dressed young man in the other boat seized a long bargepole and drove it full into the waterman's chest, tumbling him into the river. Three of the other young men in the aristocratic party had unsheathed their swords.

And then a voice Polly knew only too well commanded, "Sit down. It is only a party of Cits. Would you commit murder on this fine day? Fie, for shame, to become so incensed over the insults of such as these." It was the marquess of Canonby.

Polly turned her head away as the richly decorated barge floated past only a foot away. She sensed rather than saw the marquess as his eyes scanned their boat. She did not look round until she was sure they were past. There were screams and splashes as the Cits helped the waterman back on board.

The party resumed. At last Polly stood up and looked down the river at the retreating barge. There was a tall figure, his hand shielding his eyes, who seemed to be looking straight at her. She was sure it was the marquess. She sat down again quickly.

In vain did she try to enjoy the rest of the day. But the marquess's face seemed to dance on the water before her eyes. She told herself fiercely she was glad he had not had a chance to see her, while all the time a treacherous little longing inside went on and on, wondering and wondering what he would have done if he had recognized her.

The sun sparkling on the water was beginning to make her head ache and she was heartily glad when they finally moored alongside the pier. There was laughing and chattering as she made her farewells, and Barney proudly promised to bring her along to the next outing. He knew Polly's beauty and aristocratic bearing had made him seem even more important in his employer's eyes.

Polly declined a chair, saying she would be content to walk home. In vain did Barney and Jake outline the dangers of the London streets. There was the danger of an apprentice letting down the shutter of a shop without looking first to see if anyone was standing underneath; danger from the coal carts rush-

ing up the narrow lanes from the Thames; danger of
slops being emptied from overhead; danger in a traffic block where one might receive a cut from a whip
during a whip fight between draymen; danger from
thieves who fished for hats and wigs with long wires,
leaning out of upper-story windows.

Polly only smiled and said she was well protected
by their escort. The farther they walked from the
river, the less the memory of the marquess became.
The walk and exercise removed Polly's headache and
she was feeling tired and happy by the time they
reached home.

Their apartment was on the first floor, so as Polly
swung the kettle over the newly lit fire to boil water
for tea and heard the sound of footsteps mounting the
stairs, she assumed it was only one of the residents of
the upper floors returning home. The pounding on
the door of their apartment made the three of them
freeze. The fire crackled, the clock in the corner of
the room ticked busily, as they waited holding their
breath.

Then Barney began to laugh. "We're respectable
now," he said, approaching the door. "It's probably
one of the neighbors come to borrow something."

He swung open the door and the marquess of
Canonby walked straight past him and into the parlor.

"Good evening, Miss Jones," he said, making her
a bow.

"How did you find me?" cried Polly.

"Simple, my child. I saw you on the river, watched
where your boat moored, landed farther along and

then followed you. If you are not tired, Miss Jones, will you walk with me a little?''

"She *is* tired," said Barney truculently. "Be off with you!"

"No," said Polly. "I owe this gentleman my life. The least I can do is to give my lord a little of my time."

She and the marquess walked to the end of the street and then along a grassy path which led across the marshy fields of Bloomsbury. The evening was calm and golden, more like summer than spring. Urchins were bathing naked in the ponds and their shrill cries mingled with the lowing of a herd of cows being driven homeward by the herdsman, his blue smock a vivid splash of color against the green and brown of the marshy fields.

"Now, Polly," said the marquess gently, "why did you run away?"

"I wanted to be independent," said Polly, who had no intention of telling him she had been listening at the door of the morning room and had overheard him talking to the colonel.

"But do you not think it might have been polite to tell me? You left all your pretty gowns. I have no need of them."

"They say you did it for a bet," said Polly. "Took me from the scaffold, I mean."

"You are overnice, Polly. You were rescued. Why should the motive matter?"

Polly bit her lip and said nothing.

"But I have a concern for you," he went on, "and must ask you how you and your villains manage to afford your comfortable lodgings and how you come to be so finely robed.''

"Barney is working,'' said Polly, who briefly thought about telling him about the present of Mrs. Worthington's ring and then dismissed it. He would probably never believe her, and even if he did, she would have to admit to being at the ridotto. "He has a job of keeping the books for a tea merchant. He is highly thought of.''

"And what is the relationship of these men to you?'' asked the marquess sharply.

"I told you,'' said Polly crossly. "They used to work at the brothel, but left, and are turned respectable.''

"Why should they wish to look after you? What is their interest in you?''

"I don't know,'' said Polly candidly. "I was suspicious at first. We were all living in one room near Tothill Fields after I left you and I used to sleep with the rolling pin under my pillow, but they behave like brothers. In fact, that is part of our respectable front. I am Polly Smith and Jake and Barney are my brothers.''

"But there is no reason for this masquerade, my child.''

"What if someone should recognize me?'' asked Polly, glancing over her shoulder as if frightened that the Bow Street Horse Patrol was already bearing down on her.

"It does not matter if anyone recognizes you. If you survive the gallows, then you are free from the charge of theft!''

Polly could hardly tell him that, as she planned to

go on with her life of crime, it still suited her best to remain anonymous.

"And so this Barney manages to support you comfortably?" the marquess pursued when she remained silent.

"Yes, he is all that is respectable."

"Then I confess myself delighted. I was afraid you had returned to your thieving ways."

Polly colored. "I took certain objects from the Early of Meresly, yes, but that was because I was about to be made homeless. He has plenty of money. He need not have missed them."

"But he did," said the marquess severely. "You lack morality. What is the Meresly family to you? Are you one of the countess's family's by-blows?"

"Go away and leave me alone and take your insults with you," said Polly fiercely. "It is all very well for you to be so high and mighty. You have never been faced with starvation."

"No, but if I were, I would find work."

"You are not a woman either. What work can a woman find except that of a drudge?"

"Do not let us quarrel," he said. "You are respectable now and many a city clerk would be honored to have you as a wife."

For some reason she could not quite understand, Polly found this last remark even more insulting than being called a thief and asked whether she were a bastard. There was only a dim, half-formed realization that she would never be good enough for him. The marquess obviously considered marriage to a clerk a worthy enough ambition for such as Polly Jones.

"You are pompous and arrogant and you offend me," said Polly, picking up her skirts. "Good day to you, my lord."

She turned and hurried back along the path, leaving him staring after her.

As she reached the corner of Biddeford Row, she was so anxious to escape into her home and examine her hurt that she failed to notice the scene taking place on the other side of the street.

But a woman ran past her, shouting, "That one-eyed thief has been took."

Polly stopped dead in her tracks and looked across the street. There was a small knot of people around two men. One was Jake, clutching his brow with a handkerchief and trying to staunch a bright rivulet of blood. The other, a truculent-looking gentleman, held a stick with a silver knob and the knob was smeared with blood. He was holding Jake in a cruel grasp.

"Waiting for the parish constable," said a thin slatternly-looking woman next to Polly. "Old one-eye there stole the gentleman's watch, but the gentleman caught him and stunned him and is holding him so the constable can find the goods on him."

Polly edged into the crowd, pushing, shoving until she was standing behind Jake. Still jostling and pushing, she fell against Jake, and before she righted herself, she had slipped a hand into his pocket, taken the watch and lifted it out, her hand closed tightly round it.

"It cannot be true," cried Polly shrilly. "This is my brother. He would not steal. Do spare him, sir."

She wound her arms about the gentleman's neck. He tottered back a step in surprise but did not release his hold on Jake.

"Here's the constable," yelled someone, and the crowd, including Polly, fell back.

"This man stole my gold watch," said the gentleman, shaking the half-conscious Jake.

"He cannot have done so," said Polly stoutly. "This is my brother, Mr. Jacob Smith."

The constable hesitated, impressed by Polly's beauty and the elegance of her gown.

"We'll see about that," said the gentleman truculently. "Search in this one-eyed fellow's right pocket, constable. I deliberately left my watch on him, so he should not have a chance to weasel out of his crime."

The constable plunged his hand into Jake's pocket. Nothing. He searched all Jake's pockets. In bewilderment, he even prised open Jake's mouth and looked down his throat.

"Nothing there, sir," he said.

"Why doesn't this gentleman look in his *own* pocket," said Polly, "and leave my poor innocent brother alone?"

"Of course I have not got it," said the gentleman wrathfully. "I had it here before this fellow took it," he said, plunging a hand into a capacious pocket, "and . . ."

Then a ludicrous expression of dismay and amazement crossed his face. He slowly drew out his gold watch and stared at it.

"Monster," said Polly, giving a pathetic little sob.

"Yes," said the constable. "You should be took to Bedlam for wasting my time with your stories. Do you want me to charge him with assault, miss?"

"Oh, no," said Polly. "If I can just get my brother home, that will be enough." She smiled sweetly on the gentleman, who was still staring at his own watch. "Do not look so distressed, sir. Neither I nor my brother harbor ill feelings toward you. An easy mistake to make in these dangerous times."

"Here, let me help you, miss," said the constable eagerly, and putting a comforting arm around Jake's waist and with Polly helping, he escorted them home.

The little crowd of onlookers dispersed. The gentleman shook his head, tucked his watch into his pocket and went on his way.

The marquess of Canonby stood alone, feeling thoroughly depressed. He had followed Polly at a distance, sorry he had angered her, wondering whether he should apologize for suggesting she might be a bastard of Lady Lydia's family. He had witnessed the scene with Jake, his tall height allowing him to stand back from the crowd and yet see over their heads. He had seen Polly deftly take the watch from Jake's pocket and transfer it back into the gentleman's.

"I did society a great wrong by saving the life of such as she," thought the marquess. "Thank God we move in different circles, for it would sicken me to set eyes on her again!"

It took Jake over a week to recover from the blow to his head. He had had a great fright. In the moment that the robbed gentleman had held him fast, Jake had at last realized he stood to lose his freedom, his comfortable, happy, respectable way of life—and life itself.

For the first time it occurred to him that taking a job might be a safe thing to do.

Polly, too, had been frightened by Jake's near-arrest. She had planned to go to another ridotto as soon as the Season began and try her luck. But although the determination to steal was leaving her, it was being replaced by that old, burning curiosity about the Mereslys, and what had happened to Meg at Meresly Manor the day she died. Was she a bastard of the Mereslys? The answer lay with the earl and his family, and the only way to get close to them was to be in society. There was to be a masquerade night at Vauxhall Gardens on the following week. The social columns said all of society planned to be present. Polly took a deep breath. She herself would be there. The Mereslys had twin daughters. Perhaps she might find an opportunity of gossiping to one of them and thereby find some clue to the death of the old woman who had raised her.

CHAPTER TEN

OLLY HAD NEVER TOLD BARNEY OR JAKE MUCH about her past. They interpreted her burning desire to go to the masquerade at Vauxhall as a thieving expedition. Barney was against it. He was enjoying his newfound respectability and for the first time felt that Polly was placing his security in jeopardy.

He had promised Jake to try to get him a post as a clerk, and so Jake no longer frequented the taverns but sat each day assiduously practicing his handwriting to bring it up to the required copperplate standards of the tea merchant's business.

Vauxhall Pleasure Gardens on the south side of the Thames cut across class lines and was one of the few places where the common folk and the aristocracy mixed freely. Jake and Barney had promised to go with Polly but not to stay beside her, as the sight of the three of them together, even masked, might jog "someone's" memory. That someone was the marquess of Canonby.

Polly was too busy making preparations for the ridotto to notice that her power over her two henchmen was waning. They felt uneasily that they were becoming respectable and she was not.

The day before the ridotto was a Friday, and Barney had been given a day off. He suggested they should visit the Museum of the Royal Society in Crane Court, a narrow court leading off Fleet Street, where they would be able to see fascinating exhibits from all over the globe.

They walked slowly through the streets together, each prepared to enjoy the outing. When they reached the museum, Barney was shocked to find the catalogues cost two shillings each. With new respectable thriftiness he suggested they buy only one and share it.

All, however, considered the exhibits prime value. There was a bone from a mermaid's head, a tortoise—"his grease is good for scurvy: said when turned on his back to sigh and Fetch Abundance of Tears," a white shark, a picture of a large whale rending a boat, and a flying squirrel which the catalogue informed them "can ford a river on the Bark of a Tree, erecting His tail for a Sail." Jake and Barney gazed at these wonders with childlike awe, and Polly realized for the first time that both were actually young men, possibly only in their early twenties. Jake's tall, thin figure and hideously marred face made him seem much older, and Barney's heavy, brutish face and squat powerful figure made him look as if he had never been young. But wonder and excitement had temporarily wiped all traces of the years of villainy and hardship from their faces.

After leaving the exhibition, they walked along the Strand until a crowd gathering in Durham Court, just off the main thoroughfare, attracted their attention. They pushed forward to see what was going on.

A watchmaker had set up a booth. On a trestle, he had placed a tiny chaise with four wheels. As they watched, he coaxed a flea out of a box, and made it draw the tiny carriage. Then he set other fleas to turn watermills and march in troupes like soldiers.

Polly was clapping her hands and laughing at the antics when Jake looked across the crowd and found himself staring straight at Mrs. Blanchard. She was not looking at him. She was gazing at Polly, her expression of surprise and shock fading to be replaced with one of sheer malignancy.

"Barney!" hissed Jake. "Get Polly. It's Ma Blanchard!"

They hustled Polly away. Mrs. Blanchard followed them. But Barney and Jake had guessed she would, and they knew every twist and wynd in the neighborhood. They were panting and breathless when they finally slowed their pace.

Barney pushed open the door of a tavern and hustled Polly and Jake inside.

"Fair turned my stomach when I saw her," said Jake, when they were all seated at the corner of a long table.

"But what could she do to us?" asked Polly. "I

cannot be charged with the same crime, and she will have no interest in harming either of you.''

''Oh, yes she will,'' said Barney. ''We ran off and left her, remember? Women like her will go on hunting you down for revenge until the day they die.''

''Well, we lost her,'' said Polly. ''We all knew she was in London. We will make sure we do not go near that quarter of town again. Too near Covent Garden. Come, this is our day of holiday. Let us enjoy ourselves.'' But Barney and Jake could not seem to recover their spirits. Jake, on the threshold of respectability, thought with a shudder of his past life, and Barney dreaded Mrs. Blanchard finding out where he worked. What if she told Mr. White that he, Barney, was a thief and villain who once worked in her brothel? His job would be lost and any prospect of getting any other respectable job with it. He had heard the gossip in the city coffee houses and how quickly it spread from one merchant to another.

''Let's not go to Vauxhall tomorrow, Polly,'' pleaded Barney. ''Jake here'll get work with Mr. White, I'm sure, and between us we will be earning enough. Don't go stealing things anymore.''

''I'm not going to steal anything,'' said Polly. ''Anyway, not tomorrow.''

''Then why are you going?'' asked Jake.

''There's something that happened to a good woman who brought me up,'' said Polly. ''It's a mystery and I don't want to talk about it. But I have to get in among the Quality in order to unravel this mystery.''

They pressed her with excited questions but Polly refused to tell them any more.

"You'll land in trouble," said Barney finally. "I can feel it."

"Stuff!" laughed Polly.

" 'Strue," said Jake. "Something will happen to-morrow night and I don't want to be there to see it. You was born to trouble, Polly Jones!"

The pleasure gardens of London were at the height of their popularity, the most famous being Vauxhall, Ranelagh and Bagnigge Wells. They all boasted the same features: a concert, promenade room, a garden laid out in tree-lined walks, a fish pond with arbors, rooms for suppers, a fountain, an orchestra and a dancing floor. Vauxhall had the most dramatic enter-tainments, boasting a fireworks display, a hermit, and a lady who walked the slack wire. The entrance fee was three shillings and sixpence, but it did not deter the thieves and pickpockets who found its dark walks and groves ideal for business, or for the prosti-tutes who did a brisk trade with men drunk on the Gardens' famous rack punch.

The middle-aged might condemn Vauxhall as noisy and vulgar, its masquerades an encouragement to licentious behavior, but to Polly it was a magical place full of delights. She wished she could forget Meg and simply enjoy herself. But the Mereslys would in all probability be there, and the secret to Meg's death lay with the Mereslys.

As they approached the boxes where supper was being served to various parties, Jake and Barney

elected to leave Polly, for in one of the boxes was the
marquess of Canonby, Colonel Anderson and two
ladies. Polly, Jake and Barney were masked but they
were afraid the sharp-eyed marquess might penetrate
their disguise if they stayed together. Polly almost
did not notice their going, so intent was her study of
the marquess's fair companions. The ladies with the
colonel and marquess were very pretty and very viva-
cious. Polly felt a tap on her shoulder and whipped
about. A young man bowed and asked her to dance.
Polly shook her head and walked away and he shouted
coarse insults after her. She realized that because she
was alone and unescorted, he had taken her for a
prostitute. She was about to give up and go in search
of Barney and Jake when she saw the Meresly family
in one of the boxes.

She recognized Lady Lydia immediately. Beside
her sat the earl, and with them what must be their
twin daughters. They were younger than Polly—about
fourteen, she judged—and so bedecked with jewelry
that they flashed and glittered, the magnificence of
their jewels making them appear paradoxically drab
and awkward. Both took after their father and had
large beaky noses, rather full blue eyes, and strong,
full, sensual mouths. As Polly watched, the earl said
something and Lady Lydia shrugged and pulled a
mask from her etui and put it on, motioning to her
daughters to don their masks as well. Most of the
people in the other boxes were masked except the
marquess and his party. A group of men entered the
earl's box. Polly watched. She felt she should escape
in case some other man accosted her, but she was

rooted to the spot. The boxes were brightly lit and it was like watching a little play from a seat far away, where one could not hear the words but only make out the actions.

The men bowed to the earl and Lady Lydia. There was much laughter. The visitors flicked open and shut snuffboxes, postured and bowed. Then just as they were about to leave, Polly noticed one of the men who had been leaning at the back of one of the twins' chairs deftly detach her diamond necklace and slip it into his pocket.

Polly waited until the thief and the rest of the men had left the earl's box and then glided off in pursuit. He said a few words to them, his eyes glinting behind his black mask, and then he moved off. Polly walked behind, keeping a family party between her and the thief, for he kept glancing over his shoulder. The proximity of the respectable family party also saved Polly from insult from the gangs of young bloods who roamed the walks.

Should she pick his pocket? Polly trembled at the thought. She had not been trained as a pickpocket. If she were caught, it would be useless to accuse *him* of being the thief.

The bell rang for the fireworks display. Crowds appeared from all sides and soon the walk was a moving mass of people surging in the same direction. Polly forced her way forward until she was directly behind the thief. Before he reached the corner of the gardens where the display was to take place, the thief turned sharply right and plunged into a dark grove. Polly followed.

She shut her eyes tightly and then opened them again so as to adjust her sight quickly to the darkness. The thief had come to a stop. He felt in his pocket and took out the necklace and held it up. There was a small moon riding high above but the stones in the necklace seemed to burn with a light of their own. Polly glided behind a tree right behind him. He stuffed the necklace back in his pocket and took out his snuffbox. He was just helping himself to a pinch when Polly saw her opportunity. She darted from behind the tree and, with one quick movement, jerked his hand holding the snuffbox up with such a force that the contents went flying into his face. As he gasped and sneezed, momentarily blinded, she thrust her hand into his pocket, took the necklace and ran off, twisting quickly to right and left so that the wide panniers of her gown should not get caught in the branches.

She heard him shout and scream but his cries were soon drowned in the explosions of the fireworks cascading overhead. People were still crowding up the walk and Polly had to fight her way through the crush, back toward the boxes, wondering whether the Mereslys would still be there or whether they had not yet noticed the theft and had gone to the display themselves.

But when she arrived, panting, in front of the boxes, it was to see the Mereslys still there. The daughter who had lost the necklace was crying while the earl and his lady searched here and there on the floor of the box.

Polly took a deep breath, smoothed down her gown,

adjusted her gold velvet mask, and walked boldly up
the stairs and into their box. Her heart was hammering against her ribs.

She held out the necklace. "I think this is what
you are looking for, my lord," she said to the earl.

The daughter stopped crying and gave a glad cry.
The earl of Meresly looked curiously at the elegant,
masked figure that was Polly Jones, and said, "Where
did you find it?"

"I saw one of the men who visited your box take
it," said Polly, forcing herself to remain calm. "I
followed him and took it back."

"Which one was it?" demanded the earl wrathfully.

"A gentleman in a green silk coat and purple hair
powder."

"I remember him, papa," squeaked the daughter
who had lost the necklace. "He did not introduce
himself. He came with Torrington's party."

"Torrington is all that is respectable," said the
earl. "He will probably not even know the fellow.
He was a trifle well to go, if you remember, and
could not call to mind half the names of the men in
his company. But I shall ask Torrington in the morning if he has any idea as to the identity of the thief.
We are uncommon grateful to you, Miss . . . ?"

"Smith," said Polly, dropping a curtsy.

"I am Meresly. This is my wife, Lady Lydia
Meresly, and my daughters, Lady Emily Palfrey and
Lady Josephine Palfrey. Sit down, Miss Smith, and
join us in a glass of punch. How did you contrive to
recover the necklace?"

Polly told them and they all laughed heartily and said she was a wonder.

Even Lady Lydia drawled, "You are a most enterprising lady, Miss Smith. Have we met before?"

Polly was wearing a full mask with narrow slits which concealed the color of her eyes, and her hair was powdered.

"No, my lady," said Polly, sipping rack punch.

"And do you go about in society?" asked Josephine.

"No, my lady," said Polly. "I live in Bloomsbury, hardly the most fashionable neighborhood. I live with my brothers who work in the city."

"Indeed?" Lady Lydia's thin eyebrows rose under her mask. "Then you have found a treasure of a dressmaker somewhere, for that gown you are wearing is more modish than my own."

"I made it myself, my lady."

"How odd . . . to have to make one's clothes oneself," said Lady Lydia. "I would talk of this further, Miss Smith, but my husband cannot bear female conversation. He despises our sex, and swore he would never forgive me an I did not produce lusty sons." She waved her fan languidly in the direction of her twin daughters. "It is a wonder he did not drown these at birth . . . like unwanted kittens."

There was an embarrassed silence. Then the earl said heavily, "You must forgive my wife's jests, Miss Smith."

"I jest not," said Lady Lydia, a shrill note creeping into her voice. " 'A wife is no use to me nor shall she remain a wife of mine should she produce daughters,' that is what you said."

"I am sure Miss Smith is not interested in what I said," growled the earl. His daughters silently held each other's hands for comfort and stared miserably at the table. "We are eternally grateful to you, Miss Smith, and would show our gratitude."

"Then show it," said Lady Lydia pettishly. "Lord, but the ennui of this place fatigues me."

The earl took a large diamond stick pin from his stock and pinned it in the front of Polly's gown. It was a diamond of the first water. Polly looked down at it in a dazed way. "I-I d-don't know how to thank you," she stammered.

"Then pray do not try," yawned Lady Lydia. Suddenly she straightened her spine and one white hand rose to flick a curl of her powdered hair into place. "Canonby!" she cried, turning round with a graceful movement. "And dear Bertram!"

Her smile of welcome faded as she realized both men were looking intently at Polly. It was the first time Bertram's eyes had ever strayed to another female in her presence.

Both men bowed. The marquess had seen Polly sitting in the Mereslys' box. Masked and powdered as she was, he knew he would have recognized her anywhere. Bertram Pargeter had joined his party a moment before the marquess saw Polly. Bertram, hearing the marquess's stifled exclamation and noticing the way he quickly rose to his feet, had followed his gaze. At first he jealously thought that Lady Lydia was the focus of Canonby's interest until he saw the elegant and pretty young lady who was being entertained in their box. He would not have recog-

nized Polly, but the marquess's interest sharpened his
suspicions, so as the marquess muttered a hurried
excuse and went to join the Mereslys, Bertram had
promptly followed.

"Will you not introduce us to this charming young
lady?" asked Bertram.

"This is Miss Smith whose family is in trade,"
said Lady Lydia with a thin smile.

"Miss Smith was instrumental in confounding a
thief," said the earl with a cross look at his wife. He
then proceeded to tell them how Polly had recovered
his daughter's necklace.

A cynical smile curled the marquess's lips. "Amazing," he said dryly. "You must allow me the pleasure of a dance with you, Miss Smith."

"I am afraid I do not dance," said Polly in a
muffled voice.

"Then we shall walk and talk." The marquess held
out his arm. "Come, Miss Smith."

Polly looked to the others for help. The earl was
highly amused, Lady Lydia was angry, her daughters
were still staring miserably at the table, and Bertram
Pargeter's eyes were fixed greedily on Polly's masked
face as if the intensity of his stare could melt her
mask.

Polly meekly rose and took the marquess's arm
and moved off with him. Bertram made a move to
follow them but was restrained by Lady Lydia, who
put a hand on his arm. "Stay and talk to me, Bertram," she commanded. Bertram took a seat next to
her, casting a wary glance at the earl. But the earl
was tapping his fingers to the music on the edge of

the box. He had forgotten he had commanded his wife never to see Bertram again. One of those periods of hazy vagueness which often descended on him these days clouded his brain. He had even forgotten the theft of his daughter's necklace.

Polly and the marquess walked in silence until he turned down one of the quieter, less well lighted walks. "Now, Miss Polly Jones," he said severely, "what is all this about?"

Useless to pretend she was someone else: "It happened as the earl told you," said Polly flatly. "I returned the necklace and they invited me to join them."

"And is your reward that diamond stick-pin in your gown?"

"Yes."

"Vastly clever, Polly Jones. You take the necklace yourself and then accuse someone else of stealing it and return to collect the reward you know you will get."

"How dare you!" cried Polly, stamping her foot. "How could I take it? How could such as I simply walk into the Mereslys' box and take it?"

He stood in silence, his head bowed. "Perhaps you tell the truth," he said slowly. "But you must have been watching their box closely. What is your interest in the Mereslys? It is always the Mereslys, is it not?"

"My interest is natural," said Polly. "They own a manor on the outskirts of the village where I was brought up. I recognized them. Of course I would recognize them. I stole from them, didn't I? And nearly hanged because of it.''

"So now you make reparation. Is that the case?"

"Yes," said Polly, "so stop pestering me with stupid questions."

He took her arm and began to walk along the path. The sound of someone singing "The Gay Hussar" floated on the still night air. "And yet, I have reason to distrust you," he said. "I followed you that day in Bloomsbury and saw you save one of your villains from the hanging he richly deserved. I saw you put that watch back into that gentleman's pocket. You are remarkably nimble-fingered. But then, I suppose you have had a deal of practice."

"Since you persist in thinking the worst of me, why do you not leave me alone?" cried Polly. "Do you feel I owe you something for saving my life? You have my thanks. And yet your motives were hardly altruistic. You did it for a bet."

He shrugged. "Perhaps. Where is your cavalier? Did you lose him in the shrubbery?"

"Yes," said Polly, who did not want to tell him she had come with Barney and Jake. She desperately wanted him to think that some handsome gallant had escorted her.

He gave a light laugh. "So some city buck is beating the bushes for his fair one."

"I am not escorted by any Cit," said Polly primly. "My escort is as fine a gentleman as you, my lord."

"Then I must know him," said the earl dryly. "What is his name?"

Polly tossed her head. "None of your business, sir."

The earl caught a movement to his left. He affected not to notice and went on talking, although his eyes were alert.

"For some strange reason I cannot fathom," he said lightly, "I would feel reassured if I knew you were keeping respectable company. Will you invite me to dance at your wedding, Polly Jones?"

A black wave of depression engulfed Polly. "I wish you would go away," she said pettishly. "Your lady friend must be wondering where you are."

"I am sure Colonel Anderson is keeping both ladies amused. After all, they were his choice for the evening."

"And you have no say in the matter?"

"I am a trifle too old and too experienced to enjoy the blandishments of a couple of mesdames of cracked reputation."

"The contempt in your voice!" exclaimed Polly. "And yet it is because of men such as yourself, my lord, that such ladies carry on their trade. And believe me, I often wonder how many of these unfortunates were innocent misses when they came fresh from the country."

"Do not preach to me," he said icily. "You are hardly in a position to do so . . . thief that you are."

"You are stealing souls, sir, a much more heinous crime than any of mine."

They had come to a stop facing each other, the marquess angry and amazed at Polly's insolence, Polly hurt and furious because—although she did not yet realize it—he appeared totally unaware of her as a woman.

A twig crackled behind them. The marquess whipped about, dived into the blackness of the shrubbery and emerged, dragging Jake behind him.

Jake stood sheepishly in front of Polly, his three-cornered hat askew and bits of leaves and twigs decorating his coat.

"Here is your rich and handsome cavalier," sneered the marquess.

Polly dropped him a curtsy. "Thank you, my lord," she said sweetly. She took Jake's arm, cast a ravishing smile up into his face, and then led him away, back down the walk.

"Doxy! She is naught but a doxy," said the marquess between his teeth.

He caught up with them and walked straight past without looking at them, but so close that the cloth of gold of his coat swished against Polly's gown.

"Where have you been?" cried Colonel Anderson when he returned to his box.

"Lor', don't 'e look cross!" giggled one of the fair ladies. "I bet you're a regular Turk, my lord." Then she blushed and averted her eyes under the marquess's hot, impatient glare.

In vain did Colonel Anderson try to find out what had happened to his friend at Vauxhall. The marquess was tactiturn to the point of rudeness. The evening was a disaster. The following days proved no better. "Like an old bear with fleas," thought the colonel angrily.

Then at the end of another week, the marquess

seemed to regain his spirits. He and Colonel Anderson were to go to another ridotto at the earl of Burfield's town house. The marquess was in high spirits when they set out.

But that evening proved to be a disaster too. For the marquess, at first happy and carefree, danced with one masked lady after another. Then his spirits appeared to plunge and he began to wander from room to room, searching and searching.

Immediately after the unmasking at midnight, he turned on his heel and strode out of the house.

The colonel scratched his powdered wig. "I wonder who he was searching for," he thought.

At the end of yet another week, the marquess rode toward Bloomsbury. He felt he wanted to remind himself of what a conscienceless slut Polly Jones really was.

But when he enquired for the family Smith, he was told they had moved and not left any address.

He rode back to the West End, telling himself he was glad that the chapter in his life called Polly Jones was firmly closed, and yet his eyes kept searching the shifting, restless crowd as if looking for a girl with violet eyes.

"Here's that demned Pargeter again," sniffed Mr. Caldicott. "I'm convinced that Polly female got well and truly topped and he is only baiting us."

Mr. Barks squinted awfully through his quizzing glass at the approaching Bertram. "He's got a rose in his hat," he commented. "Rococo fop!"

"Good day, gentlemen," said Bertram. "I have news for you."

"Yes, yes," said Mr. Caldicott testily. "Polly Jones is alive and well."

"You know!" exclaimed Bertram, missing the sarcasm in the other's voice.

"No, I don't know," said Mr. Caldicott crossly. "We are weary of your tales."

"No tale this," said Bertram. "Miss Jones was at Vauxhall. Hark! She walked away with Canonby. Canonby returns alone after a while looking like death. Polly Jones was masquerading as a Miss Smith. One of Meresly's girls had a diamond necklace stolen and this Polly claimed to have recovered it although she probably took it herself and hoped for a reward. An old trick."

"And you saw her, plain as day?" demanded Mr. Barks.

"No, she was masked."

"You fool! Could have been anyone."

Bertram held up one long white finger. "Listen! After I saw Canonby return alone, I ran to the entrance gate and there I saw her with two men, one man short and squat and t'other tall and with only one eye—the brothers Smith who have a fondness for the girl and claim to have once worked for Mother Blanchard. I had met them before and made an arrangement to meet them again—an arrangement they failed to keep. I followed them close and marked their address in Bloomsbury."

"Good man!" said Mr. Caldicott. "Take us there and we will claim our baggage."

"I have taken the precaution of bringing a brace of pistols in my carriage," said Bertram. "Those two henchmen live with her and may put up a fight."

Highly excited, the three set out for Bloomsbury. Their excitement was short-lived. Like the marquess, they discovered the Smith family had left.

"Tish, I am weary of this," said Mr. Barks in disgust. "Living with those two jailbirds means she is no longer a virgin so her price on the market is now low."

Bertram stood frowning. "I think Canonby wants her," he said. "There is something there. If we keep close to Canonby, then he will lead us to her."

Mr. Barks snorted. "And then what do we do with her?"

"Why, give her to Canonby."

Mr. Caldicott's eyes narrowed. "And just what do you get out of it, Pargeter?"

"Good will toward men," laughed Bertram. "I am anxious to please you, my good friends, and return Polly Jones to her rightful place."

CHAPTER ELEVEN

HE "SMITH FAMILY" HAD NOT GONE VERY FAR
from their old address. They took up residence
in more spacious quarters in Bedford Gardens
in Bloomsbury. Jake had gained employ at the tea
merchant's. A converted criminal is perhaps just like
a converted anything else and Jake became, almost
overnight, stuffy and pompous. Polly was at first
amused to find herself becoming more and more the
subject of Jake's contempt. Then she began to become very angry indeed.

Barney was courting the daughter of one of the
clerks and he, too, had become anxious to appear
respectable at all times. The atmosphere in their home
became stilted and strained.

Polly had decided to give up any idea of thieving
and concentrate instead on finding out what had happened to Meg. The sale of the earl of Meresly's

diamond pin ensured her enough money to live on comfortably for quite some time to come.

But the very stuffiness and disapproval of Barney and Jake touched a rebellious streak in Polly's soul. Yet Polly might have come to the conclusion that stealing from the rich was morally wrong had she not lived so near the parish of St. Giles-in-the-Fields. In this parish, crammed with destitute Irish immigrants, every fourth house was a place you could buy gin. The most notorious providers were the chandlers' shops, where the poorest went to get their bread and cheese, their coal, their soap and candles. If you were desperate or miserable, and practically all of them were, then there was the standing temptation to buy cheap gin. Life was a nightmare struggle against impossible odds, and gin offered forgetfulness. Bread and cheese and gin soon became gin and bread and then gin alone. The Rookeries, the worst area in St. Giles, attracted the most depraved and destitute among the immigrants. Often thirty or forty of them would be crowded into one small house without sanitation, vermin-infested and rat-scuttling, and often lacking chimneys or windows. They frequently kept pigs in the same rooms as they lived in themselves, as they had in their huts in Ireland: the pigs fed off the rotting garbage in the alleyways, and the filth of the animals was added to the filth of the inhabitants. Typhus was rife.

The attitude toward these unfortunates was one of indifference. Only a few like Polly ached to see such misery. She lived in dread that her health would fail and that she would become destitute and be drawn into the teeming slums and lost forever. She could no longer rely on Barney and Jake to protect her. Her power over them had been waning for a long time. Now they no longer respected her, seeing her as a threat to their new existence, not realizing that their original care and championship of Polly had put them on the road to respectability, that Polly's insistence on clean linen and home comforts had been the things that had first set them on the path to a better life. Although Mr. White often asked Barney to bring "his beautiful sister" to one of the city celebrations, Barney never passed on the invitations to Polly. Although he knew that Mr. White and his colleagues were impressed by Polly's looks and manner, he was afraid they might discover her to be no relation of his and his hopes of marriage would be blasted.

Polly found their manner to her infuriating and hypocritical. Finally, she lost her temper and accused them of being poachers turned gamekeepers. For a while the atmosphere eased, only to return when Jake was promoted to head clerk.

Polly now wanted to be shot of them both, to show them that she did not need them, to show the marquess of Canonby that she was indifferent to his slights, to show the world that Polly Jones was a force with which to be reckoned. Without a word to Barney and Jake, she began to plot and plan. The poor had not enough money, the rich had too much for their own good. Polly Jones would even the balance in the favor of Polly Jones. It was a dog-eat-dog world where women were driven in droves to prostitution rather than starve.

She studied the social columns until she saw with a
fast-beating heart that a ball was to be held by the
earl of Meresly. She would kill two birds with one
stone. She would somehow get to that ball and see
what she could discover about Meg's death. And she
would see what trifles she could take.

But it was a ball, not a ridotto. She could not go
masked or in disguise. Polly decided to study the
Meresly town house. A woman loitering in the West
End on her own was sure to be accosted. It was when
Polly was looking down from her window at two
fops strolling past and thinking they looked like women
in men's clothes that she hit on the idea of disguising
herself as a man. She went to one of the better
second-hand clothes stalls and purchased a footman's
livery, took it home and altered it to fit her slim
figure. Her bust was no problem in an age where
even the servants wadded their coats with buckram.
A little padding was all that was needed to complete
the disguise. She powdered her hair and tied it at the
nape of her neck with a black ribbon, donned her
livery, and walked to Hanover Square where the
Mereslys lived.

She watched the servants come and go. There was
a great amount of bustle as preparations were made
for the ball. The livery of the Mereslys' footmen was
black velvet coat with scarlet and black striped facings on the lapels. Polly had left the square and was
still wondering how she could gain admittance to the
ball when she saw a footman in the Meresly livery
going into a tavern.

Made bold by her masculine dress, Polly strolled

in after him, noted where he sat, bought herself a tankard of small beer, and sat down next to him.

"Good day, friend," said Polly, lowering her voice several registers.

"Good day," replied the footman politely. "Do you work hereabouts?"

"No, I work in a merchant's household in the city," lied Polly. "This is my day off."

"P'raps I would ha' been better to have found employ with one of those merchants," grumbled the footman. "I don't have no time off. My lord's giving a ball and it's work, work, work, from morning till night. I'm supposed to be delivering messages, but a man needs rest."

"True, true," murmured Polly, feeling her way. "Still, it must be wondrous to see all the lords and ladies. I have never worked for a noble household. I have heard the countess of Meresly is amazing beautiful. But your tankard is empty. Allow me to refill it."

"Most kind. Thankee." The footman held out a hand. "I am Josiah Summer, second footman."

"And I am Paul Jones," said Polly.

The footman raised his refilled tankard to Polly. "Your health, Mr. Jones," he said. "You was saying about how beautiful the countess was. Harkee, friend, that one has a black soul. Always complaining."

"She has two fine daughters, I believe," said Polly.

"Pore little things. It was the earl who didn't want no daughters, but the way my lady goes on, you would think it was she who detested the female sex."

Polly looked suitably horrified. Then she said, "I come from a village called Upper Batchett. Do you know it?"

The footman nodded. "Went there a while back. Meresly Manor."

"Tell me," said Polly, leaning forward. "Do you recall an old woman who lived there called Meg Jones?"

"What? At the manor?"

"No, in the village, but she went to the manor on the day she died. Alas, your tankard is empty." Polly waved to the serving girl and ordered more to drink.

The footman thanked her and tried to remember something about Meg Jones in an effort to please this liberal footman. Then his face cleared. "I call to mind us all being given instructions at Meresly not to allow anyone from the village within the grounds. I asked the butler why and he says there was some old witch came a-calling. She had got into the rose garden and attacked my lady."

"And?" prompted Polly eagerly.

"That's all I know," said the footman. "You ask a lot of questions. Is this Meg Jones kin o' yourn?"

"No," said Polly quickly, and then added lightly, "I ask a lot of questions, I freely admit. It's because I lead such a dull life. No lords and ladies come a-calling at our place. It must be exciting to see all the jewels and all the beautiful clothes."

"Worked too hard to notice it," said the footman. "Pity you've got a job, for they're taking on extra staff for the night of the ball."

Polly's heart beat hard. "I could get away for an evening," she said slowly.

The footman stood up. "Thanks for the hospitality, Mr. Jones," he said. "But I must be off. If you're interested, call at the kitchen door and ask for the under butler, Mr. Sloane. But I think you've left it too late. They won't have any spare livery and my lord likes even temporary servants to wear his colors."

Polly sat for a long time after he had gone, lost in thought. Then she went out into the streets of London to search for a suit of black velvet. It would look odd to turn up in the hope of work already wearing the earl's livery. But if she wore a black velvet livery and pointed out she only needed to add the facings to the lapels, they might take her on.

Next day, she waited eagerly in her room until she heard Barney and Jake going off to work, donned her black velvet livery and set out once more for Hanover Square.

She was lucky. One of the hired temporary footmen had been found drunk in his room that morning and had been dismissed. Mr. Sloane asked for references and Polly produced two which she had forged during the night. To her delight, she was told she could begin her duties that day. She returned home and left a note for Barney and Jake, saying that she would be absent for a few days and that they were not to worry about her. Then she bought a few more items of masculine apparel, packed them in a bag and made her way back to the Mereslys' town house.

At first she felt like leaving, when she learned she

had to share an attic with Josiah and four other footmen. But she steeled herself to go on with the work allotted to her and leave worries about the night to come until later. As it was, it worked out very well. Josiah was too busy to be curious about this new footman who could leave a city job so easily. All the footmen, including Polly, were exhausted when it came to bedtime. The attic was in darkness when she undressed for bed, pulling a voluminous nightshirt over her head and undressing under the cover of its generous folds. As she lay down to sleep, she wondered if she could bear the smell. Despite frequent nagging, Barney and Jake loathed washing, but Polly had seen to it that their linen was fresh. But the footmen, as she discovered when she rose at dawn, slept in their drawers, and it was doubtful whether they had changed those for weeks.

But they were all as fussy about their outward appearance as their betters, brushing down their livery and arranging the frills of their shirts with finicky care on their dirty bodies. One footman had a bottle of musk which he passed around the others, and soon the attic stank of musk and sweat and something else that Polly delicately refused to put a name to.

She had already marked down some objects in the saloons and drawing room to be worth thieving. But short of an open confrontation with the Mereslys, how could she find out what had happened to Meg? Meg would not attack anyone, least of all a countess, so Josiah must have been lying.

The servants had little time for gossip and the ones who had been at Meresly Manor knew as much about

Meg as Josiah. Polly was becoming convinced she was a bastard. Her father might be the earl himself. Polly longed to find out the identity of her mother, a mother who might still be alive.

The calves of Polly's legs ached as she went about her work, for she had purchased a pair of shoes with very high heels in order to bring her up to a suitable height for a footman.

Her duties were mostly outside, delivering notes and fetching items to decorate the house for the ball. It was on the afternoon of the ball that she was told to take a basket of logs to the saloon on the first floor, for the day had turned chilly.

Polly entered the saloon and went straight to the fireplace. She did not fear discovery. She had quickly learned that neither the earl nor his countess looked at the features of their servants, any more than a farmer would study the faces of his oxen. And, in any case, she had been masked at Vauxhall. Polly did not know Lady Lydia had been at Tyburn nor at the marquess's when her cage was unveiled.

The day had turned dark and the candles had been lit. Polly was lighting a taper from one of the candles preparatory to lighting the fire when Lady Lydia said, "I see Canonby's decided to favor us with his presence." Her voice sharpened. "What is that footman doing standing there as if he wants to set the house on fire?"

Polly blushed and knelt down in front of the hearth and applied the lighted taper to the kindling.

She was aware of the people in the room behind her—Lady Lydia, the earl and their two daughters.

"I think Canonby is devastatingly handsome," said Lady Josephine. "But 'tis said he plans to marry at last."

Polly carefully picked up a log and placed it on the now-blazing fire.

"Oh? Who is the clever lady who has thus entrapped him?" asked Lady Lydia.

"Miss Caroline Ponsonby. She is quite old, mama. 'Tis said she is twenty-seven!"

"Twenty-seven is hardly old," said Lady Lydia harshly. "You there, footman, do you plan to kneel on the hearth all day?"

Polly jumped to her feet and bowed and left the room.

Canonby! But he wouldn't recognize her. He would never think of studying the features of any servant. This Miss Ponsonby was welcome to him. At twenty-seven, she would be glad of anyone, thought Polly, slamming the door of the servants' hall behind her with unnecessary force.

Mr. Caldicott was ushered into his friend's bedchamber. He stopped short on the threshold at the picture of agony that was Mr. Barks. His chest, his arms and the backs of his hands were covered with wax, which his valet was ripping off in shreds. The sounds of ripping hair mingled with the sharp yelps of Mr. Barks.

"My dear fellow," said Mr. Caldicott, putting up his glass. "Whatever is happening?"

"I am getting my hair removed," snapped Mr.

Barks, and yelped again as a long strip of wax was torn from his chest.

" 'Twould be easier to have your man shave you,'' said Mr. Caldicott sympathetically. "Why all this prettifying? Wife coming to Town?''

"Threatens to be here in a month," said Mr. Barks.

"Then why the agony?" pursued Mr. Caldicott.

"Fashion," groaned Mr. Barks.

Mr. Caldicott sighed sympathetically. It certainly was unfashionable to be hirsute, hairiness being considered next to yokelness. But men usually went in for these agonies only if there were some woman involved.

"But the lady . . . ?" questioned Mr. Caldicott with a delicate cough.

"No lady. Went to the hummuns," said Mr. Barks, meaning the Turkish baths, "and they was talking about depilatories, for some had been to Bath, and you bathe there with the ladies, you know, and men who are hairy are considered to be of low origin. One must suffer." As if to illustrate this further, he stretched out his bound feet. It was aristocratic to have small feet with high arches and so Mr. Barks's were bound like those of a Chinese woman.

Mr. Caldicott took a seat, averting his eyes from the spectacle of ripping wax. "Canonby's going to be there tonight," he said. "Pargeter's sure that Polly female will be among the guests. He says if we see her, we'll hustle her off. She can't complain because she'll have sneaked in under a false name. Mrs. Blanchard says she'll keep her locked up until

we decide what to do with her. Canonby mustn't see
us lest he intervene. She must be handed over to him
like a parcel when we feel like it.''

"I hope Pargeter's eyes are sharper than mine,''
grumbled Mr. Barks. "For with paint and powder,
it's hard to tell one female from another.''

Polly stood in the supper room behind a long table.
Her duties were to serve negus to the ladies. The
mixture of wine and hot water in its silver bowl
would be brought in just before supper was due to be
served and would be kept warm by a small spirit
stove underneath. She had worked so well and so
diligently that, although she did not know it, this job
had been given to her as a reward by the butler. It
was regarded as one of the easiest. But Polly felt
trapped. She would have no excuse to move about
among the guests.

Through the open door of the supper room, two
couples were performing the opening minuet. Polly
studied their steps. Drusilla had tried to teach her the
steps in the prison yard, although it had been hard to
achieve any elegance with leg manacles impeding
every movement. Dear Drusilla. In her heart, Polly
wished her well.

So clear was the picture of Drusilla Gentle in
Polly's inner eye that at first she thought the small,
plain, drooping figure standing outside the supper
room was her imagination at work. She blinked rapidly, but Drusilla was still there. She was standing a
little behind a highly painted lady. Must be Lady
Comfrey, thought Polly. What a fright! Poor Drusilla.

Polly had no fear that Drusilla might recognize her. As far as Drusilla was concerned, Polly Jones was dead. But the sight of the timid companion roused Polly's spirits. There *were* good and kind people in the world, and although she could not approach or speak to Drusilla, Polly felt warmed just by looking at her.

They moved away from the doorway.

Supper would not be served for another two hours. Polly longed to be able to sit down. She glanced idly out at the brightly lit section of ballroom revealed by the open door of the supper room and watched the dancers, trying to take her mind off her aching feet. Then she saw the Mereslys, the earl and countess and their daughters. The full force of the sheer silliness of her masquerade struck Polly. It was an excellent way to steal expensive trinkets but hopeless when it came to finding out anything about the Mereslys or Meg. Of course she could stay on; when she had more leisure time once the ball was over, she would be able to question the servants further. Mr. Sloane, the under butler, had indicated she could take a permanent post.

And then she stiffened. The marquess of Canonby came into view. He was wearing a long emerald-green coat heavily embroidered with gold. His shoes had emerald buckles and a huge emerald blazed with green fire from the cascade of lace at his throat. As she watched, a lady and gentleman and their daughter approached him. The marquess looked down at the daughter and smiled, a slow, caressing smile. Polly felt sick and depressed. Was this Miss Ponsonby?

And if it were, why had such a beauty managed to remain unwed at the great age of twenty-seven? Her skin was white and fair. Her powdered hair was dressed in one of the latest styles. Her white and generous bosom was exposed by the low square neckline of a dull-gold silk gown. There was a fine sapphire necklace about her neck, its blue light complimenting the vivid blue of her eyes. She was as pretty and fragile and dainty as the china shepherdess Polly had stolen from the Mereslys.

Polly felt alone and unloved. Self-pity was a new and horrible emotion. She stood with a lump in her throat and tears glittering in her eyes until the marquess and his company moved out of sight.

In the ballroom, Mr. Barks and Mr. Caldicott surveyed the scene through their long-handled quizzing glasses. Mr. Pargeter looked across at them and gave an infinitesimal shrug. No Polly Jones.

"Going to dance?" asked Mr. Caldicott gloomily, but did not appear surprised when Mr. Barks shook his head. Corsetted, powdered and pomaded as he was and with his feet crammed into tiny shoes with high heels, Mr. Barks knew he could never manage to last a whole dance. His smooth skin under his clothes felt odd and strange and itchy. He could almost feel the hair growing back in again and miserably slipped his hand inside his waistcoat to scratch himself.

"I think I shall leave after supper," said Mr. Caldicott. "Flat evening."

"Yaas," drawled Mr. Barks. "No one of interest

here,'' he added, dismissing the cream of London society.

Bertram Pargeter was in a vicious mood. Lady Lydia was flirting with every man in sight, the earl being in one of his unnoticing and forgetful moods. All the wiles which had so entranced him, which still entranced him, were being used on other men.

By the time supper was announced, Bertram did not feel quite sane.

Polly began to serve negus from the bowl in front of her. As it was the other footmen who came to her with the orders, she felt more at ease. She had taken herself to task before the guests came into the supper room, berating herself for her weakness.

The marquess of Canonby was seated well away from Polly. He was entertaining Miss Ponsonby and her parents—if that is who they were. The noise in the supper room was tremendous, a roar of voices, clattering of plates and glasses, and popping of corks.

''I would like another glass of negus,'' Lady Comfrey said to Drusilla. Drusilla looked about her for a footman.

''Don't sit there with your nose twitching like a rabbit,'' said Lady Comfrey. ''Have you lost the use of your legs? Go and fetch it yourself.''

Drusilla stood up and made her way to the end of the long serving table behind which Polly stood.

''Negus, please,'' said Drusilla.

Polly filled a glass with the hot liquid and handed it to Drusilla. She wanted to say something to this prison friend, but dared not. She looked up, thinking that Drusilla had left, but Drusilla was still standing there, gazing at Polly as if she could not believe her eyes.

Polly quickly looked down again, wishing someone else would come up.

"Forgive me," she heard Drusilla say quietly, "but you bear a striking resemblance to someone I once knew, a Miss Polly Jones. Are you a relative, by chance?"

"No, ma'am," said Polly gruffly, keeping her eyes lowered.

From across the room Lady Comfrey's voice came like a clarion call. "Come along, Drusilla, and stop making sheep's eyes at that pretty boy."

Drusilla gasped and turned away.

The marquess, who was sitting near Lady Comfrey, felt sorry for the faded companion who was making her way back through a chorus of jeers and teasing.

"Who is that awful harridan who so humiliates her companion?" he asked Miss Ponsonby.

"La, 'tis Lady Comfrey," said Miss Ponsonby. "She treats poor Drusilla like a slave. And worse! Do you know, she once had the poor thing incarcerated in Newgate!"

"But she has taken her back."

"Oh, yes, Drusilla Gentle's breeding is necessary to the scandalous Lady Comfrey. She claimed she had made a mistake and said she had subsequently found the brooch Miss Gentle was accused of stealing."

"When was this?"

"About the time of that famous hanging—you

know, the one where you snatched that body away for a wager.''

"Indeed!" The marquess's eyes blazed as green as his emeralds, and he looked across the room to where the footman was standing behind the bowl of negus. He let out a stifled exclamation, and stood up and pushed his chair back. "Excuse me," he said.

He made his way to where Polly stood. She saw him coming, half turned to flee, and then stood her ground.

"What are you doing here and dressed in those ridiculous clothes?" he demanded in a savage whisper.

"Don't know what you mean, my lord," growled Polly, dropping her voice several registers.

"Look at me when you speak to me!"

Polly kept her eyes lowered.

"Look at me . . . or I shall call Meresly."

Polly looked up and he drew in his breath. "Polly Jones. It *is* you! Thieving again? For that must be why you are masquerading as a servant. Leave here immediately or I shall unmask you."

At that moment Bertram Pargeter looked across the room and saw the confrontation. He could see the marquess's hard-set profile, he could see the blanched face of the pretty footman. It couldn't be . . . Or could it!

He made his way quickly to where they were standing. As he approached, he mentally stripped Polly of her livery and dressed her in an apple-green gown and fichu, such as she had worn on the scaffold. Jealousy sharpens the mind wonderfully, and Bertram, crazy with jealousy, knew in an instant that for some mad reason Polly Jones was masquerading as a footman.

He turned quickly. Lady Lydia was seated quite near, flirting with a young man, while the earl sat slumped in a chair on her other side, his eyes glazed with wine.

"Listen!" cried Bertram, his voice falsetto with excitement. "Hear me! The robber Polly Jones stands there. She is alive. She is that footman there. She . . ."

Polly kicked off her shoes and ran for the long windows of the supper room which overlooked the square. She twisted and turned, avoiding grasping hands. She ran out onto the balcony and leaned over it, but only for a second. She knew that if she jumped she would break both legs. Instead, she nimbly climbed over the side of the balcony, seized the drainpipe and slid down to the ground. The door of the earl of Meresly's mansion burst open and guests and servants hurtled out in pursuit.

Sobbing with fear, Polly flung herself at the brick wall which blocked off Hanover Square from the Oxford Road. She managed to swing one leg over the top and look down at the swirling mass of avid faces in the flaring light of the torches carried by the servants. That slight hesitation was her undoing. With one massive leap, Bertram sprang and seized her other foot and pulled hard, and Polly toppled back down among the guests.

Rough hands grabbed her and held her. Smiling with satisfaction, Bertram edged back into the crowd and put his arm about Lady Lydia's waist. "I thought she was dead,'' Lady Lydia was moaning softly. ''She must be dead. She cannot live.''

''Stand!'' cried a loud voice. The marquess of Canonby placed himself in front of where Polly stood, held by two footmen. ''Before you all run mad and bear this wretch, who has escaped the gallows once, back to Newgate, tell me her crime. She has played a trick on you by working as a footman, but is that so very wrong?''

Lady Lydia dragged herself away from Bertram. He tried to follow her, but at that moment Mr. Barks seized his arm, saying, ''The girl is mine. I paid for her.'' Bertram swore and pushed him so hard that he fell, then shouldered his way in pursuit of Lady Lydia.

''Well?'' the marquess was demanding. ''Has she stolen anything?'' Rough hands were plunged into Polly's pockets and inside her clothing. ''Nothing, my lord,'' said one of the footmen.

''What is that at her feet?'' cried Lady Lydia suddenly. ''I' faith, it is my etui.''

The marquess stooped and picked up the embroidered purse and looked sadly at the cut strings.

''I didn't . . .'' babbled Polly. ''You must believe me. Please believe me.''

The marquess stood looking at the purse, his face set and rigid, as two constables came to take Polly away.

''Evidence, my lord,'' said one of the constables. The marquess handed him the etui.

The earl of Meresly shook his large head as if recovering from a stupor. ''Hey,'' he called, ''is my ball to be ruined by one pretty thief? Back inside. Music! Wine! The night is young.'' Laughing and chattering, the guests began to make their way back to the house.

Lady Lydia found Bertram at her side. ''I saw you,'' he whispered. ''You cut the strings yourself and threw your etui at her feet. I saw you. You want her dead.''

Lady Lydia clutched his arm, her beautiful eyes dilated. ''You will not betray me?''

''Not if you are kind. When can I come to you?''

''Tonight. After Meresly is asleep. Tonight. He has drunk much.''

Bertram gave a slow smile. Power and satisfaction flooded his body.

Lady Lydia saw her two daughters watching her round-eyed, and snapped, ''You two have had enough excitement for one night. To your rooms.''

''But mama,'' wailed Josephine, ''we have not had our supper.''

''Now!'' shouted Lady Lydia, her voice breaking.

The constables escorting Polly were just about to thrust her into a closed carriage when a soft voice said, ''I pray you, sirs, these belong to the prisoner.''

Polly found herself looking at Drusilla Gentle, who was holding out the shoes which Polly had kicked off in the supper room.

One constable said, ''Don't see she deserves any comfort, but put them on the ground, ma'am, and she can step into them. But go careful. We have a vicious criminal here.''

Drusilla bent and put the shoes down at Polly's

feet. Then she straightened up and said quietly, "May
God bless and protect you, Polly Jones." And then
she turned and walked away.

Bertram, no longer mad with jealousy but mad
with elation, brushed aside the complaints of Mr.
Barks and Mr. Caldicott. His eyes burned as he
watched the earl of Meresly drink deep. He danced
and gossiped, but all the time he watched and watched
until he saw the earl's heavy body slump to the floor
to be picked up by two footmen and carried off.

Lady Josephine Palfrey stood at the door of her
bedchamber and watched as her father was carried
past. He groaned and came awake and vomited on
the floor. She wrinkled her nose in disgust and went
back into her room and through the connecting door
which led to her sister's room. "Hey ho," said
Josephine, sitting on the end of Emily's bed, "father
is drunk again and mama plans to cuckold him once
more."

"I would be revenged on her," said Emily. "We
could tell papa."

"You know his rages," said Josephine with a
sigh. "If he did not believe us he would half kill us,
and mama is so cautious and sly and that slut of a
French maid of hers abets her. Did you see the way
she whispered with Pargeter? He will be smuggled up
the back stairs this night."

"Hark! Papa is being most dreadfully ill."

Josephine smiled slowly. "Do you know, sis, it
just might be possible to rouse papa at the, er, critical
moment. Mama deserves a whipping for all her slights

and sneers.'' Josephine affected her mother's voice,
'What did I do to have such plain daughters?' Faugh!
She says papa is the one who did not want girls, and
yet he is kind to us. Ring for coffee. We must stay
awake.''

As he had done in the golden days of his affair
with Lady Lydia, Bertram waited at the bottom of the
back stairs leading up to her bedchamber. A red
dawn was lighting the sky outside.

He had been careful not to drink too much. Nothing must impair his lovemaking.

Then Lady Lydia's French maid appeared at the
turn of the staircase, beckoning to him.

Bertram silently followed her and entered Lady
Lydia's bedchamber. She was lying in bed, a sulky
look on her beautiful face. But Bertram felt again
that tremendous sensation of power. His hold over
her was complete. He could take her any time he
wanted.

The maid curtsied and retired. Bertram unbuckled
his dress sword and let it fall with a clatter to the
floor. ''Shhh!'' implored Lady Lydia. ''Meresly might
hear you.''

Bertram grinned. ''I know he sleeps at the other
end of the house, my sweeting. I have no fear of
being disturbed.''

Her ear pressed to the panels on the other side of
the door, Josephine heard the sword fall to the floor.
She turned to her sister, her eyes gleaming red in the
light of the fiery dawn. ''Time to wake papa,'' she
whispered.

Bertram had meant his lovemaking to be slow and sensuous. But the lifeless lack of response in the body beneath him drove him to take her hard and fast. He was mounting to a climax, deaf and blind to everything but the mad hammer of his desire, when the door burst open and at the same time Lady Lydia clawed his face and screamed, ''Rape! Rape!''

The earl of Meresly lumbered forward like an enraged bear and plunged a dagger straight between Bertram's naked shoulders.

Holding hands, Emily and Josephine crept to the door of their mother's bedchamber a moment later. The earl was holding Lady Lydia tenderly in his arms, her body wrapped in a sheet. Bertram was lying on the floorboards where he had been thrown, blood pouring from a wound in his back.

Lady Lydia lay with her eyes closed.

The earl saw his daughters. ''Go away,'' he said. ''Some fiend tried to rape your poor mother. Her great beauty inflamed some poor fool's heart. Off with you.'' He glanced at the body on the floor. ''The servants can clean this mess and call the authorities later. To your rooms, and be kind and gentle to your mother. She has had a great shock.''

Still holding his wife in his arms, he carried her off.

Josephine said a very unladylike word. The sight of Bertram did not make either of them swoon. Like the rest of their age and generation, they were inured to the sight of violence. Hanging bodies, disembowelled bodies, tortured bodies were everyday sights of London.

And then Bertram let out a faint groan.

"La!" said Emily, putting her hand to her mouth. "He lives!"

"Probably not for long," said Josephine indifferently. "That is a savage wound."

"True," agreed Emily. "But were we to bind it, to save him, mama would have a monstrous enemy. Crying rape was a pretty trick, and he would want revenge, would he not?"

"You have the right of it. Come help me. It is a wonder none of the servants have come running."

Emily sniggered. "They know better than to interfere when they hear squeals from mama's bedchamber. Let us see if we can keep this one alive!"

CHAPTER TWELVE

THE FULL GLORY OF THE STORY OF THE ARREST of the infamous Polly Jones received extensive coverage in the newspapers.

Barney and Jake, huddled together in a city coffee house, studied the reports. "Damn her," growled Jake at last. "She could ruin us."

"Ain't we going to try to see her then?" asked Barney.

"What! And have that Canonby recognize us, or that fop Pargeter? Her cell will be crowded with visitors. One of them has only to see us and cry, 'There's her confederates,' and we'll be dangling at the end of a rope along o' her. Why couldn't she let things be?"

"Seems hard . . . I mean, deserting her," said Barney.

"We can't do nothing for her," said Jake uneas-

ily. "Look, she'll die this time. No one will be
allowed near her. We stand to lose everything. Why
couldn't Polly forget that Meresly family? See here.
There is a warrant out for the arrest of that Pargeter
fellow. Tried to rape the countess. What a coil! No,
my friend. Forget you ever met Polly Jones!"

Josephine and Emily moved like small expensively
dressed ghosts through the silent rooms of their family town house in Hanover Square. Their mother was
in the grip of a raging fever and a physician and his
assistant were busy applying a drastic remedy called
Hippocrates His Heroic Treatment, which consisted
of bleeding the patient upright till she fainted, then
laying her down until she recovered, then setting her
upright and bleeding her until she fainted again, "the
which desperate course though rigorous is necessi-
tated by the quantity of effete matter rioting in the
Sanguinous System and oppressing the Vital Members."

And when they were not thus occupied, they were
busy with the earl, who had suffered a minor apoplexy following the night of the ball. His treatment
consisted of cupping. This was applying powerful
suction by creating a vacuum inside a bowl, or cup,
with a lighted taper, before clapping it to the body.

Straw had been laid down outside the house so that
the noise of passing carriages should be muffled. The
curtains and blinds were drawn.

Josephine twitched aside a curtain and looked out
into the square. "Do you think," she said over her
shoulder to Emily, "that *our* patient is still alive?"

"He was very weak and feverish when we bundled

him off," said Emily. "Faith, but I am plagued with ennui."

"Why do we not visit that girl who masqueraded as a footman?" asked Josephine. "She must be very brave. I admire bravery."

"It will take a great deal of money."

Josephine shrugged and then gave a bitter laugh. "That we have in plenty. Oh . . . no love, but plenty of money."

The marquess of Canonby was waiting impatiently for the arrival of his friend, Colonel Anderson. He had sent a note to him that morning. His footman had returned to say that the colonel was "warring" with his tailors and would be along presently. The colonel, a great dandy who ordered thirty coats at a time from Croziers of Panton Street, would kick his unfortunate tailor round the room if just one of the coats did not fit exactly.

The marquess had initially tried to dismiss Polly from his mind. She was a thief and had admitted as much. She had stolen from Meresly Manor and she had stolen from him. And yet he could not bring himself to believe she had stolen from Lady Lydia. The shock and surprise in her eyes when that etui had been found at her feet had been very real. Lady Lydia had long been finished with Pargeter. Everyone—with the exception of the earl—knew that. And yet, for some mad reason, he had been found in her bedchamber, raping her. That the marquess did not believe. Pargeter must have been there at Lady Lydia's invitation. Lady Lydia would certainly cry rape when her husband burst into the room, for had she admitted the truth she would have been cast off and all the jewels and pretty gowns which were life itself to her would have been taken away. For Pargeter to be there in the first place might argue he had some hold over her, and that hold might be that he knew Polly did not steal the purse.

The marquess tried to forget Polly Jones, but the more he tried, the more vividly her face rose before his eyes.

He looked up eagerly as Colonel Anderson was announced. The colonel was looking very fine in a coat so long, its hem reached to the knee strings of his gold-and-white-striped breeches. His white wig was embellished at the back with a long horsehair pigtail which reached to his waist.

"Bad cess to all tailors," grumbled the colonel, throwing himself into a chair and stretching out his long legs. "What's amiss?"

"Polly Jones."

The colonel's handsome face hardened. "A pretty little gallows bird," he said as casually as he could. "Desirous of a ticket from Mother Proctor for the hanging?"

"No, I thank you," said the marquess with a shudder. "The fact is, I cannot believe her guilty, and if there is any way I can prevent this hanging, then I will do so."

"My poor friend," said the colonel, shaking his head, "I have seen such things before. A man of your years, elegant and clever, avoiding the wiles of the ladies for a considerable time, only to fall slap, bang, crash for some useless piece of muslin.''

"My instincts cannot be wrong,'' said the marquess in a low voice. "I have no interest in her as a woman. But I sense a decency and honor in her. I would not see her hang.''

"Then what would you wish me to do?''

"I want you to go to see her in Newgate,'' said the marquess urgently. "I want your assessment of her character. I want you to ask her direct whether she be guilty or not. I am prepared to admit that when it comes to Polly Jones, my judgment may be clouded. And yet . . . Still, say you will do this for me.''

The colonel studied the points of his shoes. He had met Miss Ponsonby and considered her a very suitable wife for his friend. Sluts such as Polly Jones were a threat to the ordered existence of the aristocracy and were even known to wangle their way into marriage and pollute the blue blood of England with their common stock. But if he refused, then Canonby would go himself, and the jade would probably lead him into defying the law.

"I shall go,'' said the colonel, "this very day, and return with my report.''

Polly was not put in the condemned hold this time but in the "castle,'' a cell high upon the third floor above the prison gate believed to be the strongest and most impregnable part of the whole prison. Still in her servant's livery, she was chained down to the floor and fettered.

She felt stunned and numb. She did not even think that Lady Lydia might have cut off her own etui and thrown it where it would be discovered at her, Polly's, feet. She thought it had happened by accident, by evil chance. The noble visitors who crowded her cell were disappointed in her and considered her very bad value for the money, since she neither spoke nor moved.

The turnkey announced her visitors by name with all the aplomb of a butler in a noble household. Almost deaf with misery, Polly, on the third day of her imprisonment, nonetheless heard him announce Lady Emily and Lady Josephine Palfrey. The two sisters came in holding hands and staring at Polly with the same lack of pity with which they would survey a strange animal in the Tower menagerie.

They circled around her while two jailors watched to make sure nothing was slipped to the prisoner.

At last Josephine said, "We have paid a great deal of money to see you, Miss Jones. You might at least say something."

A little spark of anger in Polly's stomach grew to a flame. "I am sorry you are disappointed," she said haughtily, "but I am too busy to receive guests. As you can see, I am tied up at the moment."

"You are a lady!" exclaimed Emily, taken aback at the quality of Polly's speech.

Polly shrugged and her fetters jangled and clashed.

"If you are a lady," said Josephine, "why must you steal from mama?"

"I did not steal," said Polly hotly. "I stole nothing."

"But you must have come to steal." Emily sat down on one of the chairs provided for visitors and drew it close to Polly. "Why else were you in disguise?"

Polly looked at them steadily without replying. "Dear me," said Josephine faintly. "Have you noticed, Emily, that Miss Jones looks exactly like mama?"

"Yes," said Emily. "Are you by way of being a Berkeley bastard?"

"Berkeley?" demanded Polly.

"Mama's family name. Her brothers were very wild, you know."

Polly decided to tell these odd little girls with the old, old eyes the truth. In a halting voice, she told them of her odd upbringing and the death of her "aunt," and of how she hoped to find some clue as to what had happened to Meg on the last day of her life.

"I warm to you by the minute," said Josephine. "I have never been quite so interested in anyone before. We shall try to find out for you."

"I thank you, ladies," said Polly, "but I do not plan to live very long."

"Yes, of course, you are to be hanged," said Emily. "How vastly irritating."

"I find the thought a little annoying myself," said Polly.

"Be of good cheer," said Josephine, laying a purse at Polly's feet. "Here is money for you."

"You are very kind. But I do not need money. His Majesty's government is paying for my board."

Josephine knelt down by Polly. "Ladies!" admonished one of the jailors. "You must not pass anything to the prisoner."

"You saw us give her a purse and yet you said nothing," snapped Josephine. "Here, fellow, you take it and stand over there. I would say something private to the prisoner."

She put her lips close to Polly's ear. "If we give you a lot of money," she whispered, "could you not bribe these fellows to let you escape?"

"They dare not," said Polly in a low voice. "There is no hope."

"Never mind," said Josephine, jumping to her feet and smoothing down her brocaded skirts. "We shall come back tomorrow. Won't we, Emily?"

"Oh, yes," said Emily. "We find you vastly interesting, Miss Jones."

Despite her distress, Polly could not help feeling a certain amusement as she watched the small, stately figures making their exit, their many jewels flashing and blazing in the gloom of the prison.

Perhaps if she rallied, perhaps if she ate well and lived from minute to minute, the dread of the hanging might retreat to the shadows. The nobility who visited her cell after the Meresly twins were delighted with her and showered her with presents of money, presents which Polly instructed her jailors should be used to buy food and drink for the other prisoners.

But Polly's spirits took a plunge as Silas Brewer was ushered in, honest Silas who sat down and wept when he saw her chained to the floor.

"Oh, Polly," he sobbed. "We mourned for you when we thought you was dead and prayed for your soul, and now here you are, and in worse trouble than ever.''

Polly blinked back hot tears from her own eyes. If only she had let well alone. If only she had never stolen anything at all. If only she had met Silas before she had stolen those things from Meresly Manor. ''Don't cry, Silas,'' she said gently. ''If it is of comfort to you, then I am innocent of the crime of which I stand condemned. Oh, Silas, I have given away all the money I have received or I would give you some. How did you manage to find the great sum you must have paid to see me?''

Silas blew his nose and dried his eyes. ''It were them pearls, Polly, the ones you was wearing when you come to us in Shoreditch. We never sold them. We never had the heart to. The minute I heard of your arrest, then I sold them.''

''You would have been better to have used the money on your wife and family,'' said Polly.

''Mrs. Brewer said the money must be used to give you comforts,'' said Silas. ''I earn enough.''

''There's an important visitor waiting,'' interrupted a jailor, looking at the shabby figure of Silas with disfavor. ''Hurry up.''

''I brought you another Bible,'' said Silas. ''To comfort you.''

''Thank you,'' whispered Polly, her voice breaking.

''If you pray for help, He will hear you and comfort you,'' said Silas.

He leaned forward and kissed her cheek and then burst out weeping, and he was still weeping when the jailors thrust him out of the cell.

Colonel Anderson strode in next and looked curiously at the chained figure of the girl on the floor. Polly recognized him and her heart beat hard. The colonel's presence could only mean one thing. The marquess had not rejected her. And the marquess was great and powerful. Hope flooded her face with color and made her large eyes sparkle.

Goodness! Here is danger indeed, thought the colonel. My poor friend must be protected at all costs. Such beauty would turn the mind of most men—but not I.

He asked her politely if she were comfortable. He offered her a purse which she first refused, then begged him to send to Silas's address. He talked of the weather in the streets and the politics of the nation and the iniquities of the French. The sparkle died from Polly's eyes and her face became pale and wan. When he rose to go, she said urgently, "Is there news of the marquess of Canonby?"

Colonel Anderson looked down at her haughtily. "The only news I know is that he is ecstatically happy and is to be wed to a certain Miss Ponsonby."

"He did not speak of me?"

"My dear Miss Jones, a man deeply in love does not concern himself with the affairs of a common thief." And with that, the colonel turned and left.

Outside the grim walls of Newgate, Colonel Anderson sighed with relief. It had all been very distasteful, but it was all for the best. He mounted his horse and rode to Silas's address in Shoreditch. Mrs. Brewer was startled when a tall gentleman rudely thrust a purse at her, climbed up on his horse, and rode off without a word.

The colonel went straight to St. James's Square, where the marquess was waiting.

"Well?" demanded the marquess eagerly.

"My poor friend," said the colonel, shaking his head. "You had best sit down. This is going to be painful."

The marquess sat down slowly.

"Now," said the colonel. "I visited Miss Jones. I could not get much sense out of her, for some of her criminal friends had come to call and all were loud and drunk. She is unrepentant. She said she stole that purse and cares not. My friend, you have been sadly misled. She is a hardened criminal who consorts with hardened criminals."

The marquess put his hand to his brow. He remembered the unsavory Jake. He remembered the way Polly had smiled up at that one-eyed monstrosity. He felt sick.

"Let us put it all behind us," said the colonel cheerfully. "We go to the Ponsonbys' rout this eve, do we not? Ah, the fair Miss Ponsonby. Now, there is enchantment indeed!"

"Present my compliments to the Ponsonbys," said the marquess heavily. "I shall not go."

"Fustian, I beg you . . ."

"I said I shall not go," said the marquess harshly. "In the name of God, leave me alone!"

Next day, almost as soon as it was daylight, Polly was declared ready to receive visitors. This lack of personal privacy was, for her, the hardest part of her imprisonment. A jailor was just making a final check of her padlocks and fetters when another jailor put his head round the door and said, "It's them again. Those young ladies. Don't seem natural. Shouldn't be here and I'll swear the earl and countess don't know of it."

"Send them in," grunted the first jailor.

Polly looked up as the Meresly twins entered her cell. They were dressed alike, each wearing that informal style of gown called the Trollopee which was loose with an unboned bodice, trained overskirt and short petticoat. They both wore bèrgere straw hats over lace caps. They knelt on the floor on either side of her. "You are too near the prisoner, ladies," warned one of the jailors.

Josephine threw him a heavy purse. "Count that and it will stop you interfering in our conversation, fellow. We have brought her proper shoes," Josephine went on, unwrapping a parcel. "See, you can watch while we put them on her poor feet. The ones she is wearing have such ugly high heels, they cannot be comfortable."

The jailor untied the purse and gasped at the sight of the gold within. The other jailor joined him and they began to divide the money.

Emily took off Polly's high-heeled shoes and Josephine put a pair of flat shoes like dancing pumps on her feet. Polly winced and stifled an exclamation as she felt inside each shoe a sharp object. Josephine pinched her arm. "Well, Miss Jones," she said, "are you not going to thank us?"

"Thank you," said Polly, wondering what was in the shoes. "You are most kind, but I have little opportunity to move let alone walk."

"I am sure you will have some exercise soon," said Emily with a giggle. Polly thought of the dance of death on the scaffold at Tyburn and shuddered.

"We have not had much opportunity to help you," said Josephine. "About Meg Jones, I mean. Mama is grievous ill and papa has suffered a minor apoplexy. Our home is like the grave and just as amusing."

"It must distress you to have both your parents so ill," said Polly.

Josephine yawned delicately. "But of course," she said. "For it means we do not go to balls or parties. *Très ennuyant, je vous assure,* my dear Miss Jones. La, but we saw a monstrous funny play t'other week, did we not, Emily?"

Both sisters began to giggle and chatter about the play. Polly wondered whether they were a little mad, for they went on as if they were in a drawing room taking tea, rather than in the strongest and bleakest cell in Newgate.

At last they rose to leave, and still chattering and laughing, they made their way out.

"I feel immensely strong and brave now, Emily," said Josephine as they climbed into their carriage. "I am no longer afraid of papa or mama. Are you?"

"Not in the slightest," said Emily. "I really do not think we need be frightened of anyone ever again after what we have achieved this day."

At two o'clock, Polly's dinner was brought in. When she had finished it, her jailors checked her chains and fetters and padlocks. One of the men asked if she would like a visit later, for it was the custom to leave prisoners in isolation for the rest of the day and night once dinner was over, but they had made good money out of Polly and felt they owed her a kindness. Polly shook her head. She wanted to be alone. She was glad the day's visits were over. She dreaded to see Mrs. Blanchard's face peering round the door. She was heartsore that neither Barney nor Jake had troubled to call. She would not even admit to herself that the marquess of Canonby's absence was what hurt most of all.

When the jailors had retired, Polly slid off her new shoes. In one was a small thin file and in the other an oddly shaped key. The sudden rush of excitement and hope that Polly felt almost made her sick. Her heart was hammering so hard, she felt sure the jailors somewhere outside might be able to hear it. She took several deep breaths. Then a wave of depression as violent as the elation of a moment before engulfed her. This was some sort of skeleton key, but she was sure it would be almost impossible for anyone unpracticed in the art of lock-picking to use it. Even if she managed to unlock her fetters, this slim key would be useless on the door, which she knew was heavily bolted on the outside.

She sat for a long time, her head on her knees. Then she raised her head and looked at the Bible Silas had given her. It was a small leather-bound edition. It must have cost Silas a lot of money, thought Polly, as a ray of sun shone through the barred window of her cell on the smooth leather of the cover.

Still looking at the Bible, she fumbled with one hand for the key, inserted it in one of the padlocks and, forcing herself not to think of anything at all, she began to twist and turn it. There was a click and the padlock sprang apart. Polly took a long slow breath. Still looking at the Bible, understanding instinctively that lock-picking should be done by feel and touch rather than by sight, she began to work on the others until one by one the padlocks fell open. She picked up the file and sawed at the chain between her manacled legs. The chain was thin and not very strong and soon parted.

She hoisted the manacles up on her legs and pulled her stockings over them to hold them in place. Very slowly, she rose to her feet.

Polly walked to the window, stood on a chair and looked out. She could only see the high walls of the prison, but she knew that far below her was the street with people walking about, unfettered people, free people.

Then she got down from the chair, walked to the fireplace, crouched down and looked up the chimney. No fire had been lit in that room for a long time.

She turned round, picked up the Bible and opened it. In it, Silas had written, "To Polly Jones. God bless and keep you, Silas Brewer." Polly tore out the page with the inscription on it. If she ever got free, there must be nothing left behind which might cause the law to call on Silas.

She gave a last look round about and began to

climb. There were old rungs inside the chimney which had been put there for the use of the sweep's climbing boys. Her head struck an obstacle halfway up, and balancing on one of the rungs, she felt with her hand. An iron bar had been driven across inside the chimney.

With an almost manic strength. Polly seized the bar and pulled with all her might. The rusty bar cracked and Polly fell back down the chimney followed by a shower of broken bricks and soot.

She waited, her heart beating hard. Outside, opposite her cell, was a door leading to the quarters of the Master Debtors, who might betray her to the turnkeys. After what seemed an age, Polly slowly began to climb again.

She crawled out through the fireplace into the room above her cell. Measuring about twenty feet by ten feet and known as the Red Room, it had not been entered or used since 1716 when rebels had been imprisoned there after the defeat of the Lancashire Jacobites at Preston. Dust lay thick on the floor. The light outside barely penetrated through the tiny high window on the wall, and Polly, with her fingertips on the walls, felt her way round the cell to the door and then groped with sensitive fingers for the lock box. Hoping that this door should not prove to be bolted on the other side, she took out her key and worked at the lock. But it took almost an hour before the door finally creaked open on its rusty hinges. Polly slid quietly out into a passage. She turned left and came to another locked door. This was a door she recognized, the door to the chapel. She felt her way back along the passage in the hope of finding an easier way down, but there was no other way out. Polly returned to the chapel door.

She soon discovered that the chapel door had no lock but was barred on the other side.

Hope deserted Polly and she fell to her knees in front of the chapel door, leaning her head against the scarred wood. Then, as she knelt there, she remembered the iron bar she had broken from the chimney. One broken end had been thin and sharp. With a muffled groan, Polly got to her feet and made her way back into the Red Room and down the chimney to her cell. She retrieved the iron bar, and fear and renewed hope lending her strength, she was soon back at the chapel door. She thrust the sharp, broken end of the iron bar in the edge of the door and used it like a crowbar, wrenching with all her strength. There was an almighty crack as the nails holding the bolt plate sprang from their moorings.

Polly was now in the chapel, the chapel which she knew only too well: that macabre, forbidding room divided by high partitions topped by iron spikes into separate pens for the different classes of prisoner. It was on the top floor of the prison; there was another door on its far side leading to the passage which gave access to the roof. To reach it, Polly had to make her way through the pen reserved for prisoners condemned to death. She had been in this pen before and the very smell of it, of the whole chapel around her, was horribly familiar. She was reminded of the horrifying sermons which the prison ordinary preached from the safety of his pulpit. Before, Polly had been deter-

mined to try her best to escape, but planning all the
while to retreat back to her cell and lock herself back
into her fetters should she fail. Now, the very horror
of that chapel flooded her with the conviction that
she must escape at all costs, and should she fail, a
bullet in the back was merciful compared to a hanging at Tyburn. She climbed on top of the coffin,
placed there to remind prisoners of the dreadful fate
awaiting them, and smashed at the row of spikes on
top of the partition with her iron bar to clear a space.
The sound was hideously loud in the darkness, but
Polly knew the walls were thick and that this was a
quiet part of the prison.

She climbed over the gap she had made at the top,
jumped down on the far side and hurried to the door
at the far end.

When she touched this door in the darkness, her
heart fell. The immense iron-plated lock box was
clamped to the door with iron hoops, and beneath the
lock box an enormous bolt was fastened into its
socket by a hasp secured by a strong padlock. The
door itself was strengthened by four vast metal fillets.

For a moment she hesitated, wondering what to
do, and then she heard the clock bells of St. Sepulchre's Church chiming the hour. She counted the
chimes. Eight o'clock. She had started her escape at
three o'clock in the afternoon, after dinner. The fact
that she had come so far in five hours gave her a
steely courage. She decided that the lock could not
be picked and the bolt could not be forced, and so
she concentrated on the colossal metal fillet to which
they were both attached. Using the iron bar as a

lever, maneuvering it into position, Polly Jones looked
up into the darkness of the evil chapel and said the
soldier's immemorial prayer: "Dear God—if there is
a God—get me out of this!" Then with the strength of
a madwoman she wrenched the whole metal plate
from the door.

She pulled the massive door open and walked
along the corridor toward the roof. The door at the
end of the corridor was bolted only on the inside, so
she shot back the bolt and walked out onto the roof
and into the clean evening air.

She was now on top of the gateway. Surrounding
her on every side were high walls shutting off her
escape. She left the iron bar at her feet and climbed
onto the top of the door she had just opened, and
from there leapt to the top of the wall. She jumped
down on the far side to the lead roof beneath and,
crawling across the tiled roof of the Common Felon's
ward, she came to the parapet of the gateway. Now
she could see below her the houses and shops of
Newgate Street. The shops were still open and the
lights from the houses shone out into the street. She
judged that the roofs of the houses alongside the
prison were about twenty-five feet below the place
where she was kneeling, too far for her to jump down
to them. There was only one way to reach them.

Polly knew she would have to go back and collect
the blankets from her cell.

Back she went through the shattered door, through
the silent chapel, along the stone corridors to the Red
Room, and down the chimney. Quickly, she picked
up the two thin blankets from the floor which were

lying next to her discarded fetters. On her way back through the chapel, she used her file to saw off one of the spikes from the top of the condemned pew. She bundled up her blankets and threw them over the wall and then the iron bar.

Once more she climbed on top the door, leapt to the top of the wall and jumped down the other side.

Leaning her back against the parapet, she began to tear up her thin blankets to make a rope. With the iron bar, she drove the long spike she had taken from the chapel into the wall, tied the end of her blanket rope around it, and climbed down onto the roof of the house below—one of the many which were built right against the prison walls.

She crawled quietly along the slates until she came to an attic window. There was no light inside. She pressed her hand against the window. It was unlocked. She climbed inside and found herself in a garret. She waited, trembling, for half an hour before opening the garret door and starting to make her way slowly down the stairs. She had reached the first landing when her manacles slipped and one of the pieces of chain still attached to them gave a loud clink.

"Lord! What was that?" she heard a woman cry from a room somewhere above.

Then a man's voice answered, "A dog or cat, no doubt."

Polly felt she should retreat back to the garret, felt she should wait until all the family were asleep, but panic seized her by the throat, and hitching her stock-

ings securely round her manacles, she ran down the
stairs and out into Newgate Street.

She wanted to keep on running, but knew she
would attract attention that way. So she walked un-
hurriedly past St. Sepulchre's watch house and then
by way of Snow Hill, the Fleet Bridge and Holborn
Hill. Then she headed for the open country beyond
Gray's Inn Lane. On the outskirts of the village of
Tottenham she found a cowshed, and stretching herself out on the earth floor, Polly fell fast asleep.

She awoke at dawn, crying out at the pain in her
ankles, for they were still encircled in heavy iron
collars and were cut and bruised and swollen.

It began to rain, heavy, chill, sodden rain. Polly
lay in a daze of hunger and pain and looked out
through the cowshed door at the rain-pocked puddles
forming in the fields.

She was drifting off to sleep again when the owner
of the cowshed walked into it. Polly had rolled down
her stockings and put them back under the manacles
to ease her bruised skin and so they were in full
view.

"Who are you?" cried the man.

"Do not harm me," said Polly, speaking in as
deep a voice as she could manage. "I am a poor
young man who was clapped up in Bridewell over a
bastard child. I have just escaped."

Polly had discovered while living with Barney and
Jake in Tothill Fields that men considered the beget-
ting of bastards to be entirely the fault of the woman
and resented the law forcing them to pay support.
The father of a bastard child was required to maintain

it until it was old enough to be apprenticed. The weekly payment, usually half a crown, could be commuted into a lump sum of ten pounds on the payment of which the overseers of the parish would undertake to look after the child and release the father from his weekly obligation. As the child was not expected to live long in the care of a drunken parish nurse or at a workhouse school, the money was usually spent by the overseers on a riotous party called "saddling the spit."

"Didn't or couldn't pay, hey?" said the man sympathetically. "I have been guilty of the same thing myself in the past. But I don't want to get into trouble. You'll need to go."

"Can you get me out of these manacles?" pleaded Polly.

"I'll go over to the smith's and get a hammer and a punch," said the man, "but you must leave immediately after I free you."

Polly fervently agreed and then, after he had gone, wondered whether she was a fool to trust him. She was just about to conceal her manacles again and make her escape when the owner of the cowshed returned from the smith's with the required tools. He set to work, and after an hour Polly was free. She did not need to be prompted by his urgings to go: she fled.

She had some money in her pocket and so she bought a filthy, ragged, long greatcoat for a penny and forced herself to put it on. She herself was filthy and covered in soot and mortar dust. She made her way to a public cellar in Charing Cross and went down and ordered herself a plateful of roast beef and a pint of ale.

She ate greedily, hunched over the plate, tearing at the meat with her dirty fingers and broken nails. It was only when her hunger was satisfied that she realized that all about her were talking about the great escape of Polly Jones. It dawned on her that the whole of London was looking for her. There was a twenty-guinea reward for any information that might lead to her capture.

She was sick and weary and wondered how she could go on. And then she thought of Barney and Jake and smiled. That was one thing about consorting with villains: they would let her hide out with them.

Keeping always to the shadows, she made her way toward Bloomsbury as night fell. A dry sob of weariness shook her as she turned into Bedford Gardens. Pulling herself along by the railings, she made her way painfully home.

And then she saw Barney and Jake coming along the street arm in arm.

As they reached their own doorstep, Polly ran toward them with a glad cry.

Barney and Jake saw her, saw her white face in the light of the parish lamp—and as one man ran quickly inside and slammed and locked the door.

Polly hung onto the railings, staring at the locked door. They couldn't have locked her out. Not Barney. Not Jake.

She felt in the pocket of her livery for her house key. But it had been taken from her in the prison. She had buried the file and the skeleton key in the earth floor of the cowshed in case, were she recaptured and the implements found on her, they might torture her until she revealed the names of the Meresly girls.

Upstairs, Barney stood peering behind the curtain. "Has she gone?" whispered Jake.

"Just going," said Barney in a low voice.

"She'll ruin us," said Jake fiercely. "We stand to lose everything, even our lives, if we let her in."

"Where will she go?" said Barney, watching the drooping ragged figure of Polly as she limped off down the street.

"I don't know," said Jake. "But we'd best leave here in case she stays at large and comes back."

"Why couldn't she be respectable like us?" said Barney fiercely. "What did she have to go and get into trouble for?"

He trod on a plate of fish bones and swore dreadfully. Since Polly's disappearance, both respectable gentlemen had returned to their former low standards of housekeeping and cleanliness. When they had heard the news of Polly's arrest, they had got rid of their servant, not wanting anyone who had known Polly to be around to connect her with them.

"Oh, lor'," said Jake. "We'd better get her back."

"Who? The servant?" demanded Barney, kicking the plate across the room where it collided with a pile of dirty drinking glasses.

"No, Polly."

"But you said . . ."

"Listen," said Jake fiercely. "We're fools. If she ain't got any place to hide, if she's took and goes to that scaffold, then maybe some of them city folks like Mr. White will be at the hanging and start screeching, 'Ain't that Mr. Smith's sister?' ''

Both men hurtled down the stairs and out into the street. They searched and searched, but of Polly Jones, there was no sign.

"She'll be back," said Jake. "She's only got us."

It was two in the morning, but the marquess of Canonby was dressed and awake. He was sitting in the downstairs saloon which overlooked the square, waiting and watching. The night was dark and it had begun to rain again. Two of the parish lamps had blown out and he was grateful for the darkness.

The marquess of Canonby was waiting for Polly Jones. He had believed Colonel Anderson, and yet the idea of her being hanged became more and more unbearable. When he heard of her escape, he was faint with relief. All logic and reason disappeared from his brain, all the voices telling him the girl was a thief, a criminal, and probably a hardened one. There was some bond that bound her to him, and he hoped against hope that she might come to him for refuge.

There was a movement in the square, a darker piece of darkness. He narrowed his eyes and put his face closer to the window. There it was again.

He quietly went to the street door and opened it. He whispered into the wet and windy blackness of the night, "Come here. Come here where you will be safe." Light was blazing out from the hall behind

him. He went back into the hall and extinguished all
the lights.

Then he went back out onto the doorstep and
whispered again. "Come along. I shall not harm
you."

The piece of darkness moved and grew and resolved itself into the babbling, near-hysterical bundle
of smelly clothes that was Polly Jones.

"Shh!" he said fiercely, putting a hand over her
mouth.

He swung her up into his arms and carried her into
the house and slammed the door shut on all the
terrors of the night.

CHAPTER THIRTEEN

HE ESCAPE OF POLLY JONES FROM NEWGATE rocked London to its foundations. A new ballad about her was sung in the streets every day. People queued at Newgate Prison to see the path of her escape. At first no one could believe she had made the escape unaided, but as most of her visitors had been aristocrats, the authorities came to the conclusion that, somehow, she had managed it alone and had probably picked the locks with a nail. Silas Brewer had been too undistinguished a person for the jailors even to remember his visit.

She was reported to have been seen everywhere. *The Daily Journal* said that "the Keepers of Newgate have receiv'd certain Information that the famous Polly Jones, still disguised as a Male Servant, came a few nights ago to the Brewhouse of Messieurs Nichols and Tate in Thames Street and begged some Wort of the Stoker, which was given her, and that before the proper Officer could be got to secure her, she went off.'' *Parker's London News* reported she had been taken in Canterbury, ''her habit changed into that of a sailor.'' Another newspaper confirmed the rumor that she had been captured at Reading. But although she was apparently seen and recognized every day, and although several arrests were made of effeminate young men in servants' livery, Polly Jones remained at liberty.

Barney and Jake were surprised to find that Polly was a celebrity in the city coffee houses, and even the respectable Mr. White had been overheard to say he hoped she remained free and that anyone who turned her over to the authorities should be hanged himself.

Consumed with curiosity, Mother Blanchard joined the queue to view the route of Polly's escape and found herself next to Mr. Caldicott and Mr. Barks.

''Well, gentlemen,'' said Mrs. Blanchard. ''It seems as if we will never get our revenge now.''

Mr. Caldicott and Mr. Barks shook their heads gloomily. They shuffled forward into the prison and soon were staring in awe at the passage of Polly's escape. ''She must have been aided by the devil,'' said Mr. Caldicott in a superstitious whisper. ''No woman has the strength to go through all that.''

''Canonby would not dare give her refuge now,'' muttered Mr. Barks.

''Damme, but she must have great courage,'' said Mr. Barks, reluctantly proud of what he still considered to be his ''property.''

"And yet," murmured Mrs. Blanchard, "I would give a great sum of money to get my hands on her, *all* my money, in fact, to get hold of her. A little fun with her in the brothel and then turn her over to the authorities. Think, Mr. Barks, such a sum would buy favor at court."

"I have tried money," said Mr. Barks pettishly.

"But not a very great amount, I'll warrant," said Mrs. Blanchard.

"It will be nigh impossible to find her now," pointed out Mr. Barks. "The whole of England is searching for her."

"The Mereslys hold some fascination for her," said Mr. Caldicott. "If we remain in close touch with the Mereslys, mayhap we might discover something."

"If either the earl or countess live. Both are said to be very ill." Mr. Barks took a tiny silver shovel from his pocket, dug it into his snuffbox and applied the shovelful to one nostril.

They walked back through the chapel and then to the Red Room, staring in fascination at the sooty footprints in the dust which led from the fireplace.

"She must be hiding out with Barney and Jake, my two former servants," said Mrs. Blanchard slowly. "Find them and you will find the girl."

"That fellow Pargeter who's wanted for rape gave us an address in Bloomsbury," said Mr. Caldicott. "But when we got there, there wasn't a sign of 'em."

"Bloomsbury," said Mrs. Blanchard thoughtfully. "Now, I wonder . . ."

* * *

Mr. White sent for Barney and sat tapping the ledgers with the end of a quill pen.

"Ah, Mr. Smith," he said when Barney entered the room. "I regret to tell you that you have been making grievous errors of late."

Barney reddened. "My apologies," he mumbled. "I have much on my mind."

Mr. White leaned back in his chair and surveyed his head bookkeeper thoughtfully. "Your brother is also a trifle distracted," he said. "You have not taken any leave since I employed you. Perhaps a week . . . ?"

"Perhaps," said Barney gloomily. How could he tell Mr. White that the picture of Polly crawling away, rebuffed, was burning in his mind?

Mr. White sighed. "I am sure with a little rest you will come about. I wish I could say the same thing for our bookkeeper at our office in Bombay. Sad discrepancies in the accounts there."

Barney surveyed his employer sharply. "I could always go to Bombay and check the books for you," he said casually—as if Bombay lay somewhere at the end of Cheapside.

Mr. White dropped his pen in amazement. "My dear Mr. Smith, such a service would be invaluable. You would find me not ungrateful."

"I could take my brother with me," said Barney eagerly. "I would need his help with the work." Oh, to get away, thought Barney, from his nagging guilty conscience which would surely set him looking for Polly should he stay. And then, there was always the risk of her being recognized on the gallows by Mr. White if she were retaken.

"And when could you sail?" asked Mr. White.

"First boat," said Barney promptly.

"The *Maid of the Indies* sails from Gravesend in a week's time," said Mr. White, "but perhaps that is too little time for you to make your farewells."

"No, no," said Barney hurriedly. "Time enough and more."

"Be assured that your ladies will be waiting for you on your return," said Mr. White, meaning the ladies Barney and Jake had been courting. "And your beautiful sister will be taken care of. I shall call on her myself."

"She is no longer with us." Barney turned a muddy color. "With an aunt in the country," he added desperately.

"Very well," said Mr. White, although he wondered again why Barney and Jake, sterling fellows though they both were, should have such a beautiful and aristocratic sister.

The marquess of Canonby informed his secretary, Mr. Peter Beauly, that he had a charming lady of the demimonde in residence and did not wish to be disturbed by anyone. Mr. Beauly, ever correct, bowed his head in assent, although he was secretly disappointed in his master. It was odd that one so fastidious and correct as the marquess should decide to bring his doxy into his home.

Polly lay awake several days in the marquess's large bed, recovering from her ordeal. She had been bathed by the marquess as impersonally as if she had been a doll, fed by the marquess, and tucked into the

bed in which she now lay. The marquess slept in a
bed in the powder closet off his bedchamber.

When he judged her to be strong enough, he asked
her how she had managed to escape from Newgate.
Polly did not want to betray the Meresly girls to
anyone, even him, and so she said that one of her
visitors must have dropped a file and skeleton key
near her and the items had gone unobserved by her
jailors, who were too busy counting up the day's
takings.

"Now, you had better tell me the truth," said the
marquess.

"I have told you the truth of my escape."

"But not about the Mereslys. Come now. Why do
you haunt them? Is your striking resemblance to
Lady Lydia something to do with it?"

There was a long silence. She lay in the large bed
with her hair brushed about her shoulders. He thought
she looked little more than a child.

"You look better with your own hair, my lord,"
said Polly.

His black hair had been allowed to grow long and
he wore it unpowdered and tied by a ribbon at the
nape of his neck. He smiled. "Thank you. Now that
the compliments are over, Polly Jones, tell me about
the Mereslys."

Polly plucked nervously at the coverlet. "I was
born in the village of Upper Batchett," she said.
"The woman who brought me up, Meg Jones, I
believed to be my aunt. She was the wise woman of
the village and made potions and told fortunes. She
was good and kind," said Polly, her voice harsh with

emotion. She fell silent until she felt she had her
feelings under control. "I was wild and careless and
brought up to live a carefree life. But I was not
allowed to work or to be apprenticed to a trade, and
Meg would only say it was because she needed me to
work in the house and help brew the love potions and
medicines she sold. But I had not her art, nor could I
seem to learn it, and so she did all the work herself.

"On the day she died, she told me she was going
to Meresly Manor for she had heard the earl and
countess were in residence. I believed I knew why
she had not previously found work for me. I believed
she had planned all along to find me work as a
servant in a noble household. She had not been strong
of late and suffered from severe palpitations. But she
went off. I had slipped off to the local fair with one
of the village boys. We were laughing and singing
when we came back down the road. It was then that I
saw Meg. She was swaying at the door to the cottage, her hands to her throat. I ran and caught her as
she fell. She turned her dying eyes up to me and
said, 'Forgive me, my lady,' and then she died.

"There were cruel bruises at her neck, two purple
weals. I swear someone had tried to kill her, but I
was numb with misery. I learned immediately after
her death what had been kept from me before: that I
was a foundling and a bastard, most like, and had no
claim on the tenancy of the cottage. I went to Meresly
Manor to see if I could find out what had happened. I
knew the earl and countess had left but I hoped to
find some clue. After all, why had Meg said 'my
lady' when she was dying? She must have meant the

countess. The caretaker turned me away. It was when I went back and let myself into the manor that I decided to steal. You must see, my lord, that there were all these precious objects lying about and I was faced with starvation. I could not find work as a servant. I had no references. I should have decided to walk to London to find work. But I was desperate. So I stole from the Mereslys. At their ball, the reason I was there was because I thought I could perhaps learn from the other servants what had happened to Meg. Yes, I planned to steal. Wrong to you, wrong to God, but not wrong to me in this unfair and cruel world. But I stole nothing . . . nothing.''

The marquess's face hardened. ''I sent Colonel Anderson to see you in prison. He had my instructions to find out whether you were guilty or not. He told me you had been drinking deep with your villainous companions and bragging of the theft.''

''No!'' said Polly. ''He lied.''

''Colonel Anderson is an officer and a gentleman. I am disappointed in you, Polly. I had hoped you would be honest with me.'' He turned away.

''Wait!'' said Polly. ''Wait, my lord, and hear me. I have read in the newspapers that people can pay to see the route I took to make my escape and that my former jailors can be questioned. Go there! Ask them if I ever so much as took a drink or whether I had any villainous friends to visit me. Even Barney and Jake deserted me.''

''I will not disbelieve my friend. And why should I believe you?''

Polly sank back against the pillows and half closed

her eyes. "You are right," she said wearily. "There is no reason why you should believe a word I say."

She looked so frail that his heart gave a lurch and he said softly, "We shall talk of this later . . . when you are stronger."

The marquess gently closed the door and then strode off in a flaming temper. How could she say such a thing about his closest friend! It was not as if he had sent a *woman* to see her. Everyone knew women were fickle and prone to tell lies.

He drew on his gloves in the hall, picked up his tricorne and rammed it down with unnecessary force on his head. He marched across the square, relieved to be away from the house, relieved to be away from Polly. He was furious with himself when he found he was automatically walking toward the city. He kept telling himself he had no intention of going to Newgate Prison to check her story and he was somehow still telling himself that as he walked up Snow Hill.

The novelty of Polly's escape had not worn thin and there were many people in line, queuing to get in. He almost turned to flee when he saw ahead of him Miss Ponsonby and her parents. How could they be so vulgar? How could he ever have for one moment considered Miss Ponsonby as a suitable bride? She probably attended the public hangings.

He drew his hat down over his eyes and turned away, not wanting the Ponsonbys to see him.

At last he found himself being conducted to Polly's cell. He stood for a long moment, looking down at the pile of discarded fetters and padlocks on the floor. How could anyone who was so miserably chained down carouse with friends? He drew one of the jailors aside.

"You were present, were you not, when Polly Jones was a prisoner here?" the marquess asked him.

The jailor, a Mr. Williams, nodded. "Do you remember a certain Colonel Anderson calling?" pursued the marquess.

"Hard to recall, my lord," said Mr. Williams, "for in truth a great number of ladies and gentlemen came to see her."

"And how was her demeanor? Did any of her own villainous friends call? And did she drink with them?"

"No, my lord. I don't call to mind her having one friend. Wait a bit. There was a little scrap of a fellow. Brought her a Bible."

"And she drank with him?"

"No, my lord. She drank nothing but water, and such money as was given her she gave to me so that food and drink could be bought for the other prisoners."

"And how was her manner?"

He passed Mr. Williams a guinea. Mr. Williams tucked it away in his pocket. "You ask as to her manner, my lord? Well, there's the strange thing. She was very quiet and sad and then for a while her spirits rallied and she did her best to entertain her visitors, but more like a lady in a drawing room than a common felon. Now, if you will follow me, my lord, I shall take you to the room above and thence to the chapel."

"No," said the marquess. "I have seen and heard enough."

Outside the prison once more, he decided to get

Polly out of London as quickly as possible. His own best friend had proved untrustworthy. The marquess now saw enemies everywhere.

He did not find the colonel at his lodgings, but eventually found him in Durham's coffee house in the Temple, one of the colonel's favorite haunts.

"I am come from Newgate Prison," said the marquess, pulling out a chair next to the colonel's and sitting down.

"Didn't think you would be interested in sights like that," said the colonel uneasily.

"Why did you not tell me she was cruelly chained to the floor?"

The colonel shrugged. "Felons are always chained."

"They have leg irons, yes," said the marquess dryly, "but her confinement was exceptional. Also, her jailor said no friends had visited her, with the exception of one man who brought her a Bible and was probably, in my opinion, not a friend at all but some cracked lay preacher. Nor did she drink anything but water."

"If you will believe a jailor . . ." began the colonel huffily.

"He had no reason to lie. Had you?"

The colonel looked for a long time into the depths of his coffee cup, as if trying to read his future in the dregs at the bottom. Then he heaved a sigh. "Yes, my friend, I did lie. But she is a common thief, and your interest in such a person alarmed me. I did it for your own good. I offered her a purse which she would not take but instructed me to take it to a poor address in Shoreditch and give it to a family called

Brewer, and that much I did for her. Were she not beautiful, you, like me, would see her with clear eyes for what she is. You said she had admitted to stealing from the Mereslys. Such a connection would sully your great name. It is largely believed that she was one of the odd miracles of Tyburn and did not die and you only snatched her away for a wager. But I came to believe you had bribed the hangman to keep her alive. You must be guided by me. You . . ."

"No," said the marquess, getting to his feet. "I will not listen to you preach to me on the subject of Polly Jones. I am not a child and am well able to take care of myself. I am very angry with you."

"Stay!" cried the colonel. "I trust you have no knowledge of her whereabouts."

"Of course not," said the marquess sharply. "I am sure you went out of your way to tell her I had no interest in her whatsoever, so why should she come to me?"

He turned and walked away before the colonel could reply.

All the way back to St. James's Square, the marquess wondered and wondered what to do with Polly. He could not keep her hidden in his bedchamber forever.

Polly looked up as he came in and put down the book she had been reading. He sat on the edge of the bed and looked down at her. He took one of her hands in his, but there seemed to be some sort of charge of emotion running up his arm, and so he dropped her hand quickly.

"I apologize, Polly," he said. "You are right. The colonel did lie."

"Why?" asked Polly.

"He considers you a highly unsuitable interest for such as myself."

"Oh."

"So we will forget about Colonel Anderson for the moment, except to tell you that you instructed him to take a purse to a family in Shoreditch, which he did. What family was that, Polly?"

Polly told him about Silas.

"So you are not entirely friendless. Did you not think to go to them?"

Polly shook her head. "They have so little, and I could bring them great trouble. You, on the other hand, are rich and powerful and do not know what it is to suffer."

"Money does not protect the human race from suffering," he sighed. "But now the question is, what to do with you. My home, Hand Court, lies in Shropshire. I had originally planned to take you there and turn you over to the housekeeper for training. That will no longer answer. The dower house lies empty at the moment and you could live there, but were you to live there alone, it would occasion comment. You need a companion, some female . . ."

He sat lost in thought.

"There is Miss Drusilla Gentle," said Polly suddenly. "She is Lady Comfrey's companion and leads a most miserable existence. I am sure she would be glad to escape. She was the one who taught me ladylike manners and speech while we were both in Newgate. She had been put there because she was accused of stealing from her employer, but Lady

Comfrey subsequently said she had found the missing brooch that Drusilla was supposed to have taken and so she was released."

"And she would not betray you?"

"No," said Polly. "She is too much of a lady."

"Ladies and gentlemen can be as great betrayers and liars as anyone else," said the marquess bitterly, thinking of the colonel.

There came the faint sounds of an altercation from belowstairs. The marquess went to the door and listened. Then he hurried back to the bed and started to tear off his clothes.

"What are you doing?" squeaked Polly, pulling the blankets up to her chin.

"Shut up," he snapped. "I am not going to bed you. I am merely going to embarrass the good colonel away."

He dragged back the blankets and, dressed only in his drawers, he climbed into bed, pulled Polly roughly into his arms, tumbled her under him, forced her head down and began to kiss her with great force and energy.

"I insist on seeing your master," came the colonel's voice. "With a doxy? Fie for shame, Beauly. The master would not pollute his house with such a type."

The bedroom door crashed open.

"Darling," said the marquess passionately, and buried his firm lips in Polly's soft and trembling ones.

"Oh, the deuce," cried the colonel. "I am most awfully sorry, Beauly." The door shut again and the

colonel's voice came faintly as he descended the
stairs. "Pray do not tell Canonby of my visit. He will
kill me."

The marquess heard all this, but Polly none of it.
Her lips and breasts and body were swelling and
throbbing and burning under his touch. His body felt
cool and impersonal against her fevered skin. His
chest was smooth, hard-muscled and hairless. Mr.
Barks would have fainted with envy had he seen it.

"Well, that's got rid of him," said the marquess,
propping himself upon one elbow and grinning down
at Polly's dazed face. He kissed her lightly on the
nose and swung his long legs out of bed. He turned
away from her and began to pull on his clothes. "It's
a good thing you are *not* a lady, Polly Jones," he
said over his shoulder, "or I should find myself well
and truly compromised."

Oh, the wicked, insensitive cruelty of men!

Polly had not allowed herself to cry, not when
Meg died, not on the scaffold and not in prison. But
his words sent a rush of tears up to her eyes. She
fiercely blinked them away. There was no time to
cry. She must think of her future. She said—amazed
that her voice should sound so cool and firm, "And
so, my lord, do you think you can contrive to ask
Drusilla if she will come with me?"

"I think I can manage to do that this evening," he
said, his voice muffled as he pulled his shirt over his
head. "There is a ridotto at Lady Comfrey's this
evening. I shall speak to her then. Now, I have
various calls to make and must tell the servants I
shall be gone from town. I have given my valet a

holiday and my poor secretary will wonder why he is
left behind.''

After he had gone, Polly threw back the bed-
clothes, lifted up her nightgown and squinted down
at her naked body, expecting it to look different, to
look hot and swollen, but it still seemed the same.

Lady Comfrey looked first amazed, then furious,
and finally tried to laugh when the marquess of
Canonby asked her permission to dance with Miss
Drusilla Gentle.

''Indeed, my lord, you are too kind,'' said Lady
Comfrey, her eyes snapping behind her mask. ''But
my poor dab of a Drusilla does not dance. You
would be wasting your time. I, on the other hand . . .''

''Nonsense. I should consider myself honored,''
said the marquess, smiling down into Drusilla's frightened eyes. He led the companion onto the floor. ''I
do not really want to dance,'' he said softly. ''Is
there somewhere we can talk? It is most important.''

Drusilla gave a scared little nod. ''The library is
hardly ever used, my lord,'' she said. ''We could go
there. But I must beg you to be quick. Lady Comfrey
is not pleased with me.''

The marquess said nothing until they were inside
the library.

''Miss Gentle,'' he began, ''I am here to throw
myself on your mercy.'' He studied her weak and
trembling face, wondering whether such a poor creature would not cry out in fright when she heard he
was harboring the notorious Polly Jones.

Drusilla looked at him curiously. ''I am sure you
exaggerate, my lord. But how can I help you?''

"Do you remember Polly Jones?"

Color flooded Drusilla's face. "Indeed I do. Such a dear creature. So warm, and so good. Is is possible that you know something of her?"

"I have Polly Jones safe with me."

Drusilla let out a long slow breath. "God is good," she said simply.

"The reason I am come to you, Miss Gentle," said the marquess, "is that it is important to remove Polly from London immediately. The dower house on my estate lies vacant. She could reside there . . . but not alone. She would need a companion."

Drusilla clasped her hands tightly together. "Are you asking me to be that companion?"

"Yes, Miss Gentle. I would insure that no harm came to you, and that you would be funded with a generous pension for life."

"Oh, my lord, you are an answer to all my prayers."

"My dear Miss Gentle, the gratitude is all on my side. I am asking you to be companion to an escaped felon."

"You do not know what my life has been like," said Drusilla in a low voice. "Polly Jones is the only one who has shown me warmth and kindness. She has all the courage and gallantry I lack."

"Then I suggest you, naturally, do not speak of this to anyone. I do not wish my servants to know of this and so must leave during the night. When do you think you can get away?"

"This evening," said Drusilla. "I have only a few belongings, and can escape by the back stairs."

"You do not lack courage and gallantry," said the marquess, kissing her hand. "I feel it necessary to tell you that there is no intimate relationship between myself and Polly, nor shall there be. I am sure you will be glad to be assured on that point."

"Oh, no, my lord."

"Why? Because I am evidently a man of honor?"

"I am sure you are, my lord. But you see, I know Polly Jones to be a woman of honor."

"And yet she admits she stole from the Mereslys."

"To such as I the circumstances are understandable," said Drusilla.

"Well, we must not waste time discussing the morality of Polly's actions. I shall await your arrival, Miss Gentle, and I thank you from the bottom of my heart."

Polly received the news of Drusilla's impending arrival with mixed feelings. It would indeed be wonderful to have Drusilla as companion and friend. And yet, Drusilla's arrival meant her period of intimacy with the marquess was shortly to end.

CHAPTER FOURTEEN

OLLY HAD LARGELY FORGOTTEN THE IMMENSE social gulf which lay between her and the marquess, and so when he stopped the carriage on top of a hill, pointed with his whip and said, "Hand Court," Polly's heart gave a great lurch and a little black feeling of dismay settled in her stomach.

Hand Court lay at the foot of the valley in the golden, late-afternoon sun, power, security and wealth emanating from its every stone, from its deer park, its smooth lawns, its ornamental lake.

They had left in the middle of the night by the back stairs, and the marquess had harnessed a team to the carriage himself. No servant must be allowed to see Polly. She was now so notorious, it would be stretching the loyalty of the servants to the limit. It would be different in the country, he had explained. Such servants as he had there did not know what the famous Polly Jones looked like. She would take up residence in the dower house under her former alias of Miss Peterson.

The journey had been leisurely. Drusilla tried to maintain a sedate and ladylike front, but she was obviously elated at her escape from Lady Comfrey and inclined to worship the marquess. They had broken their journey at a posting house. Drusilla and the marquess had talked of plays and books, and Polly, smiling and listening, felt very close to him and not in the least overawed by his rank.

Now the very sight of that enormous mansion had opened up the social chasm between them again.

Far away a dog barked, smoke rose from the tall chimneys of Hand Court, and the soft air smelled of leaves and flowers.

"God bless the squire and his relations. And keep them in their proper stations," thought Polly rather incoherently. There was no breaching the social ranks in the country. That she knew. In town, beauty or novelty might give some upstart a temporary entrée into the glittering world of society, but in the country, the roots of class distinction were deep and secure.

"I shall see you settled at the dower house and introduce you to the servants," the marquess was saying, as the carriage moved forward again. "You shall take supper with me this evening and then I feel confident I can leave you to your own devices."

Polly nodded while her mind raced. Servants! She had not thought of coping with servants by herself.

But then she began to relax a little. She was not alone. Drusilla would know what to do.

The dower house stood about half a mile away from Hand Court, hidden from the drive by a shelter belt of evergreens. Polly had imagined something like a country cottage; once again she had that feeling of dismay and dread when she looked up at a large house which could rightly be called a mansion were it not set against the palatial spread of Hand Court.

A wizened caretaker answered the door and stood with head bowed while the marquess rapped out orders. A footman and three housemaids, a parlor maid and a maid of all work were to be sent to the dower house immediately. The ladies would join him for supper and stay at Hand Court for one night, then move into the dower house the following morning after it had been warmed and aired.

The marquess's carriage had been sighted on its approach to Hand Court and when they arrived, the great army of servants which serviced the stately home was lined up in the hall.

Polly and Drusilla were introduced, Polly copying Drusilla's formal manner as well as she could. Then the housekeeper led them upstairs to their rooms.

When they were at last alone in the bedroom allotted to her, Polly said, "How terrifying all this is. I do hope the servants do not take me in dislike."

"They would hardly do that," said Drusilla soothingly. "They are too much in awe of Canonby. Come, we must change for supper. I shall be your maid this evening. You must admit, all is most prettily arranged."

But Polly found the vast bedchamber intimidating with its huge four-poster bed and massive furniture. She meekly let Drusilla undress her to her shift and stood like an obedient child while Drusilla slipped a powder gown over her head and led her into the powder closet to arrange her hair.

"There are so many powders," said Drusilla. "Do you want the lavender or the pink?"

"White, please," said Polly.

Drusilla picked up the powder bellows and began to puff a cloud of scented white powder over Polly's hair after she had curled and arranged it.

Polly was then led back to the bedchamber and dressed in one of the gowns the marquess had bought her after the hanging.

It was one of the finest she had in her wardrobe. The gown was a sack dress made of kincob, very rich embroidered brocade imported from China. It was worn over a large hoop which cleared the ground to show a little of the ankle. The stomacher was of richly embroidered white silk, and the sleeves reached to the elbow and were finished with full pinked ruffles. The back of the gown consisted of two large box plaits which hung out over the hooped skirt. The square neckline was cut very low but Drusilla dissuaded Polly from using a kerchief, saying that low necklines for evening wear were all the fashion and were not considered immodest.

Drusilla herself wore a plain round gown of a drab brown watered silk. Polly protested that she must have something finer to wear, but Drusilla, who had been well schooled as a companion, pointed out

that richly dressed companions brought discredit to
their mistresses.

Drusilla then rang the bell and, when a footman
answered its summons, asked to be conducted to the
drawing room.

With head held high, Polly followed the footman
through the expensive hush of the great house with
its multitude of portraits and statuary, down the shallow marble steps of the main staircase and across the
white and black tiles of the hall. The footman threw
open a pair of double doors and they walked into the
drawing room. It was an immense room which seemed
to go on forever, a desert of carpeted elegance with
little oases of tables and chairs dotted about at intervals. The marquess was standing by the fireplace at
the far end of the room when they entered. He watched
their approach. Polly stumbled and knocked over a
chair, blushed, bent to pick it up and banged heads
with a footman who had rushed to do the same thing,
sending a cloud of scented hair powder flying up into
the air.

Quite demoralized, Polly let Drusilla lead the way.

Again, Drusilla made most of the conversation.
Polly felt miserably like a child who has gate-crashed
an adult party. They began discussing a new novel,
The Gentleman's Folly, which Polly had read and
enjoyed very much. But the marquess did not even
seem to notice her as he listened politely to Drusilla
discourse on the book's merits.

"I did not like it one little bit," said Polly loudly
and suddenly. "*I* thought it was a most stupid book!"

"My dear Miss Peterson," said Drusilla, using

Polly's alias in case some servant should be listening, "I am so sorry to hear that. Which part of it offended you most?"

Polly had enjoyed all of it. She felt trapped. "I said I didn't like any of it," she said sharply. The marquess raised his thin eyebrows, and Polly blushed and scowled fiercely at the pattern on the carpet.

Oh, dear, thought Polly. *I am become jealous of Drusilla, and yet if Drusilla did not converse with the marquess, we would all sit in silence for, somehow, I am become too frightened to speak.*

The agony went on at supper. Overawed by the vastness of the dining room and the great army of liveried servants, Polly hung her head and picked at her food. In vain did Drusilla try by every means she could think of to bring Polly into the conversation. Polly sat in agonies. She wanted the marquess to look at her. The minutes were flying by. Soon supper would be over and in the morning she and Drusilla would take up residence in the dower house. She tried and tried to think of something bright and witty to say, and no sound would come out. By the end of the meal, she had a blinding headache.

Drusilla, for all her crushed-down life with Lady Comfrey, had been brought up to be accustomed to stately surroundings. Polly desperately envied her ease of manner and the way she did not even seem to notice the existence of the servants. Twice, when a footman handed Polly a dish at supper, she smiled up at him warmly and thanked him, and then blushed beet-red at her mistake. The marquess's town house seemed a very hovel compared to all this courtly magnificence. The first time she had stayed at the house in St. James's Square, she had been served her meals in her room by the town servants, and yet that had not troubled her. She supposed that when someone has just escaped with their life, they are not apt to be bothered with social niceties. The second time, the marquess himself had attended her. In retrospect, St. James's Square now seemed like a paradise: a paradise where she had had him all to herself.

It was time to retire. The marquess bowed, raised Polly's hand to his lips, and kissed the air an inch above it.

"What a manner Lord Canonby has," sighed Drusilla when they were alone again. "So elegant, so restrained."

Polly remembered the marquess falling on top of her in the bed, holding her, kissing her. That was the way she wanted him, she thought in cold shock. But she wanted the real thing. Not a show of passion to trick Colonel Anderson. She wanted the marquess of Canonby to burn in her arms, not to drop mock kisses somewhere in the region of the back of her hand.

But none of this could she tell Drusilla. Drusilla was a lady, and ladies did not burn and sweat and ache with passion, that much Polly knew. Only women of cracked reputation lusted after men.

But tomorrow was another day; a day in which she would be witty and charming and not the least overawed.

But late next morning, she and Drusilla were conducted to the dower house by the servants. The marquess, they were told, had gone out on estate business, but would call on them in the afternoon.

Polly tried to force herself to enjoy settling in. It appeared a pleasant, manageable house after the grandeur of the stately home. The furniture was pretty and unpretentious. There were a pleasant parlor, a morning room and a dining room downstairs, all leading off a vestibule. Upstairs were four apartments, each consisting of bedroom, powder room, and tiny sitting room. Nothing to be afraid of here, Polly told herself sternly.

The servants were efficient and courteous, and Polly found herself regaining all the old ease and friendship she had experienced with Drusilla in the prison yard.

But when the marquess called in the afternoon and agreed to join them over the tea tray, he looked so remote and handsome in riding dress and top boots that Polly once more fell silent. *Cannot you see I wish to be alone with him?* her mind screamed at Drusilla. But had she voiced such a thought aloud, Drusilla would have been shocked. No young virgin was allowed to be alone in the company of any man. Drusilla did not know of the enforced intimacy of Polly's stay at the town house. She had never burned with the fires of lust and passion herself and would have been horrified and upset had she been able to guess at one fraction of the hot emotions which were coursing through Polly's wanton body.

At last the marquess yawned and stretched and as he did so, the muscles of his thighs rippled against the cloth of his breeches. Polly stifled a groan. "I must go," he said. "Pray call for a carriage should you wish to go to the nearest town. I shall have people calling to see me, but I will put it about that you are a distant relative, Polly, and no questions will be asked. You will have callers yourself, of course, the vicar and some of the local county, but I can trust Miss Gentle to deal competently with them." He stood up, he smiled, he waved, and then he was gone.

In the days that passed, Polly did receive a few callers, some of the neighbors and the vicar and his wife. She was treated with all the deference due to a relative of the marquess, and Drusilla was always on hand to add elegance to the conversation. Polly reflected wryly that the hideous Lady Comfrey had indeed lost a treasure. But she copied Drusilla's manner and ease of conversation as assiduously as she had once taken lessons from her in Newgate. The marquess had not called again, but Polly was determined that when he did, he would not find her tongue-tied.

But the reason for his absence startled her. A Mrs. Castle, a hard-featured lady whose estate was on the other side of the valley, had conceived a fondness for Polly and called several times. It was as she was taking her leave after one of her visits that she said, "I suppose I had better call at the house and present my compliments to the Ponsonbys, although I cannot precisely say I like them. But Mary Ponsonby and I were friends a long time ago and she will think it odd if I do not call.''

"The Ponsonbys!" exclaimed Polly. "Then he must mean to marry her after all!"

"If you mean Joan Ponsonby, it's she who is setting her cap at Canonby, rather than the other way around," said Mrs. Castle. "They arrived without being invited, you know. Said they guessed he had moved to the country. Of course, Joan is flying high. She is very beautiful, but when a very beautiful woman gets to the age of twenty-seven and is still unwed, one wonders why.''

"Perhaps she was waiting to fall in love," said Polly.

Mrs. Castle laughed loud and long. "You are a wit, Miss Peterson," she said, and she was still laughing when she left.

"What did I say that was so funny?" Polly asked Drusilla.

"People of the Ponsonbys' rank do not marry for love," said Drusilla, putting neat stitches in a piece of embroidery. "Only very common people do that.''

"But why not grand people?"

"If they find love, they are very lucky. But a true lady knows what is due to her family and marries suitably.''

Polly fell silent. What was going on at Hand Court?

"I am going out for a walk," said Polly suddenly.

"Very well." Drusilla put down her embroidery and stood up.

"No, Drusilla, I wish to go alone."

"That will not do," said Drusilla firmly, "and you know it."

Polly could not bring herself to say she meant to creep up to Hand Court and spy on them. She crossly went to fetch her cloak.

Her steps, however, turned toward the great house.

"I would not go too near Hand Court," said Drusilla. "Miss Ponsonby saw you when you were dressed as a footman and she might recognize you."

Drusilla's good sense was beginning to cause Polly intense irritation. If only there were some way to shake her off.

The day was warm and misty. Little drops of moisture hung like pearls on the trees and bushes. Polly looked at the sky. "I think it is going to rain, Drusilla, and it is a trifle muddy underfoot. Would you be so good as to return and fetch my pattens?"

Drusilla concealed her surprise. Polly was treating her like a servant. But, she reflected, Polly did look out of sorts and was probably not aware of what she was doing.

"Very well," said Drusilla. "I shall not be long."

Now that was wicked of me, thought Polly, watching Drusilla's drooping figure. But I shall not order her around again.

She picked up her skirts and hurried toward the great house, glad of the mist and the shelter of the trees.

She had just reached the edge of the wood which bordered the lawns in front of the house when the marquess and Miss Ponsonby came into view. They had been out riding. The marquess dismounted first

and then held up his arms to assist Miss Ponsonby
from her horse. She fell into them and laughed up at
him, pouting her full lips in open invitation.

Polly clutched a thin branch so hard that it snapped
between her fingers as the marquess bent his mouth
to that inviting one so near his own.

She knew she should turn away, but she stood
there, watching, wretched, miserable.

And then the marquess raised his head and looked
down at Miss Ponsonby with a puzzled look. Miss
Ponsonby had gone quite white. As Polly watched,
she took out a small handkerchief and scrubbed her
mouth, and then walked off into the house.

The marquess stared straight at where Polly was
standing. She was sure he could not see her but she
backed away so hurriedly that she tripped over a
fallen branch and sat down heavily on the wet grass.

"So it was you," said the marquess, standing over
her. "I had this feeling I was being watched and then
I heard a twig snap. You silly girl. Miss Ponsonby
saw you at the ball and might recognize you. You
must stay away from the house until she is gone."

He helped Polly to her feet.

"And when will that be?" asked Polly in a low
voice.

"Today, if I have played my cards aright."

Polly's eyes flew up to meet his. "I do not think
that hugging and kissing her is a way to get rid of
her," she said harshly.

"The best way. I rather took Miss Ponsonby in
dislike when I found her waiting outside Newgate to
view the path of your escape. Such vulgarity does not

appeal to me. She is an enchanting female and led me on, and yet I suspected her secret, and so moved in to frighten her.''

''I do not understand.''

''No normal female would. Let us just say that Miss Ponsonby does not like men.''

''If she does not like men, then why did she pursue you into the country?'' said Polly, exasperated.

''She did not pursue my face and figure but rather my title and fortune. Do not ask me any more questions.''

''When you kiss someone, my lord, can you tell if they don't like men as opposed to just not liking you?''

''I told you not to ask questions. If you go on I shall be forced to silence you in the way I silenced Miss Ponsonby.''

A wicked gleam entered Polly's eyes. ''Tell me about women who do not like men?'' she pursued.

He looked down at her, half amused, half irritated. She was wearing a simple, unhooped gown. Her hair was unpowdered and tied at the nape of her neck with a ribbon. Pearls of moisture gleamed in the heavy tresses of her hair. Her skin was white, almost translucent, and her large eyes fringed with sooty lashes were full of laughter.

He bent to drop a playful kiss on her nose, but she raised her mouth and he kissed her lips instead, lips that were soft and clinging. A yielding and pliant body was molded to his own. He could feel the firmness of her breasts pressed against his chest. He could smell the faint perfume of flowers from her hair.

The passion that took hold of him was so unexpected and so violent that he buried his lips deeper in hers while one strong hand came up to cover her breast.

"Miss Peterson!"

The couple broke apart. Polly looked dazed, the marquess furious with himself.

As Drusilla came hurrying up, holding a pair of wooden pattens, the marquess bowed. "Forgive me, Miss Gentle," he said. "Such behavior will not happen again."

He strode off toward the house. Polly started after him, but Drusilla caught her arm and drew her back just as Mrs. Castle and Mrs. Ponsonby appeared on the front steps.

"Have you gone mad?" whispered Drusilla, her lips trembling.

"I want him," said Polly flatly.

"Come back to the dower house," fussed Drusilla. "Have you been drinking?"

"No, I have not been drinking," said Polly, crossly. "I want Canonby."

"But you can never have him. The difference in rank is too great. He would never marry you."

"I want him on any terms," said Polly striding ahead, forgetting to walk like a lady. "And I shall have him!"

Drusilla ran after her, still clutching the pattens. "Miss Peterson," she called to Polly's retreating back, for Drusilla always called Polly by her alias when she thought there might be servants about. "Please wait until we get home and then try to listen to reason."

But when they were seated in the parlor with the door firmly shut against the servants, Polly looked stubborn and mulish.

"For the love I bear you," said Drusilla urgently, "listen to me. He can only take you as his mistress. What happens when he tires of you? You will be passed from man to man until you end up selling your favors at the playhouse for a glass of gin. I have seen it happen."

"I am prepared to take that risk."

"And what of your quest? What of Meg Jones?" For Polly had told Drusilla of her search.

"Meg is dead," said Polly harshly. "Twice I have faced death on the gallows, Drusilla. I want to live. I want to take what I want now. I do not want to be a lady. I want to be his mistress."

Drusilla began to cry. "I do not understand you, Polly."

"You do not understand me, because I am not a lady and you are," said Polly sadly. She stroked Drusilla's hair. "Do not cry. He has promised you a pension. Come now, the horrible Lady Comfrey's amours were tolerated by you."

"I had no choice," wailed Drusilla. "And I did not love Lady Comfrey."

"I burn for him, with a burning that is like a sickness, Drusilla. Cannot you understand that? The Ponsonbys are leaving. She has given him a disgust of her and they are leaving. I shall watch and wait for my opportunity to see him alone and then I shall ask him to take me. Please do not cry, Drusilla. You will be looked after.''

But Drusilla continued to sob. Polly looked at her sadly and then said, "I am not a virgin, Drusilla. I have lain with a man. You must realize that to be true with the life I have led."

Shock dried Drusilla's tears, and she stared at Polly open-mouthed. "Do not take me in dislike, Drusilla, but do not weep for me. I am no ewe lamb going to the slaughter."

"I h-had n-not r-realized," stammered Drusilla, turning brick red. "It certainly alters the situation."

"Of course it does," said Polly cheerfully. "Now just look on me as another harridan like Lady Comfrey."

"That I cannot do," said Drusilla. "Oh, it is a wicked world and men are cruel. But you must do as you see fit. I shall not stand in your way. Pray excuse me. I must go and lie down."

Polly fought with her conscience as Drusilla trailed from the room. Then she shrugged. There had been a hardening inside her since that escape from Newgate. The world was a shifting sea full of treacherous shoals. If she lived politely and carefully, she might languish in this dower house and maybe, as a great favor, be allowed to dance at his wedding.

A vision of Silas's face rose before her eyes and once more she saw the sunlight shining on the cover of that Bible on the prison floor. "Morals are for ladies," said Polly Jones defiantly to the uncaring walls. "I can't afford 'em."

*   *   *

Two long weeks passed before Polly was to talk to
the marquess again. Although she haunted the grounds,
he kept out of her way, and once, when he was
riding down the drive, he saw her, but did not stop.

Polly had forgotten about her past life, about Meg.
She was consumed with a single-minded desire to get
the marquess to herself.

But her past life had not forgotten about Polly
Jones. Jake and Barney, still en route for India,
prayed that Polly Jones would be dead and forgotten
by the time they returned. But others wanted her
alive.

Mr. Barks's wife had arrived unexpectedly in London. She was a square, mannish woman with a boom-
ing voice, and that voice of hers poured scorn on his
fashionable efforts. Her harsh laugh when she had
seen his stubble-covered chest had hurt his very soul.
But she said that if she were presented at court, then
she would have realized her life's ambition and she
would return to the country.

Mr. Barks was a desperate man.

He was sitting in Mr. Caldicott's home gloomily
wondering what to do when the butler announced the
arrival of "a person calling himself Mr. James."

Mr. Caldicott told his butler he was not at home to
persons of any description. The butler retired to con-
vey that message. The following sounds of a noisy
altercation in the hall made Mr. Caldicott seize his
sword and go to help evict the importunate Mr.
James.

He found himself looking into the white and wasted features of Bertram Pargeter.

"It is all right," he said quickly. "I know this fellow."

He led Bertram inside and shut the door on his startled butler's face.

"Why are you come?" hissed Mr. Caldicott as Mr. Barks leapt from his chair in surprise. "The Runners are still looking for you."

Bertram shrugged. "This isn't Paris," he said. "There are still many parts of the metropolis where I can stroll about in broad daylight." Unlike Paris, London did not have an official police force. Each parish of the city was responsible for its own protection, and twelve had no police at all. Westminster, which was a large area encompassing the West End, usually had eight constables, mostly tradesmen, who served for a year and went on duty every fifteenth night armed with staves and lanterns, or else hired substitutes. The Bow Street thief-takers numbered about six. There was the watch, of course, but that was made up of creaky old men who often had to rely on the good nature of the rabble to pursue and catch anyone.

And yet, thought Mr. Barks uneasily, hundreds upon hundreds were still dragged to the gallows or transported to the colonies.

"What brings you here?" he demanded harshly.

"I am confident I know where Polly Jones is."

"Not again," sighed Mr. Caldicott.

"Hark! I followed Colonel Anderson, who is a close friend of Canonby, to a coffee house. He was talking about the return of a certain Miss Ponsonby to London. This Miss Ponsonby had gone on chance to Shropshire to the marquess's home in the hope of finding him there, which they did. But whatever happened, the Ponsonbys' hopes of a marriage for their daughter came to naught.

"Miss Ponsonby had said to Colonel Anderson t'other night that she had got a glimpse of a very beautiful lady who was residing in the dower house. When she asked the identity of this lady, she was told she was a relative of Canonby. I believe this so-called relative to be Polly Jones. Now, think. We could travel there, and if it is she, we could abduct her, give her to Mother Blanchard for some sport, and then tell the marquess if he wants her back and clear of the gallows then he must pay us a large sum and find favor at court for Mrs. Barks."

"It's all a hum," said Mr. Caldicott uneasily, but Mr. Barks thought dismally of his wife and said eagerly, "It would do no harm to travel there and look."

"I will return to my lodgings and pack a trunk," said Bertram with a smile of satisfaction.

"As you will," said Mr. Caldicott. They discussed plans and Bertram took his leave.

Mr. Barks crossed to the window and watched Bertram standing in the middle of the pavement for all to see, drawing on his gloves.

And then he was witness to one of those many chances of Fate which send the hunted to the gallows. A servant in the earl of Meresly's livery ran past, stopped in his tracks, and swung round, staring

at Bertram in open-mouthed amazement. Bertram was
just strolling away as if he hadn't a care in the world.

"Oh, a pox on it," growled Mr. Barks. "The
fool!"

Mr. Caldicott joined him at the window. In silence
they watched as the servant shouted to someone at
the other end of the street. Bertram, confident in his
security, did not bother to slow his easy gait. Another servant in the Meresly livery ran up. The two
servants jumped on Bertram from behind, throwing
him to the ground and calling for help as they did so.

"Idiot," said Mr. Caldicott. "Complete and utter
idiot. Bad cess to him and Polly Jones."

"I had better go," sighed Mr. Barks. "*She* will be
waiting."

"Let her wait," said Mr. Caldicott suddenly. "She
will forgive all if you find the means to get her to
court."

Mr. Barks looked at him open-mouthed. "You
mean . . . ?"

"Yes, my friend. Oh, yes. The hunt is up!"

CHAPTER FIFTEEN

RUSILLA GENTLE BEGAN TO THINK THAT POLLY had had some sort of brainstorm over the marquess. She was distressed to think that poor Polly had lost her virginity, but on calmer reflection had to admit to herself that it was only to be expected considering the life that Polly had hitherto led. Polly was calm and pleasant and ladylike. Drusilla began to relax and enjoy their quiet and ordered existence.

She did not know that Polly was daily steeling herself to confront the marquess of Canonby.

Polly's passion for the marquess had not abated. Rather, it had grown, tormenting her during the long sleepless nights to the point of anguish.

Love can be a madness, a sickness, and poor Polly forced herself to endure the polite afternoons with the neighbors over the teacups and the long sedate walks about the estate with Drusilla—a still-cautious Drusilla who made sure Polly did not wander anywhere near Hand Court.

And then, despite the sunny weather, Drusilla caught a feverish cold. Polly dutifully nursed her until the fever abated. One afternoon when Drusilla was in a pleasant state of drowsy convalescent lassitude, Polly kissed her cheek and told her to sleep. "What are you going to do?" asked Drusilla.

"I am reading a very exciting novel," said Polly. "I think I will have a quiet afternoon indoors."

She sat beside the bed until Drusilla's regular breathing told her the companion was asleep.

Polly went to her own bedchamber and sat in front of the looking glass. With hands that trembled, she took down her hair and brushed it until it shone. She put on a pretty chintz gown and tied a lace fichu about her shoulders.

Then she made her way downstairs and out of the house, stopping only to ask the footman casually if he knew whether the marquess of Canonby was at home.

"I believe so, miss," said the footman. "He rode out this morning early but I believe I heard him return a half hour ago. A horse went down the drive in the direction of the house."

Polly stepped out of the shadow of the trees into the sunlight of the drive. She turned a corner and walked slowly toward the great house, her skirts fluttering in the light summer wind.

The marquess was sitting at his desk in the library when Polly was announced.

He had been writing letters. He put down his pen

carefully and looked warily at Polly. He was still ashamed of his behavior.

"What can I do for you, Miss Peterson?" he asked. Polly turned and shut the library door, and to his surprise, turned the key in the lock.

Then she turned back and faced him. Her gown was the new length and showed her ankles. She had very pretty ankles, the marquess thought, while wondering why on earth she had locked the door.

"I am come to offer you my services," said Polly.

"There is no need to lock us in to do that," he said, amused. "Besides, are you not comfortable being a lady? I have given up the idea of making you a servant."

"I was not offering my services as a servant."

"Then as what, pray?"

"As your mistress."

He came forward and took her hands in his and gently kissed first one, and then the other. "I am very flattered, my child," he said softly. "But you do not know what you are saying."

Polly held his eyes with a steady gaze. "I am not a virgin, sir," she said.

He dropped her hands and strode back to the desk. "Oh," he said in a colorless voice.

"Yes, you will not find me inexperienced."

Trollop! he thought savagely. *Damned slut and trollop!*

"Get out," he said. "You may stay as my pensioner but do not ever approach me again."

"Why?" Polly's puzzlement would have been funny if he had not been so enraged.

"Because, Polly Jones, I have had my fill of wantons. Get out!" He turned away.

Her lips trembled. She turned and unlocked the door. When he looked up, she had gone.

He sat for a long time in a fury. That he should have put the mantle of his noble protection over such as she! He thought of the one-eyed Jake and shuddered. She must have . . . but how could she?

And yet her lips had been so sweet. He had a sudden memory of the first evening he had met her, of turning her upside down and shaking her, and of that white and rounded delectable bottom.

He picked up the pen again to continue his writing and then looked down in dismay, for he had snapped the pen in half.

Polly sat in the parlor in blind misery while the light faded outside and the birds fell silent. She thought she would die from very shame. Why had she lied to him? But she had thought he would not touch her if he knew her to be a virgin. She had not for a moment guessed her manufactured experience would set up such disgust in him. After all, men were known to lust after impure women. The pure might gain their respect but not their passion.

The door handle rattled and Polly rose with a weary sigh. She had locked it, not wanting to be disturbed by the servants. "Wait!" she called.

She rose and went to open the door. She felt as stiff and sore as if he had beaten her.

Her footman stood outside. "His lordship's com-

pliments, miss, and he desires your presence. I shall
fetch the carriage.''

"No matter," said Polly, her heart hammering
against her ribs. "I shall walk."

Drusilla, waking at the sound of the front door
closing, called for Polly. A housemaid came in and
said that Miss Peterson had been summoned to Hand
Court. Drusilla nodded, but after the housemaid had
left, she began to pray—to pray that Polly would not
pursue her mad idea of becoming Canonby's mistress.

There was a full moon above the black lacy tracery
of the trees as Polly walked toward the great house.
Her misery had fled. The thought of seeing him
again, even though he might curse her, lent her feet
wings.

He opened the massive front door to her himself as
though he had been watching for her coming. There
were no servants about. He silently took her hand
and led her up the stairs. His face in the golden light
of the oil lamp on the first landing was taut and
strained.

Up again to the second floor and then he held open
a door and pushed Polly inside.

She found herself in his bedchamber. The huge
four-poster bed had the curtains drawn back and the
blankets turned down. A small applewood fire crackled on the hearth and a branch of candles burned on
the mantel, their steady tongues of flame reflected in
the looking glass behind.

"I have decided to take your offer, Polly Jones,"
he said. "I will retire to the powder closet to undress. You may undress here beside the fire."

Polly watched him in dismay until he had closed the door of the powder closet behind him. There was evidently not going to be any tenderness or love. She was going to be treated like the sort of woman she had pretended to be.

There was still time to run away, or time to stay and tell him the truth.

But she was so sure she could make him want her as much as she wanted him.

Shivering a little with fear, she took off her red leather shoes, then unfastened her gown and let it fall to the floor. She then unfastened the tapes of her stomacher and unbuttoned her linen undervest, and both garments joined her dress on the floor to be shortly followed by her petticoat, leaving her attired only in her thin muslin shift and flesh-colored stockings with blue silk garters.

She was standing with one foot on a chair, unrolling the first of her stockings, when he walked in.

She looked over her shoulder and then blushed. He was stark naked. Her hands shook and she looked at him blindly.

"Allow me," he said softly. He lifted her up and sat down with her on his lap and rolled off one stocking and then the other.

He eased her forward on his knees and then pulled the shift over her head and threw it on top of the little pile of clothes on the floor. The firelight flickered over her naked body, outlining the curve of her hips and the swell of her generous bosom.

If he had treated her like the trollop he believed her to be, Polly would have snatched up her clothes

and cried out the truth. But he gave a little sigh and
buried his mouth in hers, and all that pent-up passion
of Polly's grew to a searing flame. He lifted her
tenderly in his arms, still kissing her, and laid her
down on top of the bed before climbing in beside her
and taking her in his arms.

His long fingers were clever and sensitive and his
lips traced a wandering seductive course across her
body. He spent a long time exploring her mouth and
kissing her breasts and neck. Polly, one quivering
mass of sweet sensation, was barely aware that his
questing hands had moved lower. She moved wan-
tonly against him, each intimacy making her crave
more.

His searching, probing hands suddenly stilled. His
whole body went rigid. She continued to kiss him
passionately until the very coldness of his lack of
response made her stop. She looked up at him. His
eyes in the candlelight glittered with green fire. "Polly
Jones," he said through his teeth. "You are a virgin."

He rolled away from her and swung his legs out of
bed and sat with his back to her, his head in his
hands. "You would not have touched me had you
known I was a virgin," said Polly in a dry whisper.

He stood up and wrenched the coverlet from under
her and threw it over her naked body. He went to a
wardrobe and pulled out a dressing gown and shrugged
himself into it.

Then he went back and sat on the edge of the bed.

"You should not have lied to me," he said.

"Do I not please you?" Polly's eyes looked almost black as she looked up at him.

He shook his head as though to clear it. "I must try to talk some sense into you. You are still a virgin. That makes you marriageable . . . not to me, of course. If you stay quietly at the dower house for about, say, two years until the people of the neighborhood become so accustomed to your presence they will have forgotten you do not belong here, then I will provide you with a dowry and arrange a marriage for you to someone suitable."

Polly winced as though beneath a blow.

"Now, I shall leave the room and let you dress again in decency and privacy. I will then take you back to the dower house."

Polly wet her dry lips. "You cannot love me," she said. It was a statement, not a question, but he replied with a shake of his head.

He rose to his feet and went into the powder closet and shut the door.

Polly felt like the slut she had pretended to be. She had lost any chance of friendship, of respect. She put on her clothes very quickly and then sat waiting in the chair by the fire, her back ramrod straight.

He said not a word when he returned and conducted her down the stairs and out into the moonlit night. They walked down the drive in silence, each at opposite sides of it.

When they reached the dower house, Polly turned and dropped a low curtsy. "My apologies, my lord," she said. "You must find me a wearisome charge." And with her head held high, she opened the door of the dower house and disappeared from his sight.

The marquess walked away. His lips still tasted of

Polly, and his palms still tingled with the feel of all that silky skin. Never in all his long experience had he been presented with such generous burning warmth and passion. Marriage to such as she was totally out of the question. The coat of arms above the door of his home shone in the moonlight, reminding him sternly of what was due to his name.

He let himself in and walked up the stairs, trying to banish the thought of her from his mind. His bed still smelled of her perfume. There, on his pillow, had she lain, the long tresses of her hair shining in the candlelight.

He felt bowed down with an immeasurable feeling of loss. She was not only immoral, she was amoral. She stole and lied. She consorted with villains. He would talk to Miss Gentle on the morrow and see that Polly was schooled in moral values. In two years' time, she would be a fitting consort for some respectable squire or country lawyer.

Polly awoke from a fitful sleep early the following morning. She rose and dressed, suddenly anxious to escape from the house before Drusilla should wake and possibly ask questions.

She remembered a red rose bush which grew in profusion by the south lodge and decided to go and cut some flowers to decorate the parlor. She moved slowly as if just recovered from an accident. Shame and despair made her feel ill.

She walked to the south lodge, glad of the warmth of the sun on her body. She tried to face up to the thought of life without any hope of his love, but the thought was so painful it made her want to cry. Meg's face seemed to rise before her. Poor Meg. Polly shook her head, weary with shame and guilt. She hoped Meg was not able to look down from heaven and see the hopeless sorry mess her foundling charge was in.

She took a sharp pair of scissors from her apron and started to cut the roses, placing them in a basket she had brought with her. She heard the sound of a carriage approaching and resolutely kept her face turned to the rose bush. She was not prepared to face any callers.

The carriage stopped outside the gates and she heard the lodgekeeper going out to find out who it was.

She was just reaching for another bloom when she heard a sharp cry and a thud. She dropped both basket and roses and ran to the gates. On the other side stood a travelling carriage. There was no coachman on the box and no face looked out of the window. In front of the neighing, pawing horses and right against the closed iron gates lay the body of the lodgekeeper, Mr. Rathbone. Polly, thinking he must have had a seizure, ran into the lodge house by the back door and out through the front, which was on the other side of the gates.

She knelt over Mr. Rathbone and turned him over. Blood poured down from a wound on his forehead. Polly whipped around and stood up to see if there was anyone in the carriage. A movement to her left startled her, but she was too late. A cruel blow from a cudgel caught her on the side of the head. The world reeled dizzily, and then went completely black.

The marquess of Canonby rose early that morning as well. His first thought was that the sunshine of a new day would soon banish his muddled feelings and worry about Polly. Instead, he was struck by such an intense feeling of yearning that for a moment he felt he could hardly breathe.

It would not work, he told himself. Passion would burn out and leave him with a stranger who lied and stole. On the other hand, how could he bear to see her wed to anyone else? Damn his great name. He could do as he pleased. He could . . . his mind raced . . . yes, he could take Polly to, say, Italy, and there they could be married by some consul and stay for a few years until the world had forgotten about Polly Jones. He would need to change her name, to provide her with another identity, but money could always do that. He dressed quickly. There was a growing fear in the back of his mind that she might have run away.

When he reached the dower house, a housemaid told him that Miss Peterson had gone out very early to pick roses at the south lodge and that Miss Gentle was still asleep.

Relieved that he would have a chance to talk to Polly alone, he hurried in the direction of the south lodge.

The huge rose bush rioted in all its glory by the gate of the south lodge. He saw the basket of roses spilled across the drive and felt a stab of dread. It dawned on him that he had been so taken up with his

relationship with Polly Jones that he had almost forgotten she was a hunted woman.

And then he saw his lodgekeeper, lying against the
gates.

He ran through the lodge house and out the other
side and bent over the fallen Mr. Rathbone. There
were the marks of carriage wheels in the beaten earth
of the entrance. Mr. Rathbone groaned faintly and
stirred.

"Rathbone," said the marquess urgently. "What
happened?"

The man moaned again. The marquess picked him
up and carried him into the lodge and placed him on
his bed. Then he took a gun from over the mantel in
the kitchen, primed it, went outside and fired it in the
air.

He went back in and scooped a ladle of water from
a pail in the kitchen, soaked a cloth in it, and carried
both into the bedroom. A gamekeeper, who had heard
the shot, came running in.

"Rouse all the staff," said the marquess. "Send
help to me here. Then fetch the apothecary as fast as
you can. And get my hunter here as fast as you can."

He gently sponged the wound on Mr. Rathbone's
head. The man stirred again and this time his eyes
opened fully. "My lord," he said weakly. "It was
two men. They struck me down. Just before I lost
consciousness, one man said, 'No call to do that. We
could have left the carriage down the road and climbed
over the wall.' The other said, 'There she is,' and
that's all I know."

"Lie still, Rathbone," said the marquess. He went

out and looked at the marks of those carriage wheels
and then at two rose petals lying on the ground.

He returned to the lodgekeeper's side. "Rathbone,"
he said urgently. "The man who spoke. Describe his
voice."

Mr. Rathbone tried to struggle up but the marquess
pressed him back against the pillows with a gentle
hand. "He spoke like a gentleman," said Mr.
Rathbone. "I got a blurred glimpse o' them. They
were foppishly dressed. One's hair was dressed so
high it looked like a mountain, and he was wearing
pink powder. Oh, and when the other said, 'There
she is,' the first said. 'Yes.' Only he said it funny,
more like, 'Yaas.' "

There was the sound of running feet coming down
the drive and the neighing of a horse. The marquess
went out to give orders to his staff. Then he swung
himself up into the saddle of his hunter and set off,
riding hard, riding desperately, crouched over the
saddle, racing in pursuit down the long miles which
led to London.

Mr. Barks and Mrs. Caldicott were nearing London with their prize. They had taken a long circuitous
route, hiding out in hedge taverns, changing horses at
small unfashionable posting houses, but never stopping anywhere for the night. They were tired and
weary, but exultant. They had done it! And Polly
Jones lay trussed up like a hen on the floor of the
carriage.

Apart from checking occasionally to see that she
was still alive, they were otherwise indifferent to her

welfare. For a long time after she recovered consciousness, Polly was too sick to worry about anything other than the stabbing pain in her head and the heaving sickness of her stomach. The cords they had bound her with cut deep and the gag on her mouth was cruelly tight.

She heard the noise and sound of the London streets again. Hard to tell what time of day it was, for the curtains on the carriage windows were tightly drawn.

After an eternity of travel, the carriage stopped. Two men, not Caldicott or Barks, climbed into the carriage and proceeded to stuff her into a large smelly sack. She closed her eyes and feigned unconsciousness. She felt herself being lifted up and out. Then her head was bumped against a wall as the man carrying her appeared to negotiate a narrow corridor. Then she was dumped down and the sack was drawn from her body.

She peered up through her eyelashes into that all-too-familiar motherly face of Mrs. Blanchard. "What have we here?" she heard Mrs. Blanchard demanding. "What have you done with her? What a mess! Could you not have taken better care of the goods?"

"This is no way to thank us," said Mr. Barks huffily. "We have been monstrous brave."

"You had best leave her with me until I have her restored to health and prettified, else Canonby won't want her back."

Polly felt herself go weak with relief. Canonby might hate her, but he would certainly not leave her in the clutches of Mrs. Blanchard.

She continued to feign unconsciousness after Mr. Barks and Mr. Caldicott had left. Two of the prostitutes stripped her and bathed her, then dressed her in a nightgown.

Polly at last decided to open her eyes. She was in the grip of a raging hunger and did not want to be left for the night without food.

"I am hungry," she said.

"Found your voice, eh?" jeered Mrs. Blanchard. "Well, you shall eat of the best, my pretty, for you will need all your strength for what lies in store for you."

Polly was given a large plate of cold beef and a bottle of wine. She ate the beef but asked for water instead of wine. Finally, her captors withdrew and she was left alone in the high barred room she had been kept in before.

She settled herself down to sleep. All she had to do was stay alive until the marquess came to buy her back.

In the morning, she was arrayed in a stiff cream silk dress. It had a ribbed satin stripe and was embroidered with flower sprays. The petticoat was matching. The sleeves had double embroidered ruffles. They must be worried he will not want me back unless I am grandly dressed, thought Polly. She behaved in a docile manner and ate a good breakfast. She was resigned to her captivity.

When Mrs. Blanchard entered with two henchmen, Polly surveyed her calmly, although she could not help glancing at the henchmen in the hope of surprising some sympathy for her plight in their eyes. But they were small, wiry men like acrobats and their eyes were flat and reptilian.

"Now, my dear," cooed Mrs. Blanchard. "Anything you want, just ring the bell, for I am monstrous pleased with you, my chuck. You will make me a fortune."

"Canonby might not pay."

"You will have made me thousands before my lord finds out where you are."

Polly looked at her wide-eyed. "You're going to earn your keep, Polly. The men who want to mount Polly Jones are prepared to pay the earth to do so. I have six of them booked for the early evening and many more for later in the night."

"You cannot mean it," gasped Polly. "I am a wanted felon. If you have put it about that I am here, then the authorities will be alerted and you will go to Tyburn along with me."

"I know my business," said Mrs. Blanchard, "and my business is with the Mohawks."

Polly blenched. The Mohawks were gangs of young aristocratic men who roamed the London streets, tormenting, torturing and raping the poor and defenseless.

"Oh, I know what you're thinking," said Mrs. Blanchard, "that there won't be much left of you by the time Canonby comes to call. But whether he will still be prepared to pay for you or not is a small matter. You will have earned me enough to set me up for life."

She went out with her henchmen and locked the door.

Polly sat and shook with terror.

Then, after a long time, she began to think of Meg, and for the first time Polly began to feel almost angry with her kind protector. Why had Meg let her run so wild? Why had Meg never bothered to instill any rudiments of right and wrong into her young and heedless head? The answer, although Polly did not know it, was that Meg thought Polly's aristocratic blood would be enough to turn her into a lady, provide her with a fund of social manners and courtesies. Being in awe of Polly's noble birth, Meg felt it was not her place to bridle or chastise the girl. Polly's inherent good nature had managed to stop her from being as spoilt and willful as any pampered young miss. Then she thought of Silas. Silas would say she had only to ask God for help

"Oh, very well," she said aloud to no one in particular. She knelt down beside the bed and told God to hurry up and get her out of her predicament. Then she waited. Nothing happened. The door did not fly open, no angel voices spoke to her.

"Right, God," said Polly Jones. "I shall try to help myself but I wish, oh, I wish I were not so very frightened."

She paced up and down the room. She heard voices outside and pressed her ear against the panels of the door. "You stay and guard the place, Willis," she heard Mother Blanchard say. "No point in letting my girls stay idle because of our celebrity. No men allowed in until six o'clock, but I will be back long before then. The ones that wants to have Polly, take their money and cross their names off the book and

get them to form an orderly line on the stairs. I'd
have put her in one of the better bedrooms, but they
haven't got bars on the windows.''

Polly remembered Jake saying something about the
scandal of the prostitutes who roamed the parks of
London during the day under the stern eye of their
abbess. Their job was to solicit as many men as
possible, even handing out cards, like business cards,
with the name and address of the brothel.

She stayed with her ear pressed against the door
until she heard the sounds of departure downstairs.

''I think, God,'' said Polly, beginning to pace up
and down again, ''I really think I am going to get out
of here, and if I don't, I am somehow going to take
this evil building down with me, like Samson. Far
better to die clean than waste away under the hands
of those villainous Mohawks.''

She pulled at the bars of the windows, wishing she
had a file.

''Let me see,'' she said, still speaking aloud. ''That
harridan said I was to ring for anything I want. There
is no bell.''

She leaned against the door and began to scream
for help at the top of her voice. Soon she heard
Willis's voice on the other side calling, ''Stow your
whids. What's to do?''

''A spider!'' screamed Polly. ''There's a spider
under my bed.''

Willis began to laugh. He had never believed those
tales of Polly's escape from Newgate. He was sure
she had bribed her jailors to help her. Then her voice
came again, ''If you kill the spider, I will let you

have me first." Her voice grew coaxing. "I won't tell Mrs. Blanchard."

Willis half turned away and then thought what caché he would have in the underworld if he could brag he had taken her first—he, Willis, and not some lord. He held his gun firmly in his hand and unlocked the door.

Polly was standing with her hand to her brow. She looked paper-white and ready to faint. "It's under the bed," she whispered. "Please, oh, please. I cannot bear the things."

Grinning indulgently, he moved past her, still holding the gun. He took his eyes off her for one moment to glance toward the bed—and that was his undoing.

Polly Jones brought a heavy earthenware chamber pot round from behind her back and brought it down with all her force on his head. It gave a satisfying crumping sound as Willis slumped to the floor.

She bent over him and detached a ring of keys from the belt at his waist.

Holding the gun, she ran downstairs, toward freedom. But she stopped short before she reached the street door. Why should this evil palace of sin be allowed to stand? thought Polly. And what would hurt Mrs. Blanchard most? Why, loss of property and loss of money. She searched the downstairs, opening up the locked doors with the keys she had taken from Willis, until she came on Mrs. Blanchard's parlor. There she found a strongbox. She put the gun in her petticoat pocket and then heaved the box up in her arms and carried it up and up, and dumped it out on the roof by climbing through an attic window.

Polly intended to set fire to the house. If anyone to do with the brothel came running, the first thing they would do would be to rescue the money, but the money Polly intended to melt in the flames. She could not escape through the streets for fear of discovery. She would escape over the roof or go to her death with the house. At that moment, Polly did not care whether she lived or died, provided she was able to strike a blow against her tormenter.

Valuable time was lost tying up Willis and bumping his body down the stairs and heaving it out to a stone wash house in the back yard where she locked him in. At least there was a chance he would not be burned to death.

Driven by Furies, Polly returned to that parlor, found a tinder box on the mantel and lit a taper. There was a lurid pornographic book lying on a table. Polly ripped it into shreds, page by page, and then set it alight.

She walked from room to sordid room, emptying the contents of oil lamps on the floor. Then she retreated up the stairs as the blaze began to take hold.

CHAPTER SIXTEEN

THE REVEREND JOHN CARPENTER WALKED UP and down outside the Mereslys' mansion in Hanover Square and wondered what to do. His visit to England was nearly at an end. He had called at Upper Batchett, and there, to his horror, had learned that Lady Mary Palfrey, or Polly Jones as everyone knew her, was as famous as the king. He heard how she had stolen, escaped the gallows, only to masquerade as a footman and steal again.

His heart went out to the Mereslys. He had learned that the earl and countess were now completely recovered from their illnesses, and yet he had not the heart to tell them of Meg's letter. Surely Meg must have been rambling. Like Meg, Mr. Carpenter idealized the aristocracy and thought that any child with blue blood in its veins must, despite surroundings and upbringing, grow up to be a lady, mysteriously endowed with the right accent and a gift for playing the harpsichord and executing pretty watercolors. The fact that there were tales of the dissolute goings-on of the aristocracy in the newspapers every day did not alter his opinion. Set against all this was his sharp and clear recollection of Meg as a thoroughly good and dutiful woman. Yet surely the Mereslys would be better left in ignorance of such a child.

"There he goes again," said Lady Emily Palfrey to her sister Josephine. "Round and round the square. Do you think he is looking for our escaped Polly?"

Josephine looked over her sister's shoulder. "It is almost as if he is debating whether to call or not. Ah! See. Here he comes. Quickly, let us belowstairs and hide behind that screen in the hall."

They had just managed to get into hiding when the knocker on the door sounded.

"I am Reverend John Carpenter, and I wish to see the earl of Meresly," came a man's voice.

"I will take your card to his lordship and see if he will grant you an audience," answered the butler.

Then Joseph and Emily stiffened as their mother's voice sounded from the upper landing.

"You must not trouble Meresly with every stray visitor. What is this person's business?"

"My business concerns your daughter. I trust I find myself addressing Lady Lydia Meresly?" said Mr. Carpenter.

"My daughter?" The countess gave a thin laugh. The twins heard the swish of her skirts as she came swiftly down the stairs. "Come into the library, Mr. . . . ?"

"Carpenter, my lady. The Reverend John Carpenter, of Boston."

The twins heard the library door shut behind them.

"Quickly," hissed Josephine. "I must hear what goes on."

They darted back behind the library screen as the butler came out and Lady Lydia could be heard saying, "I am not to be disturbed by anyone." The door closed again.

Back out came the twins, and pressed their ears against the door.

Fortunately for them, Mr. Carpenter had a resonant voice, used to giving sermons from the pulpit of a large church.

"If you will read that letter, my lady," they heard him say, "you will see that one Meg Jones of the parish of Upper Batchett claims that the girl she brought up as her niece, Polly Jones, is in fact your first and legitimate daughter, Lady Mary Palfrey."

There was a long silence while the listening sisters gripped each other and exchanged startled glances.

There was a crackling of parchment and then Lady Lydia laughed. "My dear Mr. Carpenter. Do you know who this Polly Jones is? A convicted thief, an escaped felon!"

"I am aware of that, my lady, which is why I have taken all this time to dare to approach you."

"The whole story is wicked nonsense. Take yourself off, Mr. Carpenter. A man of the cloth such as yourself should be bitterly ashamed to waste my time with such a tale."

There was a heavy step on the stair above and the

earl's voice said, "What are you young ladies doing eavesdropping?"

"Oh, papa," cried Josephine. "There is a reverend gentleman in the library who claims that Polly Jones is mama's legitimate daughter."

"What!" The earl pushed past them and lumbered into the library.

Lady Lydia turned white. "This gentleman has just been asking for a donation for his church," she said, throwing Mr. Carpenter a warning look.

"You are lying, mama," said Josephine gleefully, "and you know that lying is wrong. You see, we know Polly Jones is our sister."

"We do?" asked Emily faintly and got a savage pinch on the arm from her sister in reply.

The earl was in one of his clearheaded and lucid periods.

Mr. Carpenter silently handed him Meg's letter.

"Are we talking about the notorious Polly Jones who stole from me and escaped from Newgate Prison?" asked the earl.

"Oh, yes, papa," said Josephine. "But she had to steal, for she was destitute. We visited her in Newgate and she begged us to find out what happened to Meg, for Meg Jones had two bruises on her neck the day she died."

"This is wicked nonsense," said Lady Lydia savagely. "When and where am I supposed to have given birth to this child?"

"We worked that out," said Josephine. "It would be when papa was away at the wars."

"Listen to me, Meresly," begged Lady Lydia, her

eyes swimming with tears. "You must believe me.
There is no proof."

"Yes there is," said Josephine, crossing her fingers behind her back.

"There is?" exclaimed Emily, staring at her sister
in awe.

Josephine looked at her mother and thought of all
the beatings and snubs and cruelty. "I found a poacher
from Upper Batchett," she lied. "He was there the
night you had that baby." For Josephine had cleverly
guessed that if Meg lived in Upper Batchett and had
taken the baby away, then Lady Lydia must have
given birth to it at Meresly Manor.

The earl looked down at his trembling wife. "You
will tell me the full story, Lydia. You will tell me the
truth. If you do not, then I shall have you arrested for
denying your own daughter her birthright."

Lady Lydia seemed to crumple up in the chair and
grow small. "I did it for you, Meresly. You would
rant and rave and say you must have a son and that
women who bred only daughters were not women at
all. You said if I did not bear you sons, you would
cast me off. After you left for the wars, I found I
was with child. I travelled to Meresly Manor. I had
cleverly concealed my condition. I told the servants I
was going to visit Lady Jeffries in the north. I quar-
relled with the servants before I left and insisted on
hiring a carriage and renting grooms so that the
household servants would not know where I went.

"I remembered Meg Jones. I met her first when I
was a little girl visiting my parents' friends in
Hackminster and she told my fortune. I told her I

would pay her well to deliver me of the child in
secret. If it was a girl, she was to kill it. But she did
not. She came to me on the last day of her life. She
had learned I had subsequently given you twin daughters and you had not turned me off. She begged me
to accept Polly as my own. I was frightened. I told
her I would kill her and the girl if she came near me
again. I thought you would never forgive me for
concealing the birth or for ordering the child to be
killed. I put my hands round her scrawny old neck
and shook her and shook her. It was only to frighten
her. Why do you all look at me so? I could not do
anything else.''

"Your etui," said the earl heavily. "She did not
steal that purse. You threw it at her feet.''

Lady Lydia nodded.

"And Bertram Pargeter, who is to hang next week?''

"He saw me,'' said Lady Lydia in a dry whisper.
"He said I must let him lie with me or he would
tell.''

The earl slumped down and buried his head in his
hands.

"I think, papa, you would find some action cheering,'' said Josephine.

"Oh, yes, indeed,'' said Emily, putting an arm
about her sister's waist.

"You must issue a proclamation that Polly is your
daughter and innocent of the crimes against her and
you must drop the charges against Mr. Pargeter.
There is no need to wash poor deranged mama's dirty
linen in public. You must simply say Polly was
snatched away by gypsies and found by this Meg

Jones who kept her secret until after the grave, when a letter she wrote to Mr. Carpenter reached him.''

Mr. Carpenter looked uneasily at the two Meresly daughters as they stood with their arms twined about each other's waists, at their happy shining eyes, and felt that, in their way, the twins were far greater monsters than their mother.

Mr. Barks was sitting with his wife on his knee. She was so heavy that he was sure the blood had stopped circulating in his legs, but he felt he could bear it all. Mrs. Barks was pleased with him and had called him ''her clever, little darling.'' For, without going into details, he had told her that Canonby would be shortly calling to provide her with an entrée to the royal drawing room.

She kissed his cheek and admired his pink hair, which was piled up in a tall sugar-loaf shape on his head. Only the week before, she had been shouting at him that he looked like an idiot.

''A little brandy perhaps, my sweet?'' he murmured.

She coyly got to her feet and simpered down at him. ''I shall fetch it with my own fair hands.'' She waggled her fingers at him, then blew him a saucy kiss and lumbered from the room.

Mr. Barks let out a sigh of pure satisfaction. All was well with the world.

The door opened again—but it was not his wife who stood on the threshold. The marquess of Canonby stood with a face like the devil and a drawn sword in his hand.

''Where is she?'' demanded the marquess.

Mr. Barks quailed and then rallied. After all, he held all the aces.

"Wouldn't you like to know," he jeered.

The marquess's sword flashed once. It sliced right through Mr. Barks's pink hair. The top flew off and went sailing across the room in a cloud of pink dust.

Mr. Barks, his face a muddy color, stared at the marquess. The cushion over which his hair had been piled stuck up exposed on the top of his head.

"Now," said the marquess, "let's see what other little bits I can slice off." He drew back his sword and pointed it at the most vulnerable part of Mr. Barks's body.

"No!" screamed Mr. Barks. "I'll tell you. She is at Mother Blanchard's."

The look in the marquess's green eyes was so terrible that he was sure his last moment had come.

But the marquess turned on his heel and collided with Mrs. Barks. "Oh, Lord Canonby," she twittered.

The marquess pushed her rudely aside. "Get out of my way, silly old woman," he said.

Mrs. Barks stood with her mouth open and then slowly her eyes narrowed and turned in the direction of her shaking husband.

Polly Jones stood high on the roof of the blazing brothel. Dimly through the smoke, and far below her, she could see the anguished face of Mrs. Blanchard. Polly tugged at the lid of the strongbox and to her surprise it opened. It was full to the brim with gold coins and jewels.

Acting as if in a dream, Polly picked up handfuls

of coin and jewels and sent them down to the crowd
below, handful after handful, until the smoky sky
seemed to be filled with rubies and pearls, sapphires,
emeralds and diamonds and a rain of gold coins.

The fire engine of the Sun Fire Insurance Company came charging into the street, driving through
the milling crowds who were scrabbling in the cobbles for jewels and guineas. The firemen in their blue
liveries and silver badges seemed like angels to the
desperate Mrs. Blanchard. The fire chief climbed
down from the engine, patted the nose of one of the
great Shire horses harnessed to it and unclasped a
leather-covered notebook. "Name?" he demanded.

"Blanchard, you fool," screamed the frantic abbess.

"Blanchard. Let me see, Bingham, Bland, ah,
Blanchard. Sorry, you ain't paid any insurance for
the last year. Come along, men."

The fire engine swung about and began to make its
way off with Mrs. Blanchard weeping with rage and
hanging onto the back of it as if she were trying to
pull it back.

"Polly Jones, Polly Jones," muttered the crowd,
the mutter swelling and growing louder. The prostitutes had talked.

"Polly Jones," they yelled. "Three cheers for
Polly Jones!"

The marquess pushed his way down the street. The
crowd was laughing and cheering and pointing up to
where a still figure stood veiled in thick smoke on the
roof.

The marquess ran for the door of the brothel but
was beaten back by the flames. He ran into the

evacuated premises next door, kicking down locked door after locked door until he reached the skylight at the top of the stairs and smashed it open with the hilt of his sword.

He heaved himself through it.

Polly was standing at the edge of the roof, watching the crowd. She seemed dazed and her eyes were blank.

He edged his way toward her.

"Come along, Polly," he said.

She gave a tired hiccuping sigh. Part of the roof fell in and a wicked greedy tongue of flame leapt up.

He seized her round the waist and she came to life and fought him off with mad strength.

"Leave me to die!" she cried. "Newgate waits below for me."

"I will fight for your life. I will marry you. Polly, you must come with me."

"No," said Polly, holding her arms tightly round her shivering body. "Leave me to die."

"I love you," he shouted.

"What?"

"I love you!" yelled the marquess of Canonby.

She wound her arms round his neck and kissed him full on the lips, while the crowd swayed and cheered.

He lifted her up in his arms.

The building he had entered to get to the roof was now ablaze as well, although the Royal Exchange Assurance Fire Brigade was dealing with it, the owner having, unlike Mrs. Blanchard, paid up his dues.

Stumbling over the tiles, he walked across the
rooftops. He came to an open attic window and lifted
her gently through it and then followed her.

"We will face them together," he said. "Come."

As they made their way down, shots sounded from
the street, followed by a great silence.

He opened the door and led her out, then stood,
grim-faced, with his arm about her shoulders. The
militia were holding at bay the angry mob who,
without the restraining presence of the militia, would
have carried Polly off to freedom. There were four
Runners, three constables, and a magistrate. The constables held fetters and manacles and chains at the
ready.

In a clear voice, the magistrate began to read out a
long list of charges.

The marquess held her tighter, wondering what to
do. He should never have brought her down. He should
have tried to escape across the roofs to safety with
her and then tried to get her out of the country.

"The charges have been dropped by the earl of
Meresly," cried a shrill voice from the end of the
street. The magistrate stopped his recitation and looked
up in surprise. There were shouts of, "Let them
through. Polly Jones is pardoned."

The crowd parted, the militia opened their ranks
and the earl of Meresly, shambling and shocked, and
supported on either side by his daughters, walked
toward Polly. The marquess thought he looked like
King Lear.

"It is true," said the earl heavily. "This is not
Polly Jones, but my long-lost daughter, Lady Mary."

"You may kiss us, sister dear," said Josephine primly.

All the tears she had kept back for so long came gushing out of Polly's eyes as she fell weeping into her sisters' arms.

Emily and Josephine exchanged startled glances and then pushed Polly away.

"Really, Polly," said Josephine severely. "If we had guessed you would turn out to be so *miss-ish*, we would not have bothered to help you!"

EPILOGUE

N̶O ONE IN THE WHOLE OF LONDON WAS MORE
relieved and delighted than Silas Brewer to
read of Polly Jones's pardon. Ever since her
escape from Newgate, he and his wife had lived in
fear and dread of a knock at the door and a voice
accusing Silas of helping the notorious criminal to
escape.

He did not learn of it until a week after Polly's
dramatic descent from the roof. He had been out on
the road in his cart.

His wife had saved a newspaper for him and he
read the account of her pardon over and over again.
"She'll have left that Bible I gave her," he said,
putting down the paper. "Reckon I'll buy her another
as a wedding present."

"You'll do no such thing," said Mrs. Brewer
sharply. "The weather's turning and the children

need shoes. Besides, she's Lady Mary Palfrey now, and soon she'll be the marchioness of Canonby. A great lady like that'll have forgotten your very existence, Mr. Brewer.''

Silas sniffed and picked up the newspaper again and barricaded himself and his dreams behind it. He thought wistfully of how grand it would be if Polly had not forgotten him and would invite him to dance at her wedding. There was money enough left over from that purse that gentleman had given his wife to buy the children shoes. Then he shook his head. His wife had the right of it. Polly could now buy scores of Bibles and never know the difference.

There came a tremendous knocking at the door. Silas jumped to his feet and clasped his wife in his arms and they both stood trembling. Then he put her away from him with a shaky laugh.

"You forgit, Mrs. Brewer," he said, "we have nothing to fear now."

He opened the door and stared up in amazement at the tall figure looming over him. A gentleman dressed in a green coat heavily encrusted with gold embroidery stood smiling down at him. He took off his gold-laced three-cornered hat and made Silas a courtly bow. "Mr. Brewer?"

"Oh, yes," gasped Silas, putting his wrinkled work-worn hands to his mouth and looking for all the world like the monkey that spoke no evil.

"My name is Canonby. I am come to invite you to my wedding."

Silas gaped at him. Then he saw the street was crowded with all his neighbors. He puffed out his thin chest and stood back. "Pray step inside, my lord," he said.

The marquess ducked his head and walked into the dark little kitchen, where the children hid behind Mrs. Brewer's skirts and peeped out at him.

"This is the marquess of Canonby," said Silas, his voice trembling. "He's come to ask us to his wedding."

Mrs. Brewer tried to speak but only a strangled sound came out. The marquess was so tall and so magnificent. Their one tallow candle on the kitchen table sent sparks of green fire shining from the emerald he wore among the cascades of fine lace at his throat.

"Get his lordship some ale," said Silas sharply. The marquess drew out a chair and sat down. Silas collapsed into a chair opposite him.

The marquess drew out a heavy purse and placed it between them. "There is gold for you," he said. "It will go to furnish wedding clothes for you and your good wife. Lady Mary wishes you and your family to move to my estate in Shropshire, where there is a cottage in the grounds for you and your family."

Mrs. Brewer shyly put down a mug of ale in front of the marquess. He smiled and toasted her health.

Silas found his voice. "I don't know rightly how to thank you."

"The thanks are mine," said the marquess, tossing off the ale. "You have been very kind to Lady Mary. After the wedding, my secretary shall call on you to make arrangements to transfer you to the country."

"And Lady Mary is well?" asked Silas.

"Very well," said the marquess, getting to his feet.

"Tell me," said Silas. "It said nothing in the paper about that wicked woman, Blanchard. What happened to her?"

The marquess turned to go. "The mob hanged her from a lamp bracket at the end of the street."

But as he drove off, the marquess reflected that he did not think Polly was very happy. As befitted her new position, she had taken up residence in her family's home in Hanover Square. Drusilla had arrived from the country to join her. Every time the marquess called on Polly, she was chaperoned strictly by Drusilla, which was just as it should be, but he longed to get her alone and find out what was causing those shadows under her eyes.

Certainly, the Meresly town house did not have a particularly joyous atmosphere. The outwardly exonerated but privately damned Lady Lydia remained isolated in her apartment with only her French maid for company. That odd pair, Polly's little sisters, always seemed to be jumping out of corners. At times, the marquess wondered whether they were quite sane.

He presented his card at the Meresly mansion and was ushered into the drawing room.

Polly was looking listless, a piece of embroidery lying idle on her lap.

"Would you care to come driving with me, Lady Mary?" said the marquess abruptly. "The air would do you good."

Drusilla rose to her feet. "I shall fetch our cloaks,

Lady Mary," she said and went out, carefully leaving the door wide open.

The marquess seized Polly's hand. "Come!" he said. "Now!"

"But Drusilla . . ."

"Damn Drusilla."

He pulled her out of the room and then hustled her into the street.

"I shall not be driving this time," he called up to his coachman on the box. He opened the carriage door, helped Polly inside, and then climbed in after her. Then he shouted through the open window, "Drive off quickly, man."

"Where to, my lord?"

"Anywhere."

The carriage rolled forward and turned around the square just as a breathless Drusilla appeared on the step, clutching cloaks.

"Poor Drusilla," said Polly. "She will be most shocked. Everything I do seems to shock her. She used to be my friend and now she moralizes from morning till night."

"That was my fault, my love. I instructed her to try to instill some moral sense into that criminal brain of yours. My apologies, my sweetest gallows bird. Is that what is making you so miserable?"

"Everything in that terrible house makes me miserable. Meresly—I cannot bring myself to all him papa—wanders about muttering and mewing. The girls torment me daily, telling me that I am so dreary and such bad value they wish they had never rescued me. I can tell you now it was they who left me a skeleton key and a file in the prison. It has also dawned on them that as the elder daughter I might inherit the bulk of the Meresly estate and Josephine makes jokes about poisoning me and then they both giggle and put their heads together. Lady Lydia refuses to see me. I was better off without them.''

The marquess raised the trap on the carriage roof. ''The Mayfair Chapel,'' he called.

Then he settled back and took Polly's hand in his. ''We shall go to Curzon Street and pay that reprobate, Dr. Alexander Keith, a guinea to marry us.''

Polly gasped. ''But it will not be a real marriage,'' she said. ''Dr. Alexander makes his living marrying people without banns or license or parental agreement.''

''We will be married properly at the date on our wedding invitations,'' he said. ''Married again, that is. But this day I am taking you home with me as my bride. Drusilla can be sent to the country to wait for us. I shall have you all to myself. We shall bar the doors to all comers.''

Polly sighed with relief and rubbed her cheek against his coat. ''I am so tired of them all. Your friend Colonel Anderson called.''

''I have not yet forgiven him,'' said the marquess. ''What did he want?''

''He apologized most prettily. He says he is considering getting married himself.''

''To whom?''

''To Miss Ponsonby.''

''Serves him right,'' said the marquess of Canonby.

Lady Lydia's French maid whispered in her ear

that a gentleman was waiting to see her at the foot of the back stairs.

"Are you mad?" cried Lady Lydia. "Those days are over."

"But it is Mr. Pargeter," said the maid, comfortably aware of the weight of an enormous bribe nestling in her bosom.

"Madder and madder. He is no doubt come to slit my throat."

"Listen, my lady, he says he has come to take you away. Out of the country."

Lady Lydia's eyes narrowed and then she said, "I have nothing to lose. Show him up."

Bertram came in and stood watching her with hungry eyes. He watched her rise and stretch out her hands to him and saw the smile of welcome on her still-beautiful face. He knew his plan was going to work. He would take her to Italy and, once there, he would abandon her. She would be left friendless and alone, as friendless and alone as he had been in Newgate.

He caught her to him and kissed her passionately, savoring all the while the thought of her humiliation to come.

Fat and swollen with drink and dysentery, Jake and Barney sat on the veranda of their home. Both heartily wished for the hundredth time they had never volunteered to go to India.

"Wonder where Polly is now," said Barney.

"Probably dead," said Jake savagely. "I've told you not to speak of her."

"Well, I will speak of her," said Barney furiously. "I wish we had let her in that night. We wanted respectability and what have we got? Heat and flies and the flux."

"I've written to Mr. White asking him to recall us," said Jake.

"Why wait?" said Barney. "Let's take the next boat back. Let's just go. Say he's mad and we lose our jobs, we can still see old London again. Maybe look for poor Poll."

"Forget her," said Jake impatiently. "She's probably dead."

Mr. Barks and Mr. Caldicott sat in an inn at Bristol. They were bound for America and were racking up for the night, waiting for a favorable wind. Although the marquess had brought no charges against them for the abduction of Polly or the attack on his lodgekeeper, they felt it was just a matter of time before he did so. They did not know the marquess had judged his beloved had suffered already from too much notoriety to bother bringing them to trial.

Mr. Barks was wearing a Campaign wig to cover the ruin of his hair. He had shed his corsets and was wearing a large roomy coat and generously cut breeches.

Mr. Caldicott was also plainly dressed. Both were attired in the guise of tradesmen.

"You know," said Mr. Barks, "I could almost find it in myself to be grateful to that Polly female. I am a free man. No Mrs. Barks, and these common clothes are uncommon comfortable.'' He raised his glass. ''Here's to a new, free life.''

''May I join you gentlemen?'' Both looked up. A soberly dressed man stood over them. ''May I present myself? I am Jonas Hammer, at your service. I am in a generous mood and of a mind to buy a fine bottle of wine.''

The pair brightened visibly and invited him to sit down. Mr. Hammer snapped his fingers and a bottle was produced.

''Thank you kindly, Mr. Hammer,'' said Mr. Barks. ''What is the celebration?''

''Tell you in a minute. Is that not a fine wine?''

Mr. Barks and Mr. Caldicott drank deep. The wine was very strong and very sweet.

''Now,'' said Mr. Caldicott. ''What is the nature of the celebration?''

''Another glass and I shall satisfy your curiosity.''

Mr. Barks and Mr. Caldicott drank again. Mr. Barks reflected hazily that all he had drunk that evening must have suddenly risen to his brain, for Mr. Caldicott's face was beginning to waver and change as though it were under water.

Sharper than his friend, Mr. Caldicott seized the edge of the table and tried to haul himself up. ''The wine,'' he croaked. ''Don't drink any more, Barks.'' He collapsed back into his chair and his eyes closed.

Mr. Barks saw Mr. Hammer reach forward and press something into Mr. Caldicott's palm. Then he felt something pressed into his own. He looked down blearily—and winking up at him was a bright new shilling.

"And that," said Mr. Hammer, "is the reason for the celebration. Captain Hammer at your service, gentlemen." He blew a whistle and the room was soon full of sailors.

"These two have taken the King's shilling," said Captain Hammer. "Load them on board." The now-unconscious figures of Mr. Barks and Mr. Caldicott were carried out. Captain Hammer followed with a grin on his face.

"Welcome to the King's navy," he called.

Mr. Barks and Mr. Caldicott had been press-ganged.

Polly and the marquess sat facing each other across the dining table. Polly had talked to him as she had always wanted to talk, freely and without social restriction and embarrassment. They laughed over her adventures and over poor Drusilla's brave attempts to be the very model of a strict chaperone. But Polly had now fallen silent. She stared at the wine in her glass, turning the glass this way and that, refusing to meet the marquess's eyes.

"Nervous?" he asked softly.

"Yes," whispered Polly.

He rose and went to stand behind her chair. He bent and kissed her neck.

He helped her rise and took her hand and led her from the room. But he could not wait to get to his bedchamber before he started kissing her and so he seized her when they were halfway up the staircase and kissed her breathless. He sat down abruptly and pulled her onto his knees and kissed her breasts above the square neck of her gown. "The servants," whispered Polly against his mouth.

"Told to say downstairs and make sure they stay there. Kiss me again, my wanton."

Polly sighed against his mouth. She untied the ribbon which held his long black hair at the nape of his neck and then ran her hands through his thick curls. Then she kissed his ear. He groaned and pulled her hard against him, overbalanced, and they both rolled down the stairs and fell with a crash in the hall.

"Oh, my love, are you all right?"

"Yes," sighed Polly. "Kiss me again."

The marquess's butler was the toast of the servants' taverns for weeks to come. Mr. Durrell felt he was not relating scandalous gossip, for my lord and my lady had now been twice married. And everyone wanted to hear of how my lord and my lady took over an hour to get from the hall to the bedchamber and how they had stayed in that bedchamber for two whole days, having their meals served on a tray and left outside the door.

Besides, Mr. Durrell had suffered a terrible earache after having spent an hour with his ear pressed to the keyhole of the back-stairs door which led onto the hall.

He was a devoted servant but felt his little moment as a celebrity had been well earned.